BODY BLOWS

BODY BLOWS

BODY BLOWS
A Joe Grundy Mystery

Marc Strange

A Castle Street Mystery

DUNDURN PRESS
TORONTO

Project Editor: Michael Carroll   Design: Courtney Horner
Copy Editor: Allison Hirst   Printer: Webcom

Library and Archives Canada Cataloguing in Publication

Strange, Marc
      Body blows : a Joe Grundy mystery / by Marc Strange.

ISBN 978-1-55488-390-5

      I. Title.
PS8637.T725 B63 2009   C813'.6   C2009-900497-6

1   2   3   4   5   13   12   11   10   09

Canada   Conseil des Arts   Canada Council   ONTARIO ARTS COUNCIL
          du Canada   for the Arts   CONSEIL DES ARTS DE L'ONTARIO

We acknowledge the support of The Canada Council for the Arts and the Ontario Arts Council for our publishing program. We also acknowledge the financial
support of the Government of Canada through the Book Publishing Industry
Development Program and The Association for the Export of Canadian Books,
and the Government of Ontario through the Ontario Book Publishers Tax Credit
program, and the Ontario Media Development Corporation.

Care has been taken to trace the ownership of copyright material used in this
book. The author and the publisher welcome any information enabling them to
rectify any references or credits in subsequent editions.

J. Kirk Howard, President

Printed and bound in Canada
www.dundurn.com

Dundurn Press   Gazelle Book Services Limited   Dundurn Press
3 Church Street, Suite 500   White Cross Mills   2250 Military Road
Toronto, Ontario, Canada   High Town, Lancaster, England   Tonawanda, NY
M5E 1M2   LA1 4XS   U.S.A. 14150

for Karen

acknowledgements

As much as I might like to think that I accomplish these things on my own, it is essential that I thank the following people: Fred Petersen, Sarah Strange, Lisa Murray, and Ian Sutherland, without whose continuing support and encouragement very little would ever be completed.

To a large extent, a series such as this is a leap of faith, and it is of immeasurable help when one isn't the only person who thinks it's worth doing.

chapter one

The fifty-million-dollar renovation of the Lord Douglas Hotel is complete, only nine months behind schedule and twelve million dollars over budget, which, I'm told, isn't all that bad these days. With the scaffolding gone, the venerable inn once again faces the public with dignity and grace. An elegant awning shelters the arriving guests, a new red carpet paves the way to the famous brass doors (*not* new, always gleaming), and it's even better inside. All the SORRY FOR THE INCONVENIENCE signs have been removed, the Gabriola Ballroom has been reopened, Floor Eleven has a new floor, the Champagne Baths swimming pool, spa, fitness, and pampering centre is now fully operational, PROVIDING RELAXATION AND REJUVENATION — 24 HOURS. The elevators are swifter, the rooms are Internet-friendly, and the Lower Mall has added a six-screen Multiplex, a

Gap, a dojo, and a chiropractor. The Lord Douglas has reclaimed her time-honoured reputation as a bastion of refinement while adding those embellishments so vital to the modern traveller. That's a direct quote. There are brochures everywhere.

It is in recognition of this effort that Leo Alexander will receive the Hotelier of the Year Award — an honour that isn't necessarily bestowed every year. The tribute is overdue but Leo keeps a very low profile and has managed to avoid personal publicity for some time. This evening's arrival at the Royal Lotus Ballroom on the other side of town will mark his first public appearance in eight years, at least as far as I know. Wallace Gritchfield is happy to point out that I don't know everything, but if Gritch has other information, he isn't saying. On the subject of our boss we all tend to be discreet.

There is a Toronto woman, very stylish, name of Hiscox, who's been trying to get some of the staff to open up about Leo Alexander. She claims to be writing a biography.

"Authorized?" I ask her when she finally tracks me down.

"It's meant to be a surprise," she says. We're sitting in the Street Level Sports Bar; she's drinking a martini. She would have been better off having Barney make it for her down in Olive's. Barney is a traditionalist; his martinis are stirred, not shaken.

"So Leo doesn't know about it."

"Not yet."

"Are you a guest of the hotel?" I ask.

"Oh, yes," she says. "Nice little suite, not wild about the wallpaper, but then I wasn't consulted."

"I really don't have much I can give you," I say.

"You'd think he was Sicilian," she says, "the way people clam up around here."

Roselyn Hiscox is a long-legged blonde with a flawless manicure. She isn't taking notes and I don't see a tape recorder.

"Truth, Ms. Hiscox," I say, "not many people in the hotel really know him. He hasn't been seen below the fifteenth floor for quite a while."

"Is he like Howard Hughes up there, growing his fingernails and saving his urine?" She laughs, stylishly, but without mirth.

"Not at all," I say. "He lives a very comfortable, normal life."

"Comfortable, yes," she says. "Normal? People with money and power live on a somewhat more elevated plane than the rest of us." She inspects the olive. "He's been a major player in some very big deals." She has good teeth; the olive pit is immaculate when she produces it. "But careful to stay in the shadows." She smiles.

"I will go on record as saying that Leo Alexander is a good boss and I'm happy to be in his employ. How's that?"

"Very helpful." She stares off into space and I see something in the set of her jaw, determination perhaps. "This isn't a hatchet job, Mr. Grundy," she says, not looking at me, still watching something playing out in her mind. "Your boss has had a very interesting life. I have material that goes back as far as 1959. The only section that's skimpy is the time that he's been hiding out in his hotel."

"I think he's just enjoying the fruits of his labour," I say. "A comfortable semi-retirement."

"Fine," she says. "I just want some details — what's the penthouse like, state of his health, people he's still in contact with."

"Why don't you give him a call?"

"I told you," she says, "it's going to be a surprise."

"One thing I can tell you without breaking any confidence," I say, "Leo doesn't much care for surprises."

Gritch had a turn with her as well.

"I told her he was up there changing lead into gold and plotting world domination," he says. He's following me through the lobby. I'm headed in the general direction of our offices and my personal quarters on the far side of Accounting.

"More interesting than the story I gave her," I say.

"Yeah, well you were probably trying to be gracious. It's one of your failings."

"I'm not telling her what brand of soap he uses, even if I knew, which I don't."

"She's not the first," he says. "Your pal Gormé's paper tried to do a piece on him a few years back. I think the *Emblem* got a case of libel chill."

That stops me briefly. "A piece about the hotel?"

"Nah, something to do with his ranching days.

Before your time."

"Everything's before my time," I say. I'm trying to decide whether I need to check into the office or forego the pleasure in favour of a hot shower. "If it doesn't involve the hotel, I don't want to know."

"Invincible ignorance," Gritch says. "Can't beat it."

"It's invincible," I say.

"And ignorant."

"If you'll excuse me, I need a shave and a shower."

"Oh, yeah," he says, "you've got a big date."

Leo's tailor is a man named Han Chuen Chu who is about the same age as Leo and has been making fine suits in Vancouver for forty years. I have three presentable suits in my closet but Han Chuen Chu didn't build them and it's easy to tell the difference.

About a month ago Mr. Han measured me for a tuxedo. He did it at the same time he was measuring my employer. Leo and I stood side by side, in his penthouse high atop the Lord Douglas Hotel, in our underwear, while Mr. Han called out measurements to an assistant. Leo insisted that our outfits be of the same quality. Not the first time he's done that. I've learned to be careful about complimenting Leo on anything as it usually means that the same model, in my size, will be delivered within twenty-four hours.

"We'll be sitting at the head table, Joseph," Leo explained. "Can't have my XO looking like he doesn't belong."

"At least I'll be wearing the right uniform," I said.

"Never underestimate the power of good tailoring," he said. "A Han Chuen Chu tuxedo is as potent as four stars on a general's epaulets."

"Five stars," said Mr. Han.

My "soup and fish," as Morley Kline used to call evening wear, arrives in a royal blue garment bag with a gold chop which probably translates as "if you have to ask, you can't afford it." Maurice brings it back to my office personally. Maurice has been recently elevated from bell captain to concierge and he's taking a while to settle in to his new position. As bell captain, he knew a hundred ways of skimming the surface of anything flowing his way. Learning how to exploit his new title to its fullest extent will take him a while. I'm sure he'll figure it out.

"Hope that thing came in a Brinks truck," says Gritch. He's sitting in the corner fondling an unlit cigar and counting the minutes until Rachel Golden goes off shift and he can light up.

"Two of them," says Maurice. "I just took the other one up to the old man. Tonight's the night, right?"

"Limo at the front door, eight p.m.," I say.

"He's going out through the lobby?" Maurice is surprised.

"Yeah," says Gritch. "Might want to cover the roulette wheels."

"Is he going to want some acknowledgement?" Maurice wonders. "Line up some of the staff, show him out the door with ceremony?"

"I don't think so," I say. "He'll be happy if his house

is running the way it's supposed to."

"Probably be a few people want a look though. Most of them have never seen him."

"Line 'em up," says Gritch. "They can sing 'Hail to the Chief' as he walks by."

Maurice goes off to check the parade route and I carry the fancy garment bag through to my bedroom to hang it up. On the bed are laid out the other elements for tonight's costume — shirt, studs, links, suspenders, bow tie (I may need some help with that).

"Nice material," says Gritch. He's followed me. He does that.

"I could have rented one," I say. "Leo wouldn't hear of it."

"Host the Oscars in a tux like that."

"I'll try not to get gravy on the cuffs."

"They're letting you eat?"

"I'll be sitting at Leo's table. They have to put a plate in front of me. It wouldn't look right."

"Will the tiny perfect newswoman be there?"

"Not at the head table. I did promise to acknowledge her existence, should our glances meet."

"Big of you."

"She thought so. Don't know what she'll be doing there. No sectarian violence, no bullets flying."

"Don't be too sure. Last time you took the old man on a date you got more than gravy on the outfit."

I remember.

Eight years ago, almost exactly. I remember it was spring

and it wasn't raining, and I was working for Louis Schurr at the time. He called me into his office, cluttered room with two desks and one chair with a wonky castor, and he said, "Got a dark suit?"

Louis was always a sharp dresser but he wasn't well that spring, the thing that was killing him had left him frail. His own dark suit was much too big for him.

"The one I wore yesterday," I said.

"No, that won't do," he said. "Take a walk over to Manny Bigalow's on Granville and tell him I sent you. Tell him you need an outfit."

"What do I need an outfit for?"

"You have to watch somebody's back for a few days, there'll be functions and receptions. The guy travels in some classy circles. You don't want to look inappropriate."

"Heck, no," I said.

I went to see Manny Bigalow. He's not with us any more. Neither is Louis Schurr come to that. Two of a kind in a way. They both had strong opinions about shirts and shoes and appropriate lapels. My new suit had the proper lapels. Manny held up a few ties against a few shirt collars and made certain I was supplied with enough haberdashery to cover a week of bodyguarding among the rich and famous. He told me to hang the suit up every night. I promised him I would. I haven't always lived up to that one either. Manny Bigalow impressed upon me how important a well-made, unwrinkled suit was to how the world perceived me. "First impression is everything," he told me. "You show up at Leo Alexander's office looking good, he's going to be reassured."

So, one spring morning I went to meet Mr. Alexander, wearing a fine dark suit of medium-weight wool, a shirt that fit around the neck and a silk tie that was far too good for me.

Eight years ago Leo ran his various interests from a suite of offices with a view of the water. His two sons, Theo and Lenny, had offices in the same building but on separate floors. They didn't like each other very much, even back then. Alexander and Co. (not Alexander and *Sons* you will note) had framed architectural renderings on the walls, and models of buildings in glass cases. Leo favoured the look of growth they suggested. He was equally fond of model sailboats.

I had to cool my heels in the outer office for half an hour. I was told that Leo was in a meeting. The meeting was loud enough for me to overhear a few words from time to time. "Take responsibility —" was clear enough, as was the instant retort, "— take the damn clamps off!" It went on like that for a while. I pretended to be fascinated by a drawing of a shopping centre.

The man who eventually stomped out of Leo's office looked like a well-fed politician; his waistcoat snug across a barrel chest, his cheeks and nose rosy from frequent liquid lunches, his eyes small and mean. He reminded me then, as he does now, of a prize Berkshire hog. He glared at me as he passed by but didn't bother to compliment me on my choice of neckwear.

Leo was sitting behind a splendid walnut desk, a yachting magazine open in front of him. He seemed entirely unruffled by whatever had just transpired. He looked me up and down and I got the impression that Manny Bigalow's merchandise was being scrutinized as much as I was.

"Sorry to keep you waiting, Mr. Grundy," he said.

"Quite all right, sir," I said. I think he approved of the tie.

"That was my son," he said. "Theodore," he added. "He doesn't think his allowance is generous enough."

"He looks quite successful."

"He eats too much," Leo said. He took a last look at whatever sailing vessel he'd been thinking of buying and closed the magazine. "Louis Schurr tells me you're someone I can rely on," he said.

"What would you want me to do, Mr. Alexander?" I asked him.

"Stay close, not too close, close enough to see who's heading in my direction and get a read on them."

"Would I be looking for anyone in particular, sir?"

"No one I could point out."

"You could ask for police protection," I said. "I mention that because I'm only licensed to carry a gun if I'm protecting money or valuables, current provincial law doesn't believe humans qualify."

"I don't think a gun will be necessary," he said. "I'd rather just have a large presence at my back. All right if I call you Joseph?"

"Of course, sir."

Leo was, and still is, one of those men who appear taller than they are; it's a matter of bearing, and attitude. Leo is a patrician, silver hair, deep-set steel grey eyes, the weathered face of an ocean racer, or a cattleman, both of which he was reputed to have been at one time or another. And a very sharp dresser. Manny Bigalow's suit was good; Leo Alexander's suit was the best.

He was such a man-about-town in those days that he needed a social secretary, a buoyant woman named Madge Killian — Betty Boop lips and a permanent perm. Madge made itineraries and kept Leo's dance card organized. He was much in demand. He was a bachelor, he was rich, he was charming, and he knew which fork to use. An unattached man who doesn't drink out of the finger bowl is an attractive option for someone making up a guest list. The suit paid for itself the first week I worked for him. We went to the opera and the reception after the opera. We went to a gala fundraiser with an orchestra and dancing. I wasn't required to dance, although I was asked. We even went to a garden party where my new dark suit wasn't quite appropriate, but I stayed in the background with the caterers and parking attendants and didn't stand out too much.

Leo never told me why he was expecting trouble. I got the impression that it was a recent development and that prior to hiring a bodyguard, he had functioned quite comfortably with only Madge to tell him where his next meal was coming from, and if he was expected to send flowers.

On the ninth day of my employment we were to attend a thousand-dollar-a-plate dinner supporting the candidacy of a man running for federal office. Leo bought me a place at his table. He was flanked by attractive women on either side, neither of whom looked like they wanted to harm him. The gentleman beside me was an inebriated gasbag and the twitchy younger man on his right was trying to avoid a scene. Neither looked to be a threat.

Both of Leo's sons were in attendance, albeit not at their father's table, nor seated within twenty paces of each other. I hadn't detected much paternal pride or filial warmth when he introduced me. I felt he was establishing his perimeter rather than being polite. Theodore, whom I'd already encountered, was accompanied by his wife whose name I learned somewhat later was Gloria. She looked tiny and apprehensive beside her walrus husband. I couldn't blame her. Theo looked like he squashed things without thinking much about it.

His greeting was curt. "Hiring muscle, Pop?"

His wife wasn't given the opportunity to shake my hand or say hi.

Leo's other son, Lenny, was a different sort. He had the look of a man who'd risen from the ranks. Although a head shorter and fifty pounds lighter, he braced me with a pugnacious scowl and a nod that said "I back down from nobody." I believed him.

His wife, Jackie, as it turned out, was cute and flirty. I don't think her fluttering endeared me to Lenny.

When coffee was served Leo excused himself to do some mingling and I rose to accompany him. Not too close: a large presence at his back.

Leo schmoozed his way through the gathering with elegance and nimble feet. He didn't have a date that evening and felt free to lavish charm on the neglected wives he encountered, never lingering long enough to start a rumour, just pausing sufficiently to earn a flattered titter from a matron or a proprietary glance from a preoccupied husband.

People were standing now, moving from table to table, a small orchestra began tuning up across the dance floor. Leo pointed at, and then started moving toward the French doors leading onto a terrace. He wanted a cigar. I had the cigar case in my Manny Bigalow jacket pocket. Leo didn't want his silhouette to bulge.

I was two steps behind him as we passed through the French doors, reaching inside my jacket for Leo's cigar case. Leo turned, already gesturing with two fingers for his after-dinner panatela, and I saw him spot someone over my shoulder, saw a change come over his face. With my left arm I swept Leo to the side as I swung around. Sharp snapping sounds. I took a bullet through my left trapezius which clipped my collarbone, another went through the fatty layer of my left exterior oblique muscle, and a third scorched across my chest and tore Leo's cigar case to shreds an inch from my fingertips. There were two other shots fired but by this time I was down, dragging Leo with me. I heard screams and shouts and turned just in time to see a dark figure disappearing over the terrace wall. Leo hadn't been hit. I'd been very lucky by about half an inch. Manny Bigalow's suit was ruined.

That was our last date.

I spent some time getting well, then went to work full time for Leo as head of security for the jewel in his crown, the Lord Douglas Hotel. Leo stopped going out.

He sequestered himself in the penthouse suite. He says he likes it up there. It's comfortable enough, and it requires a special key to visit. The shooter was never apprehended. Neither of Leo's sons hastened to our aid.

chapter two

Rachel Golden helps me with the bow tie.

"You can get ones that clip on," Gritch says. "It's the latest thing."

"Pay no attention," says Rachel. "He's jealous because he wasn't invited."

"Are you going home soon?" Gritch wants to know.

Rachel took over as manager of JG Security a while back and since then things have run smoothly. Rachel looks like the chairperson of a PTA committee, but she's ex-Army and I've seen her escort a large drunken man onto the street by merely taking his hand. She had two of his fingers pointing in an unnatural direction at the time and he was trying not to blubber, but you get the picture. Hiring Rachel has made my life a lot easier. She handles the details I was never good at, and a few I used to think I'd be good at but never actually attended to. I still make my grand tour mornings and evenings, still handle complaints when a measure of beef is indicated, still keep my uncashed paycheques in the hotel safe, but I've become more of a presiding entity than a day-to-day administrator.

Even Gritch grudgingly allows that Rachel is much better at running the operation than I ever was. Still, her presence rankles. "The Presbyterians," as Gritch insists on calling her four new staffers, are excessively well-groomed and polite for his taste. He was more comfortable when the Lord Douglas had ashtrays in the lobby. Gritch is an indispensable part of the security system but doesn't fit any designation that Rachel is familiar with. He's not part of any shift, he sets his own hours, and he refuses to acknowledge her authority. Except on the subject of cigar smoke in the office — Gritch can't light up until she clocks off for the night.

"There," she says. "You look like a million bucks."

"As long as you're wearing clean gonch for the trip to Emergency," Gritch says.

"Okay, *Grinch*," she says. "I'm heading home to suburbia. You can fire up that thing. Remember to turn on the ventilator."

"Thanks for the bow," I say.

"You look great," she says. "Don't get chicken-ala-king down your frock."

"Prime rib," I say.

Rachel heads out and Gritch waits the obligatory five seconds then lights his cigar. Gritch doesn't smoke the same brand as Mr. Alexander. No one on a salary does.

"You going upstairs or waiting for him down here?" Gritch asks.

"I'm invited for a drink," I say.

"This is a big step for him," Gritch says. "Been seven years, almost eight."

"Eight exactly," I say. "This time eight years ago a doctor was explaining how fortunate I was."

"He say why, now?"

"He says he wants to try out his tango lessons."

"He has a date?"

"Oh, yes," I say.

Leo's date is a woman some years his junior, closer to my age. She has diamonds at her throat. Leo introduces her as Vivienne Griese but she corrects him immediately and explains that she's reverting to her pre-divorce name of Saunders. Vivienne Saunders is wearing a gown the colour of black roses. It rustles as she crosses the room.

"I've just heard all about you," she says. "Leo says you used to be a prizefighter."

"Sometimes he tells people I was an astronaut," I say.

Leo hands me a small whisky, which he knows I won't drink. Forget about the fortune in Italian wool I'm wearing, I'm on the job. He can refer to me as his Executive Officer, or his good friend, or an astronaut if he wants. I'm still what I was the last time we went to a party — the large presence at his back.

"Sometimes I embellish," Leo admits. "Telling the same stories over and over can be a bad habit at my age."

"Hiding up here for so long was a bad habit," says Vivienne. "I'm thrilled you've decided to rejoin the human race."

"I guess the timing was right," says Leo, with a puckish smile. I can't be certain but he may have winked at me.

"My divorce was final as of yesterday," she says to me sideways.

"I'm never sure," I say. "Are congratulations appropriate?"

"In this case, definitely," she says.

"Be a shame to waste half a bottle of Veuve Clicqot," says Leo. "How are we for time, Joseph?"

"It's your night," I say. "It can't start until you show up."

Leo refills Vivienne's flute and his own with the flourish of a man handy with champagne. I take my half-finger of whisky and retreat a few steps. Three's a crowd. Vivienne is telling Leo about a tango club in Buenos Aires. I notice that Raquel, Leo's housekeeper, is preparing canapés in the kitchen.

¿ Cómo está usted esta noche, Raquel? I ask.

She smiles at me. "*Muy bien, Señor Grundy,*" she says. She lowers her voice. "He looks fine tonight, does he not?"

"Very fine."

"It is good to see him like this," she says.

"I didn't know he was taking tango lessons."

I'm almost certain I catch the flicker of a smile as Raquel turns to check her *mis en place*. There are serving dishes and shiny glasses standing by.

"Are guests coming back here after?" I ask.

"He says it is possible. If there is anyone he is still friends with. You know how he talks. I have things prepared."

"Then I'll see you later," I say.

She holds up one finger and looks around the corner to make sure Leo is occupied. She gestures me closer.

"Could you do something for me?"

"I'd be happy to," I say.

"I have bought a little gift for Señor Alexander," she says. "I wonder, could you pick it up for me? It's a secret. I don't want him to know until his birthday."

"Where do I go?"

"The cigar store on Robson. You know the one? Austin & Davies?"

"That's where Gritch wants to go when he dies."

"It's all paid for." She checks to make sure the coast is clear, then hands me a folded piece of paper. "The receipt," she says. "You are kind to do this."

"Tomorrow," I say. It takes me a moment to come up with the correct phrase. "*Tengo tiempo*."

"Very good. You have time." She grins. "*Gracias*. I am relieved."

"It will be my pleasure," I say. "*Hasta luego*."

"*Si*," she says with a lovely smile. "*Hasta pronto*."

She's always pleased when I get it right.

"All set?" Leo is beckoning from across the room. Vivienne is adjusting her wrap, black roses with a crimson lining. I glance back at Raquel. She is ignoring the elegant woman with the perfect hair and the diamond necklace. Leo hands me his cigar case and gold lighter. "Hold these for me will you, Joseph?" The case is three-barrelled, Spanish leather, primed with Cuban extravagance. The lighter is a Colibri. Han Chuen Chu's tux has a special inside pocket to hold both items

without ruining my silhouette. Leo no doubt has the
same pocket but chooses not to burden himself.

It crosses my mind that Caesar Augustus would have ap-
preciated the regal decorum of Leo's passage through the
lobby. Maurice has imposed a level of restraint on the
personnel, no palm fronds waving or ram's horns blow-
ing, but, had Leo deigned to raise a finger in benediction,
twenty people would likely have genuflected. To most of
the hotel staff, whether customer service or support, Leo
Alexander is a mythic figure, the unseen power who lives
on Olympus and controls their destinies. Have to admit,
tonight he looks the part.

Andrew, our doorman, himself resplendent in gold-
braided livery, opens the polished brass door with perfect
timing and Leo exits the Lord Douglas and inhales the air
at street level. Give him credit, he doesn't swivel his head.
That's my job. I checked the faces of everyone on the
interior parade route and I'm checking the street in both
directions and I even look up at the portico ceiling in case
someone's hung an anvil. Our limo driver is holding the
passenger door open. He has a moustache and a stubby
ponytail. I'm half-expecting a brass band to give us a
sendoff. I hear a restrained "whoop whoop" as we turn
onto the street and I think Leo just winked at me again.

chapter three

A few hundred of Leo's "closest personal friends," most of who have had to introduce themselves, are spilling drinks and waiting for the dinner doors to open. So far I haven't noticed Leo being particularly convivial with anyone, but I'm impressed by the restraint he's showing with some puffed-up middle-management-type from the Fairmont chain.

"I hear you finally changed a fuse in that mausoleum of yours," the guy says. "Ever get elevator three moving again?"

"Oh, sure," Leo says. "Of course the people inside had long since starved to death, but we comped them anyway."

Then I see his eyes light up at the approach of a pretty face. I'm almost certain I told Connie Gagliardi that I'd be working tonight and didn't want to be distracted, nonetheless she's put on an emerald gown which shows off her nice shoulders and she's wearing the cheeky smile that always makes my face crease. I can feel Vivienne's temperature drop as Connie sifts through the pre-dinner reception throng. I admire the way she dips those nice shoulders, like a running back weaving toward the end zone.

"Mr. Alexander," she says. Touchdown. "How nice to meet you at last. I'm Connie Gagliardi, Channel 20."

"You've smiled at me from your news desk often, Ms. Gagliardi," Leo says, bending over her outstretched hand. "Be assured that I was smiling back."

"Have you missed me? I'm on in the morning now."

"And I thought you'd gone to Hollywood." A charmer when he wishes to be.

"I'm hoping I can sit you down for an interview. At your convenience, of course."

"Maybe we can discuss it over lunch sometime soon," says Leo.

"Better make it quick," I say. "She's trying to hitch a ride to Afghanistan."

Connie tilts her curly head in my direction. "Will *he* have to be there?" she wants to know.

Leo begins his acceptance speech with generous thanks to all concerned for the great honour. He even manages to look flattered by his profile in *bas-relief* on the mandatory brass plaque they've stuck him with.

"The Lord Douglas is one of the last, great, fully independent hotels," Leo says, looking out at the audience of well-fed innkeepers. "I know that many of my peers and competitors look forward to the day when either old age or red ink forces me to become a link in some global chain ..." (He pauses to allow for the expected chuckle) "but I advise them not to hold their collective breath. Autonomous innkeepers may be a disappearing breed, but we ain't extinct. Hell, some of us aren't even on the endangered list." (Another chuckle.)

So far I haven't seen a hint of anything suspicious or out of place. The affair has been catered like clockwork. The three-hundred-plus guests all received their prime ribs hot and their *crèmes brûlée* crunchy on top and creamy in the middle. Connie Gagliardi is at a table somewhere off to the side. She's been chatting with a quarterback from the Seattle Seahawks who's up here for some charity golf tournament. Drake something-or-other. It's either Drake-something, or something-Drake, I forget. I've heard Connie's wicked laugh ring out more than once. Even so, I'm staying focused.

And finally, after the applause and the benediction and another round of convivial schmoozing, the doors to the dance floor are opened and Leo Alexander and Vivienne Saunders get a chance to try out their moves.

"Not dancing?" A familiar voice at my shoulder.

"Hmm? Quarterbacks don't dance?"

"Ho," she chortles. "You *were* paying attention."

"I'm working," I say.

"Your boss is getting away," Connie says. "Couldn't you do a better job from the dance floor than the stag line?"

"He's picked up some nifty moves, got to admit."

"Come on," she says. "We'll head him off by the fountain."

"I'm pretty rusty."

"Where have I heard that recently?"

I don't think I'm as good at this job as I once was, and it isn't just my two-step that's rusty. I'm losing my edge. I've been enjoying myself far too much.

After a while Connie says, "I think he's flagging."

"It's the new hip," I say. "It's only good for an hour of ballroom."

The dancers pause in place to applaud the last number (a mambo, I think, I've let Connie set the tempo and chauffeur me around) and we cross the parquet floor to join Leo and Vivienne.

"Isn't he terrific?" says Vivienne. "I haven't had this much fun since Argentina."

"I'm about ready for a splash of brandy and a cigar," Leo says. "Ms. Gagliardi, would you care to join us?"

"I'd be delighted," she says.

"How many more are coming, sir?" I ask.

"Just us," he says. "I haven't met this many horse's asses since the last time we went out together. See about getting the car, will you, Joseph? I'll make a few obligatory good-byes."

"Don't like leaving you alone, sir."

"Pish-tosh," he says. "I have two lovely escorts. What do I need you for?"

I get the impression that Ms. Saunders isn't completely thrilled that Connie has joined the select circle, but she smiles nonetheless, give her that. I head for the main entrance and tell the valet to order up Leo's limo. I do all the tipping. Leo doesn't carry cash either.

Leo's obligatory farewells must include everyone in

the ballroom because wherever he is it's behind a wall of backs and heads. I start across the room toward the largest flock and one of the organizers comes running up, a man who introduced himself near the start of the festivities but whose name I've misplaced. He looks upset.

"Excuse me, you're Mr. Grundy, is that right? Mr. Alexander's assistant?"

"That's right, ah, Mr. —" he's wearing a nametag "— Trueller."

"Tulley," he says.

I should get contacts.

"What can I do for you, sir?" I ask politely.

"It's … ah, most embarrassing. The … ah, memorial plaque, the bronze, rosewood frame, engraved —"

"Yes, I saw it. It's very handsome."

"It's been defaced," he says sadly. "Someone ruined it."

"Where is it?"

He leads me back to the head table. The speaker's lectern has an inner shelf where speeches and jokes and names to remember were kept, where Leo's Hotelier of the Year Award is evidently still waiting to be picked up. The plaque has a big hole where Leo's right eye used to be.

"Leave it," I say. "Don't touch it. Could be fingerprints."

"Should I call the police?"

I leave him to decide that on his own time and give myself a mental smack on the head. I knew it. Happy-go-lucky, feeding my face, cavorting with the rich and semi-famous, forgetting what my job was. Where the hell is he? I'm crashing through a thicket of gowns and starched shirtfronts — "Excuse me, pardon me, let me through, please" — trying not to look like I'm panicked.

Finally. He looks safe enough, quite pleased with himself, in fact. Doesn't look like he needs rescuing.

"Ah, Joseph," he says. "There you are. Past my bedtime is it?"

"Car's waiting, sir," I say.

The ever-vigilant Connie Gagliardi has caught something in my face, or heard something in my tone. Maybe it's the faint reek of dread still clinging to me.

"Hi there," she says. "How're ya doing, big guy?" It's not an idle question.

"Just fine," I say. "But it's time we hit the road."

Connie and Vivienne each take an arm and begin shepherding Leo toward the exit. I try not to bowl anyone out of our lane. There are smatterings of applause as we pass, a little bantering, an occasional mutter, genial farewells. Leo evidently has kissable cheeks.

The limo is waiting; our driver is holding the door. He has a moustache. He doesn't have a stubby ponytail.

chapter four

W e're in a Yellow Cab, the first one in line at the taxi stand.

"What was wrong with the limo?" Vivienne wants to know.

"Joseph is overly cautious," says Leo. "But I trust his instincts."

That's true enough. He didn't protest or balk at being swung sideways, past the open limo door and into the back seat of a well-used Chevy. He's tucked himself into the corner. I'm on one cheek in the middle, scanning through the rear window. Ms. Saunders is avoiding the imagined stains by sitting on the edge of her seat. Connie's in front with our driver whose photo-ID declares him to be Josip Stanishevski. He looks like his photograph, and he drives like a cabby, and we're out of there before the bon voyage crowd has stopped waving at the empty limous

"Did it break down?" Vivienne is trying not to be flustered.

Connie has the cellphone. She's dialing Gritch for me.

"You should program the number," she says. "You'd only have to push one button. Ringing … Here."

She hands it back and I manage to find the flap where the sound comes out. "Gritch. We're in a cab. We'll be coming in through Olive's. Check the street, check the lobby, post a Presbyterian, secure an elevator."

"Somebody chasing you?"

"Make sure nobody's waiting for us."

"I'm on it," he says.

"Seriously," says Vivienne. "Are we in danger?"

"No, Ma'am," I say. "I probably over-reacted to a change in chauffeurs. I'm sorry if you were startled."

"Different driver?" Leo asks.

"Yes, sir."

It's ten blocks to the Lord Douglas. A high-revving Suzuki motorcycle zings by us and disappears down the street but I don't spot anyone following us.

Gritch himself is there to open the cab door. Josip accepts two twenties with a smile. He was worth every penny. One of the Presbyterians, Roland is his name, a gentle soul, a bodybuilder, walks like he's wearing armour plate under his blue suit, ushers the party to Olive's front door. Gritch looks me up and down as I hit the sidewalk.

"Least you're walking," he says.

"I got spooked," I say. "Gotta talk to the limo find out why they switched drivers."

"I can do that."

"Let's get Leo upstairs first."

But Leo has no intention of going upstairs in a hurry. He's bought a round for the house, he's greeted people he hasn't seen in a while, and he has the sumptuous Olive May wrapped in a big hug. He looks right at home.

"I'd forgotten what a great place this is," he says.

"I've got an elevator waiting, sir," I say.

"Let's stick around for a nightcap, shall we?" he says. "Olive's going to play my favourite tune."

"Which one is that, sugar?"

"Any number you sing will automatically become my favourite," says Leo.

He commandeers a table near the bandstand, Vivienne returns from the powder room with her aplomb adjusted, Olive May and her bass player, the stalwart Jimmy Hinds, ease their way into a medley of Cole Porter perennials, and Connie Gagliardi is tugging my coat.

"Everything okay, big guy?" she asks.

"Looks like," I say. "For now, anyway."

"What spooked you?"

"Missing ponytail. Could've been a shift change. Probably a logical explanation. Maybe he had a haircut. Maybe he lost his rubber band. I didn't need to find out."

"I mean before that. When you came looking for us."

"Bad practical joke." I notice that I've started whispering out of the side of my mouth, bending closer. "Someone defaced Leo's award."

"Oh, that's terrible," she says. "Graffiti, bad words, what?"

"A hole. Right through the eye."

"Wow. Nasty."

"Solid bronze. Must've used a drill press."

"Or a .44 Magnum," says Connie Gagliardi the nascent war correspondent. I worry about her. I'm going to buy her some Kevlar for Christmas. Maybe sooner than that.

Gritch returns from wherever he's been. "Who's got a .44 Magnum?"

"Dirty Harry," she says.

"You find out anything?" I ask.

"Limo service says the guy hasn't checked in yet. Name's —" he looks at a piece of paper. "— Starr. Dimitar Starr. Reliable driver, supposedly, been there five months."

"Maurice booked the limo," I say. "Check with him. See if we've used this outfit before."

Olive swings into "You're the Tops."

"Look at him," I say. "We'll never get him out of here."

Leo and Vivienne are sipping brandy while Olive sings to them. Ms. Saunders has adopted the tolerant air of a slumming duchess but Leo is in his element. He's enjoying himself. For the first time tonight he looks relaxed. I'd been aware of a constant hum of tension all evening but assumed that I was the one generating it. I can see now that attending the ceremony required an act of courage on Leo's part.

Vivienne has demurred on the offer of a further nightcap in Leo's lair and I'm escorting her to a taxi. I could have given Gritch the chore, but after insisting that Leo stay inside, he asked me as a personal favour to make sure his date was sent safely on her way. Andrew has signalled up a slightly spiffier vehicle than Josip's cab and is holding the door.

"Do you tango, Mr. Grundy?" Vivienne asks.

"Not according to Ms. Gagliardi," I say.

She sniffs at the name. Her night hasn't unfolded as smoothly as it might have. She gives me a thin-lipped smile and takes the fifty-dollar bill. Cab fare.

Andrew looks me up and down. "That's a splendid suit," he says.

"Hope it likes mothballs," I say.

A large man is weaving across the street in my direction.

"Didn't waste any time, did she?" he yells at the departing taxi.

"Who would that be, sir?" I ask.

"My slut wife," he says. "You the new one? Hope you've got lots of money. She likes money."

He's on my sidewalk now, close enough to breathe bourbon on my face.

"I assume you're referring to Ms. Saunders," I say.

"Shit!" he says with disgust. "Saunders already, is it? Christ!"

"Excuse me, sir," I say, "I have to get back to work."

He takes a lazy loopy swing at me, well off the mark, not worth blocking, and sits down heavily on the curb.

"Would you like me to get you a cab, sir?"

"I don't need you to get me shit," he says.

"Perhaps not, sir, but I can't leave you sitting on the curb, the police will take notice. Why don't you head on home?"

He snuffles. "Why don't you just piss off!"

I can see Andrew signalling to a taxi and coming forward to take charge of the situation. He can handle it from here.

Olive has finished her set and retreated to her private corner banquette. Connie and Leo are missing.

"They went up, sugar," Olive says to me. "Two minutes ago. With Gritch and the Impeccable Bulk."

"I told them to wait."

"Leo was feeling mellow. I think he wanted to show your girlfriend his mansion in the sky."

"I used to be good at this job," I say.

"You're still good, Joey darlin', but you need to loosen your tie."

Olive tugs one end of the bow and unbuttons my collar.

"There. Now you look like Frankie Sinatra. With muscles." She gives me one of her throaty chuckles.

"I'd better get up there," I say.

The evening has given me a bellyache. I could use a cold beer and a quiet place to sit. Someone went to a lot of trouble to mess up Leo's memento. That is worrisome. Not that Leo sets much store by such things and would probably have stuffed the plaque in a closet, but I wouldn't want him to see it in its present condition. And the missing limo driver is gnawing at me as well.

One way or another I need to find out what that was all about. At least Leo had a pleasant interlude in Olive's. By now he's probably helping Raquel serve canapés, pouring champagne....

Wrong.

Connie is waiting as the elevator doors open and her expression tells me more than I want to know.

"Joe," she says.

Leo is sitting on the floor with one leg bent under him. He's leaning against the wall. His eyes are closed. Gritch is on the phone. Roland is standing in the kitchen doorway.

I cross the room and look past the young man. Raquel is lying on the kitchen floor. Her canapés are scattered. Her shiny plates and glasses are smashed. Her blood is pooled under her.

"I just checked for a pulse, Joe," Roland says. "Didn't touch anything else."

"Oh, Jesus Lord," I say.

"Cops are on the way," says Gritch.

Connie is sitting with Leo.

"My fault," he says. "My fault. All mine."

"Fire stairs?" I ask Gritch.

"Locked," he says.

"There's a blood smear on the key pad," says Roland.

"Got a pencil?" Roland hands me a ballpoint pen and I use the button end to punch in the security code and open the fire door. Seventeen flights of steel stairs straight down, poorly lit. And faintly echoing.

"Could be somebody going down," I tell Gritch. "See if we've got a man on the ground floor who can get around to the back."

"You chasing?"

"If my knee holds out."

Not an idle concern. Since tearing the anterior cruciate ligament in my left knee over a year ago, I've been careful not to make the joint do more than it wants to. Fore and aft it's working fine, but thumping down an endless metal stairwell is a heavier workout than it's ready for.

I can't hear the echoes any longer. If there *was* anyone they're probably on the street by now. Whoever it is, I'll never catch them anyway. What the hell, it's something to do. Christ! She's dead. Raquel is dead. Lying on the kitchen floor.

By the time I get to street level my knee is throbbing, my shirt is sticking, and I needn't have bothered. The street is deserted, no squealing tires, no fading footsteps, nothing to do but make the long hike around to the side entrance. No more stairs tonight if I can help it.

At the corner I meet Todd, another of Rachel's hirees, clean-cut, competent, and confused.

"Joe? Who am I supposed to be looking for?"

"Todd, I have absolutely no idea. Nobody ran past you?"

"Not a soul."

"Okay. There'll be police showing up pretty soon. Give Gritch a call, he's up in the penthouse, he'll have to come down and escort them. Go ahead. I think I'll take a look down the block."

"What's going on?"

I don't really want to tell him. "Call Gritch."

The backside of the Lord Douglas runs north-south. Across the street is the parking garage with a skywalk to the mezzanine directly overhead. To my left are the hotel's loading docks, dumpsters, service entrances, and at the far end, the fenced construction site where the Warburton building once stood and where a huge hole in the ground has been waiting for Leo and his son Lenny to work out who will own what percentage of whatever they decide to build there some day. Leo has a controlling interest in the property but the hotel's costly renovations have forced him to hold off on a start date.

The covered walkway along the fence has grilled portholes for sidewalk superintendents to check on progress. Since the hole was excavated there hasn't been much to look at. The giant crane which stood idle and wasting money for three months has long since been relocated to a going concern and now, except for sporadic pumping sessions to get rid of rainwater, the site is essentially abandoned and resembles an immense square-sided bomb crater with a wide ramping slope at the far end.

And something or someone, in motion, near the top.

I can't see much through the narrow grill. Just a shadow, a shadow that shouldn't be there, moving with some purpose, lifting something, or hiding something, or shifting a piece of machinery.

My new size thirteen dancing pumps have given me a blister on my right heel and my left knee feels like it's swelling up. Whoever is down there isn't going to wait around for me to creep along. I was never much of a creeper anyway. Not a great runner either.

The truck entrance is around the corner, wide chain-link gates, padlocks, and numerous signs insisting upon hardhats and safety shoes and absolving Streiner Construction of liability for injuries incurred by unauthorized visitors who are correspondingly threatened with criminal prosecution for unlawful entry.

The gate is ajar, the chain hangs loose.

I can hear him now; he's near the top of the ramp. He'll have to get by me if he wants to leave.

I'm ready for just about anything except the sudden appearance of a motorcycle roaring up the ramp, scattering a roostertail of mud and gravel and heading straight for me. I make the mistake of trying to haul the rider off his saddle as he powers by and get knocked off my feet by a flying elbow to the side of my head.

As I'm rolling down the muddy ramp I can hear the bike bouncing over the curb and howling away in the general direction of Stanley Park. I stagger almost to the bottom, shaking my head to clear it and manipulating the jaw sideways. Both actions are painful. I don't think anything's broken but I've taken left hooks from professionals that hurt less. Han Chuen Chu's creation will need dry-cleaning.

Almost pitch black down here. There's a half-moon and scattered street lamps visible, and on the far side of the pit the north side of the hotel shows a few lighted windows, but precious little illumination makes it all the way down. The floor of the excavation has the look of a giant child's construction project abandoned in favour of a trip to the circus. Random, bound stooks of rebar jutting from truncated concrete pilings, meandering trenches, massive stacks of pipe and lumber, plywood walkways to nowhere in particular. All of it without apparent plan or purpose.

The south edge of the pit rises like a cliff face and above the rim the Lord Douglas looms like a second mountain range. Leo's aerie is a faint glow high above. And, if I trace a line directly down from the penthouse, a plunge of probably twenty stories in total, I arrive at the dead man impaled on jutting rebar on top of a piling.

In the darkness I can't make out features or details except that he's lost a shoe, and his blood is staining the concrete.

chapter five

The detectives who catch the case are both men, Geoff Mooney and "Looch" Pazzano. Mooney is the senior guy, about fifty, mournful features, bags under his eyes, quiet and careful the way he moves around. His partner is in his thirties, a bruiser, bristly black hair, thick neck, small feet. There are two uniforms in the room as well — first officers on the scene. One is a woman. She's Asian, possibly Chinese, I'll know soon enough. Her partner is a guy I met some years back. His name will come to me. I'm not thinking very straight right now. The four cops have taken over the living room and the kitchen. We're all in the elevator foyer. Leo is sitting beside Connie. He's looking straight ahead, his eyes reaching for somewhere else he'd rather be.

"That's a good-looking bruise," Gritch says.

"I hope he broke his elbow." I'm still a bit woozy.

"At least I think it was his elbow, might have been a handlebar."

Gritch is keeping his voice down. Roland is behind him, leaning over his shoulder to catch the words.

"Knew something was up as soon as the elevator got here," Gritch says. "The armchair was on its side. I told Leo to hold it. The living room was trashed, the TV, the French doors. Roland checked down the hall, I went across to the kitchen."

"Nothing down the hall," Roland says. "Bedrooms, bathrooms, nothing."

"Whatever happened, happened in there," Gritch says.

Mooney comes out of the living room and looks in my direction. He comes over.

"Joe Grundy, right? I'm Detective Mooney."

"I chased somebody down the fire stairs, Detective," I say. "Don't know if they started from this floor. And someone had a motorcycle stashed at the construction site."

"Get a look at it?"

"Went by in a hurry. Wasn't big. Sounded like a dirt bike, 250cc, something like that. And you've got a dead body at the bottom of that construction pit. Hard to tell anything in the dark. He could have come straight down from the railing out there."

"Oh, Christ," he says sadly. "Wait here."

Mooney goes off to make arrangements for more police.

"Tell who it is?" Gritch asks.

"He's stuck on top of a pylon or something. Twelve

feet off the deck."

"Be tricky getting him down," he says.

Roland says, "Somebody fell from here?"

"Or got tossed," says Gritch.

Mooney looks around at the crowded foyer. More cops are arriving. "Can you arrange for another room?" he wants to know. "We'll have to seal off this floor."

Gritch gets on the cellphone and tells Raymond D'Aquino, the night manager, what needs to be done.

"What does it look like to you, Detective?" I ask.

"Tell you one thing," he says. "Looks like she put up a helluva fight."

I don't find the statement comforting. The image doesn't sit well.

The Lord Douglas has almost a full house tonight and Leo won't inconvenience guests. Raymond did the best he could. We're on the eighth floor, in a small suite that hasn't yet reopened because the new shower stall was damaged during installation. Leo looks completely out of place, sitting at the writing-desk/vanity/entertainment centre, doodling on hotel stationery with a hotel ball-point, diamonds and Xs and checkerboards, now and then looking at his face in the mirror, looking his age, not liking what he sees.

Gritch is standing in the hall giving a statement to Pazzano. Roland has been released to continue his shift. Connie comes to me, puts her arm through mine, we stand side by side squeezing each other's upper arms.

"You okay, big guy?"

"Oh, yeah, I'm fine. Might want to restrict kisses on the right cheek for a few days."

"Aww, that's my favourite." She glances at Leo. "He going to make it?"

"It's killing him," I say.

"You knew her, didn't you?"

"She was always there."

She looks up at me. I know what she's asking. She has eloquent eyebrows. I shrug.

"After you talk to the detectives why don't you head home?" I give her arm an extra squeeze. "I've got a lot to do. They might want to bring us down to the station for statements."

"Why?"

"I was his bodyguard. Obviously he was concerned about his safety. They're going to want to know what he was concerned about."

"But you don't know."

"I never did," I say.

She pulls her arm free, turns to stand in front of me, hits me softly on the chest with the flat of her hand.

"This is a story, you know," she says.

"Do your job, Connie. It'll be okay. It's going to come out. I'd rather you set the tone than the front page of the *Emblem*."

Mooney talks to Leo inside the suite while I have a chat with Pazzano in the hall. It's four a.m., we've agreed to show up at the station in the morning for a more detailed statement. Right now, all Pazzano wants are the basics:

when did we leave, when did we come back, who was she? That's the question that hits the hardest. Past tense. She was. She isn't any longer.

Raquel. Mendez. Raquel Esperanza Mendez. She lived up there. She had her own suite. She was Leo's housekeeper. I don't know if she had any family. I don't know if she and Leo had "a thing."

My own questions are met with the usual police reticence. The body hasn't been recovered from the construction site, no identification, and no motorcyclists have been apprehended, and when we know, you'll know. Maybe. I won't hold my breath.

After Mooney and Pazzano quit for the night I check on Leo. He's taking off his tux and putting on a hotel robe.

"I'll need a suit for the morning," he says.

"I'll get it, sir," I say.

"In the morning."

"Yes, sir. Just tell me what you want."

"In the morning," he says.

"Are you going to be all right in here? Raymond says he can move you into the Ambassador Suite tomorrow."

"You get some sleep, Joseph."

"I could stick around, sir, if you want to talk or anything."

"No. I'd rather be alone now."

As I head for the door he stops me without raising his voice.

"Joseph?"

"Yes, sir."

"I need to know who did this."

"The police will take care of it, I'm sure," I say. "It looks like a robbery that went sour."

"Maybe," he says. "Maybe that's what happened."

The lobby is almost deserted — exhausted late arrivals checking in, a vacuum cleaner pushed along the far wall. The police presence is evident but low-key — one marked cruiser still near the entrance, one further down the block. I feel weary. My knee hurts. Too much dancing probably.

Gritch follows me around as I climb out of the overpriced soup and fish that I can't imagine ever wearing again.

"Might want to get those pants sponged and pressed," says Gritch.

"I suppose."

"Tiny perfect newswoman gone home?"

"She has," I say. "Unless she decides to do a special report from the front steps."

"Think this will be a big story?"

"Not to her," I say. "She'd rather be dodging RPGs around Kandahar."

"Damn," Gritch says. "I never checked back on that limo driver."

"It can wait," I say. "I'm hoping there's nothing."

"You mention it to the cops?"

"No."

"You going to mention it to the cops?"

"Sure. Sooner or later," I tell him.

"What are you being coy about?"

"I'm being careful. I don't know what's going on

with Leo. Has he got himself into something? We still haven't had a straight talk about any of this."

"You know anything about the demon biker you haven't told the cops?"

"Nope. Strangers in the night," I say. "I know he was in a hurry to get out of there."

"Don't blame him," says Gritch. "I don't like people unexpectedly dropping in either."

As I'm hanging up my jacket I feel the extra weight in the pocket. Three fine cigars sheathed in leather, and a heavy gold lighter.

"Check the other pocket," says Gritch. "Maybe there's a ham sandwich."

Gritch and I sit for a while in my "private space," the small office between the main office and my living quarters. I sit at Louis Schurr's old desk, in his creaky oak chair with the one wobbly castor, and Gritch sits on a chair that he drags in. We light up a hundred dollars' worth of Cohibas and fill the confines with expensive smog.

"All connected, right? Gotta be." Gritch is being hypothetical. "Two is coincidence, three is conspiracy. What they say. Got the trashed award plaque thingy, got The Case of the Missing Ponytail, and then there's —" I know what just went through his head ... the first two are absurd, the last was tragic. "— what happened upstairs," he finishes carefully.

"*Could* be connected," I say.

"Damn right could be. And don't forget what happened seven years ago, eight years ago. *That* could be connected. Whoever did *that* is still running around loose."

"As far as we know," I say.

"We know diddly. Except we *know* nobody got arrested for that little caper, and we *know* Leo was still being careful about something, otherwise why would he drag your carcass to a fancy-dress ball?"

"He was tense. All evening," I say. "He handled it well but I could tell. Like he was waiting for something."

"Been waiting for the other shoe to drop for eight years," says Gritch.

Eight years ago.

Leo didn't come to see me. I would have checked myself out of the hospital by the third day but he insisted that I take my time. His personal GP was keeping an eye on me. Madge Killian bounced in with flowers and a fruit basket and magazines. She seemed really proud of me, kept patting me on my good shoulder. She told me that Leo had arranged for someone named Wallace Gritchfield to provide security for me.

"He should keep it for himself," I say. "Until whoever did it is caught."

"He's in a secure location," she says. "He wants you to come and see him when Dr. Markle releases you. Not a day before."

"I will," I say.

Wallace Gritchfield didn't look like a bodyguard. He was short, round, balding, and looked like he'd stopped a few pucks with his nose over the years.

"Hi," he says. "Call me Gritch. Leo wants me to park myself in the hall overnight, make sure nobody tries to finish the job. 'Course if they come through the window, you're screwed."

"I don't think it's necessary. They weren't after me."

"If he really thought you were in danger he'd have a platoon of rent-a-cops at the main entrance. The old man doesn't fool around."

"You work for him?"

"I do security at the hotel."

"What hotel is that?" I ask.

I didn't know much about the Lord Douglas back then. I'd never stayed there. It was out of my price range. My manager, Morley Kline, liked to have a drink in the Press Club once in a while, shoot the breeze with the sportswriters, Hap Reynolds sometimes gave us a promo for an upcoming fight. I guess the hotel was showing her age, had faded somewhat from her heyday. Still, she had that look, the look that grand hotels have — a lobby as big as a ballroom, lofty as a cathedral, crystal chandeliers, washroom attendants, and mahogany doors on the water closets. If the Persian rugs had a wide pathway worn from entrance to elevators, and the leather sofa cushions sagged a little in the middle, there was no mistaking the era, or the refined sensibility of the people who had built the place. The Lord Douglas wasn't a rush job. She wasn't poured concrete, she was cut stone.

"The house dick, Ceece Lund's his name, had a thrombosis about, I don't know, six months ago maybe," Gritch is telling me. "I was working for him for seventeen, eighteen years, so I've been filling in. I don't think he's coming back. Ceece."

"Shouldn't you be over there?"

"I'm not the only guy working," he says. "I've got

assistants. Don't know their asses from their elbows, either of 'em, but Leo knows where I am if something comes up."

"What kind of stuff comes up?"

"What doesn't?" he says.

Leo was reopening the original owner's penthouse above the Fifteenth Floor and was planning on living there. When I arrived there were workmen all over the place — plumbers, glaziers, electricians. Leo was personally overseeing every phase of the operation. He had already established a small office complete with phone, fax, computer, and a leather couch where he was spending his nights pending completion of his bedroom.

"Joseph," he says. "How are you feeling? How's the arm?"

"I've healed up just fine, sir," I say. "How are you?"

"Very busy, very busy, Joseph."

"I can see that."

"I don't mean all the hammering," he says. "I'm retrenching, circling the wagons so to speak. Backing away from a number of interests, going to concentrate on getting the Lord Douglas back on her feet."

"That's nice, sir. She's a fine old hotel."

"And I want you to be part of that."

"In what capacity, sir?"

"Hotel security. There's a job opening."

"Working for Mr. Gritchfield?"

"No. He'd be working for you."

Gritch had spent much of his working life sitting

between a fern and a palm tree in the lobby of the Lord Douglas, from which observation post he surveyed every entry and departure. He was a married man, but his wife maintained that he was a bigamist and that his first wife was the hotel.

In the old days Gritch would lift whatever newspaper he was hiding behind to sip from a flask but when we first teamed up he told me he was on the wagon.

"I've been sober for three years," Gritch told me. "Three years, three months, and one, two, three days, hey, no, it's after midnight, four days."

"Congratulations," I say.

"No mean feat," he says. "I was never a binge drinker. I was a steady, well-schooled, dedicated souse, ambulatory and capable of coherent discourse. I was a pro."

"What made you stop?"

"Oh, you know, wife."

"Oh."

"She said there were three things in my life: the hotel, the booze, and her. She said I was going to have to drop one of them."

Louis Schurr retired a few months later, died a few months after that, and I started work at a job I wasn't particularly well-suited for, running a small staff of less-than-stalwart operatives. Nonetheless, I managed to make a go of it, predominantly because of Wallace Gritchfield.

That was eight years ago.

"How many special keys are there anyway?" Gritch wants

to know. "Keys that will get you up to the penthouse?"

My expensive cigar suddenly tastes foul. Extravagance is an acquired habit. Gritch seems able to deal with it.

"One in Lloyd's office. We've got one."

"You carry that one all the time. Is there another one in this office?"

I shake my head. "Maurice has one I think."

"Nope. Maurice has to get the one from Lloyd's office."

"Got to be more than two, right?" I say. "Leo has one. And Raquel. She must've had one."

That brings a moment of silence.

"Housekeeping," I say. "Mrs. Dineen."

"Yeah. Her too," Gritch says. "And there's the fire door."

"Someone went out that way," I say. "Why didn't the bells start ringing?"

"Maybe they knew the security code."

Right, I'm thinking — keys, security codes, but no cameras.

"Should have had cameras up there," I say. "The place just got outfitted with security cameras on every floor. Why didn't Leo install them up there?"

"Privacy," says Gritch. "He's a bear for his privacy."

chapter six

First thing in the morning, before toast and coffee, I check in with Lloyd Gruber and Margo Traynor, manager and assistant manager respectively, in Margo's office (Lloyd doesn't like me in his office, he worries that I'll break something). Their reactions are predictable. Margo says, "Oh, my God, that poor woman. Is Leo all right?" And Lloyd says, "Christ, the papers will have a field day!"

He can put his worries on hold for a few hours at least. The morning papers haven't yet picked up the story. I have a look at the *Emblem* in the Lobby Café while Hattie butters my toast.

"It's true, Joe?" She doesn't want to believe it. "Raquel?"

"Yes."

"I can't believe it," she says. "Such a nice person."

"Yes."

"What happened?"

"The police don't know, I don't know, Leo doesn't know. It looks like someone broke in somehow."

"Up *there*? How?"

"That's what they're trying to find out."

"Who would do a thing like that? Such a nice person," Hattie says. "She gave me a Christmas card last year. She said Mr. Alexander always spoke well of my mother."

"Yes, she was very thoughtful," I say. I've just remembered that Raquel wanted me to pick up something for her. Where's the receipt? Still in the pocket of my tux, likely. Leo's not going to feel much like celebrating a birthday tomorrow, but I suppose I'd better attend to it anyway. I promised.

"Is there going to be a funeral?"

"I'll let you know, Hattie," I say. "The police haven't released the body yet."

"Oh, the poor dear," she says. "Such a sweet person."

The uniformed cop who lets me into Leo's closet is impressed with the array. For someone who never went out, Leo has a long clothes rack. I follow Manny Bigalow's old-school rules. "No cufflinks until evening ..." White shirt, charcoal grey suit, striped tie. "Always appropriate ..." Plenty to choose from — black shoes, dark grey socks. I get the socks and fresh underwear from one of the dressers in his bedroom. I've never been in here before. King-size bed faces a big-screen television, reading material on both side tables, an ashtray on the left side, a Martha Stewart magazine on the right. Leo's linen is perfectly sorted and aligned in the dresser drawers. I can sense Raquel's careful attention to detail. And something more. She smoothed these stacks of laundry with her hands before she closed the drawer. I can feel it.

The policeman lets me stare into the living room for a few seconds before he gets twitchy about my presence. The French doors are smashed. Possible point of entry. But from where? The floor below? I'll need to get out on the terrace to see if it's possible, but that isn't going to happen on this trip.

"Sorry, sir. The Crime Scene Unit will be up here pretty soon. They want everything the way they left it."

"Sure, I understand," I say.

Dark sky, no sunrise, rain starting to fall. The air is unnaturally warm and humid. Leo stares through the windshield, doesn't say a word, his mood as dreary as the clouds moving in across the water. When he gets out of the car I give him my arm. He has no strength this morning.

"Did you get anything to eat, sir?"

"My stomach's in a knot," he says.

That makes two of us.

Mooney and Pazzano tag-team the interviewing sessions, me in one room and Leo in another. Pazzano drops in to start things off.

"How long you been working for Leo Alexander?"

"Eight years."

He's shorter than I am, broad in the shoulders, heavy-browed. He shuffles around the room restlessly. I get the feeling he wants to show me he can take care of himself. "How'd he come to hire you?" he asks.

"I was available."

"As his full-time bodyguard?"

"Supposed to be for a week or so.

"Then you took a couple of bullets for him."

"Not on purpose."

"That's pretty loyal for a guy on a short-term contract," he says. "I guess he felt he owed you something, giving you a job, place to live, good salary."

Mooney comes in and they play it together for a while. Mooney sits across from me, hands folded on the table. Pazzano stays on point.

"Pretty much locked himself up there for eight years, right?"

"You could say that."

"Like he was afraid whoever took the shots might come back to do it right."

"You'd have to ask Leo," I say. "He's a private man. He never told me what he was thinking."

"Or who to watch out for?"

"Nope."

"Or why someone might hate him that much?"

"Nope."

"Makes your job a lot harder, doesn't it?"

"These days my job is hotel security."

Mooney finally speaks up. "Except last night," he says. "Last night you were back to being a bodyguard."

The two of them pay Leo a visit and I sit by myself for a while, writing up a statement. I don't much like being in a police station; you're never there because you want to be; you're either suspected of something, or a witness to something, or waiting for the cops to be finished with someone you know. Any minute I'm expecting them to start asking about the ruined plaque, or the switched drivers. I haven't written those details down and I won't bring them up until they do. Withholding information of this kind probably isn't covered by any recognized confidentiality privilege and at some point no doubt I'll pay for it, but right now my concern is strictly for my boss. I haven't told him about the plaque either.

Mooney comes back to resume our conversation.

"Castle in the sky, right?" Mooney says. "Any ideas how the guy got in?"

"Your guess is as good as mine, Detective."

"I figure he must've had an elevator key. Don't you?"

"Could be."

"Unless she let him in herself."

"That's another possibility."

"Which means she would have known him."

"Or her."

"Yeah, right, or her, or *them*."

They trade off. Mooney goes back to Leo, Pazzano steps into the room. He looks like he's run out of questions. He waggles his head a couple of times as if to loosen his thick neck.

"We've got some fighters on the force," he says. "Boxing club."

"You part of that?"

"Oh, yeah."

"What do you fight at," I ask sociably. "One-ninety-five?"

"Ninety-nine," he says. "You?"

"Fighting weight was two fifteen," I say. "I'm up about five, give or take."

He's looking me up and down, wondering. He's about ten years younger, belongs to a boxing club, works out regularly. Only natural for him to speculate.

"You should maybe come down sometime, put the gloves on, give us a free lesson." He rolls his shoulders. "Weed says you used to be pretty good."

"Quit before I lost too many brain cells," I say.

"You ever meet this Vivienne Griese before?"

"Saunders. She said she was going back to her maiden name. And no, I'd never met her before." I've just remembered something. "Her husband was around last night. Outside the hotel. Drunk. Angry."

"Hey now. Pissed-off husbands go to the top of the list," Pazzano says. "'Course, in your boss's case that would make for a long list."

"I wouldn't know, Detective."

"Oh, yeah," he says. "Word is your boss had lots of lady friends. Three wives, at least. Who knows how many mistresses, or unsatisfied wives, or hotel maids for that matter." He pretends to smile. "I hear you were pretty friendly with the deceased yourself. She was giving you Spanish lessons."

"Mostly correcting my pronunciation."

"Teach you any new words?"

"Sure."

"Such as?"

"Let's see, *Puede usted donde el aeropuerto?*"

"What's that?"

"Can you tell me where the airport is?"

He likes that. "Were you two planning a trip?" He glides back in my direction. "You ever see her outside the hotel?"

"You mean socially?"

And now he's in my face. "I mean any way at all, in the kitchen, down in your room. Private lessons so to speak." He smiles a nasty smile. I repress the urge to wipe it off his face. "Anything going on between you and Miss Chimi Changa?"

My turn to smile. "Once fought a guy from East L.A.," I say. "Now *he* was a trash talker. He'd say just about anything to make you lose your temper, nasty remarks about your girlfriends, always mentioned the size of his penis. I never understood that."

He nods his head. "You should really come down sometime. Put on the gloves, just for a 'friendly.'"

"I never thought of it as recreation, Detective. It was my job."

The door opens. Mooney pokes his head in. "You signed that statement?"

"Barring any spelling mistakes, it's as accurate as I can make it," I say. I avoid adding that it's somewhat incomplete.

"Got that motorcycle business in there?"

"Makes for one short paragraph," I say. "You find out the name of the guy who fell?"

Mooney declines to answer. Typical cop. "We'll be talking to your boss for a while longer," he says. "You can wait out there."

When I stand up, Pazzano braces me for a moment. I can see that he's considering things.

"Nice to see you two getting along so well," says Mooney.

I say, "Detective Pazzano was just inviting me down to the Police Boxing Club."

"Some tough guys down there, Grundy," Mooney says with a grin.

"I'm sure there are. Wouldn't have to fight them all, would I?"

"Just the toughest one," he says.

"And who would that be?"

"That would be me," says Pazzano.

"Figured," I say.

A familiar face is coming into the detective's room. Sergeant of Detectives Norman Quincy Weed is wearing his finest green suit. It must be getting close to St. Patrick's Day. He's wearing a brown tie and brown shoes. He looks like a hedge. Norman has his own sense of style.

The detective's room has a new Bunn-O-Matic. They're very proud of it. It grinds fresh beans every time.

"Did you get a coffee?"

"I could use another one," I say. "I didn't get a lot of sleep."

Weed sips, makes a face. He misses the old hotplate. "You want stuff in that?" He offers me a sugar packet.

"Just the caffeine," I say. The coffee tastes fine to me.

He checks out the bruise on my jawbone. "You been brawling again?"

"Chasing shadows," I say. "One of them tried to run me over."

"Where's your boss?" he asks.

"Interview room. It's hit him pretty hard."

"Un hunh," he says. He doesn't sound too sympathetic. "They were close, weren't they?"

"I think he was closer to her than anyone in his world."

"Got any ideas?" he asks.

"Not a clue. It looked like a break-in, all the damage. She was a fighter. She probably threw one of them over the side."

"Anything stolen?"

"I wouldn't know," I say. "They didn't get into the safe. I don't think they were up there to rip off the TV-set."

"Tough place to burglarize," Weed agrees. "You need a special elevator key, don't you?"

"It was a fortress," I say. "See if you can find out how they got in, will you?"

"Not my case, Joe."

"I know that. But when it won't break the rules or kick you back down to crossing guard, you might pass me the word, right?"

"Sure, Joe," he says. Norman's a friend. He's also the ranking detective in this room.

"You identified the other guy?"

"I wouldn't know."

"But he was up there, right?"

"I'll wait till I get a report from my detectives," he says. "After that ... I might not tell you anyway."

"Thanks," I say. "The lead guy, Mooney, he's competent?"

"Oh, yeah," Weed says. "So's his partner. They'll do a good job."

"Leo *really* wants to know who did this."

"Sure he does. And if he asks you to meddle, pretend you didn't hear him."

"I'm just trying to watch his back," I say.

"Mmm hmmm." My response hasn't satisfied him much. "How much do you know about your boss?"

"Not that much. He's a private person."

"Yeah, well, he's got a lot to be private about."

"Meaning?"

He sips his coffee, adds more sugar. "You're working for a pirate, pal," he says. "That's all I'm saying." He tries his new coffee combination and deems it passable. "A real buccaneer."

I remember him saying something similar when I first met him.

Eight years ago.

Second day in the hospital, a sleepy-eyed guy rolls into the room wearing an orange and green tie and a cerulean blue suit. He sits down beside the bed without being asked and helps himself to my juice box.

I say, "Help yourself."

"Were you drinking this?"

"Hadn't started."

"They'll get you another one. The doc tells me you missed getting your ticket punched by about an inch and a half."

"I don't think it was that close."

"Close enough," he says.

"You're a cop."

"Detective," he says. "Norman Weed, middle name Quincy for some reason. My mother was coy on the subject."

"I never got a look at the shooter," I say. "He was over the wall by the time I turned around."

"Yeah. People are either staring at the gun or diving for cover. Your boss says he saw the guy's face but didn't recognize him. A stranger, he says."

"Anyone else get hurt?"

"One guy got dinged in the leg by a ricochet. Not serious. He'll be dancing again in a week."

"Any leads?"

"Yeah, well, that's the thing, isn't it? Whoever it was, he was there to shoot your boss, but your boss isn't very forthcoming."

"About?"

"About why someone would be gunning for him."

"I don't think he was expecting anything that serious."

"Because?"

"He just wanted someone to watch his back."

"Because?"

"Didn't say. I asked him what he was worried about, just so I'd have some idea what to look for, and he said he'd had a phone call."

"That's it?"

"That's it. I assumed it was a threat of some kind but he wasn't specific."

"Mysterious guy."

"Wish I could help you. First time anybody took a shot at me."

"Five shots. Three of them drew blood."

"Suit was too good for me anyway."

He stands up and puts my empty juice box back on the tray. "Here's my card if anything comes to mind."

"All right."

"Nice talking to you."

"You know Manny Bigalow?" I ask him.

"Who's he?"

"Sells suits," I say. "He told me never to wear bright blue. It doesn't go with anything."

"Yeah, well, I have my own sense of style," says Norman Quincy Weed.

Leo is coming out of the interview room. He's not the same man I saw doing the tango with the classy divorcée last night. He's running low on vital juices, folding inside himself, not as tall.

Leo and Weed don't shake hands.

"Sorry for your loss," Weed says to Leo.

"She was just the best person," Leo says.

Pazzano is standing in the background, watching us. Mooney is already at his desk, transcribing notes, making phone calls.

I take Leo's arm and start to move him toward the exit. I can feel his shoulders shaking.

Margo Traynor is waiting to escort us to the Ambassador Suite. She has Leo's messages collated according to import and substance, all neatly clipped together. "Nothing that can't wait," she says. "And I'd be happy to attend to any responses you don't want to make personally."

"Either of my sons call?"

"No, sir. They may not have heard. Would you like me to get in touch with them?"

"It can wait." Leo has a look around the suite, his home away from home. "They did a passable job with the decor, don't you think?" He checks out the bedrooms, the new fixtures in the master bath, doesn't appear impressed. "Fifty million doesn't buy a lot these days," he says wearily.

Margo says, "The police have assured me they will be finished with the ... finished with your floor by this afternoon, sir."

"I can't go back up there," he says. "Not for a while."

"Of course. But we'll be able to collect anything you might need and have it brought down here."

"Joseph can do that," he says. "I'll give him a list. I want him to check things out."

"In the meantime," Margo says, "Anything else you might need ..."

"Thank you, Ms. Traynor," Leo says. "May I say that I'm grateful you handled this yourself. I don't think I could have borne Lloyd Gruber's ministrations just now."

"He did ask me to convey —"

"Of course," says Leo. "Tell him, tell him whatever you want to tell him."

He crosses the room, stares out at the building across the street. Margo looks in my direction. I try to gesture that she's done well, that things will settle down, that Leo's okay. I'm not sure I manage to get that across. I'm even less certain it's the truth.

"Thank you for stocking the bar," he says.

"I wasn't sure what —" Margo begins.

"You covered all the bases."

She finally manages to complete a sentence. "May I offer my own sympathy for this terrible loss."

Leo looks at her with what might have been an attempt at a brave smile but comes off as a grimace of pain.

"I appreciate it," he says.

Margo gives me a glance that suggests general helplessness. I show her to the door.

"He'll be okay," I whisper.

"Everybody's shaken up," she says. "Downstairs. They'll do anything. Even Lloyd."

"Best thing is, keep the place running like nothing's happened."

Margo leaves.

Leo pours himself a drink. I wait for orders. It's a long wait. Two minutes is a long time if you're waiting for someone to speak, if you're watching a man in pain pull himself together by an exercise of dogged will.

"Is there anything I can do for you, sir?"

I can see the tendons in his fingers and I worry that he's going to crush his whisky glass, but his voice when he finally speaks is as cold as death. "Yes, there is, Joseph. You can find whoever did this ... thing."

"The police —"

"The police will do what policemen do," he says. "*If* they catch the bastard they'll charge him with second-degree murder which will probably get knocked down to manslaughter or aggravated assault and he'll be a free man in seven years if the courts are feeling really tough that day."

"I suppose that's possible."

"I'm seventy-four years old, Joseph. I may not *have* seven years to wait. Otherwise I could plan how I'd kill the sonofabitch as he walked out of prison." He has a sip of Scotch and smiles at me. It isn't a friendly smile. "You think I'm joking?"

I choose my words with care. "I think you're understandably angry and that you want whoever did this to be punished."

"I don't want them punished. I want them dead."

"One of them is."

"Good," he says. "It's a start."

chapter seven

Rachel gives me a sad smile when I come into the office. She looks likes she wants to give me a hug. I'm not in a huggy mood but I open my arms enough for her to get close, accept a quick squeeze.

"You okay, slugger?" she asks.

"Oh, sure," I say.

She steps back and checks me out. "We had the same name you know," she says. "Raquel, Rachel. It's an ancient name."

"You should hear it in Hebrew," Gritch says. He's sitting in his corner. "How's the old bugger doing?" he asks.

"He's okay I guess. His doctor came by, checked him over, gave him something to help him sleep tonight."

"Hit him hard," Rachel says.

"He kept saying how we should have gone straight

up, that she was waiting for him to come home, that he shouldn't have been downstairs listening to music."

"Wouldn't have made any difference," Gritch says.

"Maybe not."

"Seriously," he says. "I was talking to one of the uniforms. The pretty one?"

"Chinese?"

"That's the one. Melody Chan. Nice kid. Wants to be a detective."

"What did she have to say?"

"Says it probably happened between midnight and one."

"She tell you anything else?"

"Well, I had to chin for a while, bits and pieces, she's pretty sharp, had her eyes open. She says there were at least two intruders, maybe three."

"She knows this how?"

"She doesn't *know* it, she thinks it. *Maybe*. Says she saw footprints from the terrace, dirt tracked in, and a different set with no dirt. Maybe. She was just spitballing. Cop talk."

"Regular Chatty Cathy," says Rachel. "You must've turned on the old Gritchfield charm."

"Hey, she was stuck guarding an empty hallway. We were comparing notes. Technically, I was first on the scene."

"What the hell were they after?"

"Beats me," Gritch says. "If they were looking for something, they either found it in a hurry or quit looking. They didn't go down the hall."

"Maybe they were after her," says Rachel. "Lot of

talk this morning. The general opinion is she was more than his housekeeper."

"She was," I say.

"Ahh," says Rachel.

"Do me a favour," I ask them both, "check out where the brothers were. They both had invitations to the dinner, neither one showed up."

"Not a lot of togetherness," Rachel says. "We had twenty-seven at our last family gathering, and not everyone could make it."

"They all get along?" Gritch asks.

"Heck no," she says, "but they came. It's family."

Housekeeping is located on the third floor, east side, close to the service elevators — supplies, equipment, lockers and dressing rooms for the maids and cleaning staff, and Mrs. Dineen's office, from which she rules every aspect of the Lord Douglas's domestic management. It isn't a part of the hotel I have need to visit often.

Two women in uniform are emerging from their cloister at the end of a corridor. The murmured conversation can only be about one subject.

"Hi," I say. "Is Mrs. Dineen in?"

"She's there," says a woman whose name is, I think, Christine.

"It's Christine, right?"

"Mr. Grundy," she says in reply. "Yes. We've met. Twice."

"Better than my average," I say. "Usually takes me four meetings to put a name to a face. I'm not all that quick on the uptake. I'm sorry, I don't know your friend's name."

The other woman has more important things to attend to than loitering in the hall with an interloper. She's already headed for the service elevators.

"That's Tricia," says Christine, who is moving past me. She looks over her shoulder toward Mrs. Dineen's closed door and I know that the last thing on earth she wants is for that door to open.

I follow her to the elevators where Tricia (I'm repeating the name in my head in a conscious effort to memorize it) is checking supplies and consulting a list of room numbers with notations of checkouts and special requests — extra towels, more coffee filters.

"Hi, Tricia," I say. "I'm Joe Grundy, you've probably seen me prowling the halls. You know what happened last night, I guess."

Tricia's hair is cut short and square across the front; she keeps her voice down but speaks clearly. "We don't *know* anything, for sure. Raquel was killed up in the penthouse. That's all."

"Must be a hundred rumours going around," I say.

"Just gossip," says Christine.

"Mrs. Dineen doesn't encourage gossip," says Tricia.

"I'm investigating a murder," I say, although I'm certain Mooney and Pazzano would characterize my intrusion otherwise. "What sounds like gossip right now could be helpful later on. May I talk to you for a minute?"

"Get on," Tricia says, as the elevator doors open.

The two women wheel their service carts aboard and I join them.

"Nine," Tricia says. "In back." She presses 9. Christine stares at the numbers climbing. Tricia looks directly at me. "Can you be trusted?" she asks.

"Yes."

"I don't mean as a human being," she says. "That would be asking too much. I mean can you be trusted that as far as Vera Dineen is concerned, this meeting never took place?"

"Scout's honour," I say.

"I'd prefer something a bit more binding," she says. "My brother was a scout. I wouldn't trust him as far as I could toss him."

"Raquel was my friend," I say. "I liked her."

I hear a sudden sob from Christine and see her burying her face in both hands. The rear doors of the car open and Tricia ushers us into an empty corridor. "This way," she says.

A *cul de sac* around the corner, a small window facing the parking garage across the street, a table and a pair of plastic chairs, and an ashtray, hidden (poorly) behind a sad, potted cactus on the sill. Christine sits in one of the chairs. She is wiping her eyes with a wadded Kleenex. Tricia remains standing, facing me.

"Tell us what happened, first," she says. She lights a menthol cigarette in defiance of at least three of Mrs. Dineen's edicts. I take it as an affirmation that she's decided to trust me.

"Leo and I went to the award dinner at eight last night, got back to the penthouse around two a.m. Raquel was dead, in the kitchen. It looked like she'd been stabbed. Things were broken. The police said she put up a fight."

Christine sobs again.

"That's all?" Tricia asks.

"There was evidence that people were on the terrace, and someone ran down the fire stairs, but we don't know who that was, or if they had anything to do with anything. And there was a body at the bottom of the Warburton excavation. It could have fallen from the terrace. I don't know that for a fact. The police haven't released any details."

"Did they do anything to her?" Christine asks.

"Do anything?"

"Was she ... molested?"

"No. I don't think so," I say. "No, I'm sure not. It looked like a break-in. Maybe she surprised some burglars."

"That's good," says Christine. "Not *good*, but good. She was a very moral person."

"She was living with him," Tricia says.

"I know," says Christine, "but she really loved him, and it was the best she could get."

"I'm not judging her," says Tricia. She exhales a plume of smoke. "I don't blame her. She's not the first maid got invited to the penthouse."

"She's the first one who moved in," says Christine firmly. "Five years. More. It was serious, not like the other ones."

"So," I say. "What's the gossip?"

"Her husband murdered her."

"Her husband?"

"She was married. He's an American, he was never around, but he wrote letters here, he made phone calls. He was after money."

"She was giving him money?"

"Maybe. He'd stop harassing her for a while, then it'd start up again. Once she moved upstairs the letters didn't come to Housekeeping any more, so I don't know. They might have been delivered straight up, if there were any."

"Do you know his name?"

"Ramon or something," says Christine.

"It was Ramon." Tricia is certain. "Ramon Mendez. The postmarks were California."

"The gossip is that her husband came here and killed her?"

"He went up there to kill her and Leo. Catch them in bed together. The Unwritten Law. Very Spanish," says Tricia. "A question of honour."

"Have either of you ever seen him? Know what he looks like?"

"Not a clue," says Tricia.

"She had his picture in her locker for a while," Christine says. "She took it down after a while. I never got a good look at it. He had dark hair. He was wearing a suit."

"Any other rumours circulating?" I ask.

"Mrs. Dineen did it," says Christine, then immediately clamps a hand over her mouth and giggles, then sobs.

"Wouldn't put it past her," says Tricia.

"Why would she do a thing like that?" I'd like to know.

Tricia laughs. "Spite," she says. "She was Number One, for a while. He didn't live here then, but he visited a lot."

"Mrs. Dineen and Leo?" I'm shaking my head at the image.

"There was a time ..." says Christine.

"Lady Muck," says Tricia. "Queen of towel cupboard."

"And Raquel supplanted her?"

"Oh, she was supplanted long before Raquel showed up." Tricia butts her smoke in the hidden ashtray. Grabs a can of air freshener and gives the air a spritz. "What was the next one called?"

"I don't remember," Christine says. "Vera fired her."

"I guess my boss was more of a ladies man than I knew," I say.

"Ladies man?" Tricia snorts. "He thought he was a sultan or something. Housekeeping was his harem."

Mrs. Dineen reminds me of a nun who used to smack my knuckles with a yardstick. Sister Clarissa was a world-class knuckle-smacker; humourless, chilly, and fully informed of all your secret sins. Vera Dineen has that same look. When she sees fit to spare me a frosty glance, I'm certain I missed a spot shaving.

"Mr. Grundy? Something I can do for you?"

"Yes, Mrs. Dineen, there is. You've already spoken to the police, I suppose?"

"Oh, yes, they were here."

"Checking on who had access to the penthouse?"

"That's correct. I explained to them that I personally hadn't had occasion to visit Mr. Alexander's private chambers for some time."

"I've been trying to add up how many special elevator keys there are."

"To my knowledge there are seven. One held by the manager, Mr. Gruber, one in your possession, one here in Housekeeping, Mr. Alexander kept two, one for himself and one for Mrs. Mendez." She gives me a pointed look. "You knew she was married?"

"I didn't know her all that well," I say. "Nothing about her personal life."

"I never met her husband," says Mrs. Dineen. "I believe he lives in Spain, or Mexico, or somewhere. I take it they were estranged, had been for some time. She no longer wore her wedding ring."

"Oh."

"Was there something else, Mr. Grundy? I'm quite busy."

"Let's see. Lloyd has one, Security has one, Housekeeping one, Mr. Alexander, two. That makes five. You said *seven*?"

"I believe I did."

"And the other two?"

"Mr. Alexander's sons, Theodore and Leon."

"Oh. That's a surprise. I didn't think they were all that welcome upstairs."

"Perhaps not. Nevertheless ..." She starts rearranging her desk, straightening already straight piles. "If there's nothing else ..."

"No. That's it. Thank you for your time, Mrs. Dineen."

Leon? I always thought his name was Lenny.

Gritch has the same reaction when I see him in the lobby. "*Leon*?" he says. "You ever see him up there? You ever see either of them up there?"

We start heading back toward the office. I should eat some lunch. My stomach isn't happy.

"You'd think the wives at least would've jumped at the chance to go to a fancy-dress ball," he says. "Get their hair done, hire babysitters, get out of Burnaby or wherever."

"One lives in West Van, one in North Van."

"Gee, lemme guess," says Gritch. "Theodore is high up the British Properties, and 'Leon' is on the wrong side of the Capilano."

"Hard to believe they're brothers," I say. "They don't look anything like each other."

"Half brothers," Gritch says. "Theo's from the first marriage. Lenny's arrival was, shall we say, unsanctioned."

More evidence, if I needed any, that I know precious little about the man I work for. In fact, I may know less than anyone in the hotel.

"You find out why they didn't put in an appearance?"

"Theo's out of town, according to his wife. Las Vegas or L.A. Playgrounds of the rich and famous. Probably accompanied by his 'design consultant,'" he throws in. "Mrs. Theo sounded a wee bit sarcastic when she mentioned that part."

"The 'design consultant' is female?"

"Impression I got," he says.

"What about Lenny?"

"Ah, that too is interesting. Lenny, or Leon if you prefer, has moved out of the hacienda, current whereabouts unknown. Wife Jackie says as long as the support cheques show up, she couldn't care less."

"I guess I'll have to track him down."

"Lenny's a thug but I can't see him doing something like that," says Gritch.

"The rumour, in Housekeeping anyway, is Raquel's husband did it."

"Husband, hunh?" He shrugs philosophically. "He living nearby?"

"American. California. Ramon Mendez. A couple of the maids say he was sending her threatening letters, hitting her up for money."

"Yeah, yeah, that could be," Gritch says. "She lets him in, figures they're gonna sort it out, pay him off, or cut him off, turns into a domestic, violence ensues."

"Another rumour is that Vera Dineen did it."

"Ha!" Gritch barks. "Lordy, do they hate her guts up there or what?"

"Did you know she once had a thing with Leo?"

"Oh, yeah, I heard that. Ancient history, but it lasted a while," he says.

There is a delicious aroma lingering in the office that gets my stomach talking to me again. Grundy, the starving sleuth, is almost certain there's something to eat in here. Rachel recently hired a bookkeeper, a woman named Mariah who hails from a place where the waters are bright blue and the sun shines every day except during hurricane season. Mariah wears bangles and vivid colours and Gritch likes it that she doesn't look the least bit Presbyterian. She also makes the neatest numbers I've ever seen. Mariah shows up once a week for a couple of hours to keep JG Security solvent, legal, up-to-date, and square with the taxman. Something else I always planned on doing. Sometimes she brings food.

"Anything that needs my attention?" I ask Rachel. Don't want to look too desperate.

"Not a thing, boss man," Rachel says. "We've got a convention of florists. How much damage can they do?"

"You'd be surprised," Gritch says.

"Joe?" Mariah is crooking one of her tangerine fingernails at me. "Excuse me for saying, my dear, but you really must start depositing your pay cheques and not leave them lying around."

"I keep meaning to do that," I say.

"There's a new bank down in the mini-mall. No excuse. It is very bad for the accounts."

"Never spends a nickel," Gritch says. "Parsimonious as a Dundee bank clerk."

My stomach rumbles are clearly audible. Also, my mouth is watering. I open the office refrigerator. "What's this?" I ask in all innocence.

Mariah looks up from her perfectly aligned columns. "Jerk ribs," she says. "Try one. I don't make them too spicy for first-timers." She has a wicked smile.

I have a bite. The metabolism signals that I've done a wise thing. "Delicious," I say. They are. Also *muy picante.* I can feel beads of sweat breaking out on my forehead. "Lordy! How spicy do you make them for veterans?"

"Lethal," says Mariah.

"Don't dribble on your tie," says Rachel.

"Right," I say. "I've got errands to run."

"Such as?" Gritch wants to know.

"Pick up the award we forgot to collect last night, and while I'm doing that I thought I might drop by the limo company and see about the mixup with our driver."

"Let the police handle it," Rachel says.

"He hasn't told the police," Gritch says.

"You haven't?" Rachel is looking at me with disapproval.

"Probably some disgruntled innkeeper making a comment," I say. "Not everyone there was a fan."

Rachel, Gritch, and Mariah are all looking at me with stern expressions.

"Okay, all right. I probably should have mentioned."

"*Definitely* should have mentioned," Rachel says.

"And should I find that the organizers have no reasonable explanation for why Leo's award was trashed, I'll hand it over to detectives Mooney and Pazzano. And should the mixup with the limo drivers turn out to have sinister implications, I'll be certain to pass that along as well. Otherwise, I won't complicate their investigations with inconsequentials."

"You buying this cow-pucky?" Rachel asks Gritch.

"Ankle-deep and rising," he says. "You'll be up to your knees by suppertime."

"Any more of those ribs?" I ask.

"Will you promise to deposit your pay this month?" Mariah is insistent.

"I used to run this joint," I say. "Remember, Gritch?"

"Those were the days," he says.

chapter eight

The two construction men are taking their mandatory coffee break before tackling whatever job they've been assigned. They note my arrival with the considered interest of men with not much else to look at.

"Hi," I start. "Name's Joe Grundy. I do security at the hotel next door." I offer a handshake to show that we're all on the same team.

"Hey," says the older one, a big man with a moustache which he obviously cares for.

"Hi," says the other guy. He has a half-eaten cruller that he has to transfer to his coffee cup hand in order to shake mine. I can feel the sugar on my fingers.

"Cops all finished down there?"

"Finally," he says, licking his thumb. "Didn't get the body down until ten, spent another couple hours taking measurements."

"Don't know what they were measuring," says the big guy. "They don't have a tape measure stretches that high."

"I almost got run down by someone on a motorcycle who was inside here last night," I say. "Mind if I have a quick look before you lock up?"

"Better wear this," says the big man. He hands me his hardhat. "I've got about ten minutes worth of coffee left."

"Easy," says the other guy.

"Appreciate it," I say. "Any idea how he might've got in?"

"People been camping out down there. Construction company's had to run them off more'n once."

"Somebody sawed through this chain," says the big man. He shows me where one link has had a chunk removed and used as a hook to keep the length together. The missing piece was masked with a wrapping of black tape.

"Wasn't the jumper," says the other guy. "He got in a different way."

I step through the gate and start down the incline. The ramp is wide enough for massive heavy equipment and I doubt that the police learned much from a chewed up surface that has obviously supported a few thousand trips by haulers, cement mixers, backhoes, and earthmovers. A Harley FatBoy wouldn't have made much impression, let alone a dirt bike.

It's a lot easier finding a path in daylight. The area around the pylon is still ringed with Do Not Cross tape but I can get close enough to see the blood smears on the rebar spears.

I skirt the police zone and make my way around the perimeter. In the far corner of the pit, near a careless pile of plywood forms, I can see grease spots on the concrete pad, and narrow tread marks, a little too wide for a ten-speed, just about right for a dirt bike.

Back of the pile, plywood sheets have been braced together into a crude A-frame. Inside are a bedroll, a duffel bag, cigarette butts in an empty paint can, fast-food wrappers. Home sweet home, for someone.

I should probably leave a thorough search to the police, but since they didn't bother to check this far into the site, and in all probability the homeless person who's been squatting here doesn't have any connection to what happened atop the adjacent mountain, and as long as I'm rationalizing, I might as well have a quick look at what's in the place. The concrete floor is covered with layers of flattened cardboard boxes. A metal toolbox contains a hacksaw, electrician's tape, pliers, a hammer, and nails. The duffel holds wads of not particularly sweet-smelling laundry which I don't feel like pawing through. I upend the thing and dump the contents onto the cardboard carpeting. A couple of paperbacks, a web belt, grubby sneakers, and the last item, a torn and twisted length of ribbon threaded through what looks to be a U.S. Army Bronze Star. The ribbon is knotted to a white plastic fob of some sort, possibly a small flashlight. On closer inspection I recognize it as a MedicAlert tag. I pocket both items.

"Someone's been squatting down there," I tell the men as I return the hardhat.

"Streiner should be collecting rent," he says.

The Royal Lotus Ballroom is in the ultra modern (and somewhat garish to my taste) new waterfront palace called The Singapore Garden, one of the baubles in a string of sparklers circling the Pacific Rim under the banner of a Hong Kong-based chain called Peak Haven Hotels. I have to admit that it's an impressive joint. Bigger than the Lord Douglas by at least three hundred suites, indoor fountains, heliport, charter boats, "Olympic-size" swimming pool, escalators at every rise. One step removed from a trip to Disneyworld.

The concierge, an immensely pleasant man named Ko, tells me that Mr. Tully can be found in the Events Coordinator's offices, a mere two escalators up and a few hundred metres along a skylighted walkway with a grand view of the inner harbour. I am pleased to find that Mr. Tully is exactly where he's supposed to be. He has company.

Detective Mooney is holding the plaque. He's holding it by the corners. He looks me over as I come through the door.

"Look who's here," he says. "Mr. Tully tells me you saw this thing last night."

Busted. "I figured it was a prank from some disgruntled innkeeper," I say.

"Uh hunh." He sounds unconvinced. "Pretty elaborate prank. Big hole through the eye."

Pazzano steps forward. "Heard you were in a hurry."

"Leo told me he was ready to leave."

"Yeah? Word is you kinda rushed him outta here."

"People were crowding around."

Pazzano comes closer. "You grabbed a cab."

"That's right." It occurs to me that since I knew this was all going to come out I should have been better prepared. "The limo driver wasn't the same one who brought us. I probably overreacted."

"Okay," Mooney begins. "Let me get this straight: You see that your boss's award's been trashed and that's enough to get you hustling him out of here, then you see that your driver's been switched and that's enough to make you look for alternate transportation, and then you get home and find out your boss's girlfriend's been murdered and somebody did a half-gainer off the balcony." He smiles. I hate it when cops smile. "And it didn't occur to you that those things might be connected?"

"It has since occurred to me," I say. Better to look slow than devious.

"I bet." Pazzano isn't buying it either.

"I wanted to tell Leo first," I say, deciding to at least state the obvious. "My first responsibility is to his safety. *If* these occurrences were somehow connected to what happened to Raquel I would have, and Leo would have *insisted* that I report it to you."

"Oh, that's okay then," says Mooney. I hate it when cops are sarcastic. "Sure, because we're merely involved in a homicide investigation, whereas *you* are concerned with protecting your boss's reputation. Am I right?"

"I take your point," I say, with as much rue as I can muster for the occasion.

"You've got a good friend down at the shop," Mooney says. "Otherwise I might consider making your life miserable for a few hours. Maybe even overnight."

"I appreciate your restraint," I say.

"Don't be a wiseass," Pazzano throws in. I get the distinct impression he'd like to go a round with me. I don't like the odds; he has a badge, a gun, and handcuffs. "Weed says you're not to be trusted."

Mooney moves in. He's probably had to defuse similar situations involving his partner. He holds the plaque out for my inspection. "You got any idea who did this?"

"No."

"If you *get* any idea who did this what'll you be doing with the information?"

"I'll be passing it on to you," I say.

"You check into the missing limo driver?"

"With no satisfaction, so far," I admit.

"Well then," he says, patting me on the shoulder. "How be you let us take it from here? Okay?"

"Certainly," I say.

"Good," he says. "We understand each other."

Pazzano glares at me for a long moment before turning for the door.

"Did Weed really say I wasn't to be trusted?"

Pazzano looks back. "What he said was, 'give him enough rope and he'll hang himself.'"

"Doesn't sound like you guys are giving me much rope."

"Hang yourself somewhere else," Pazzano says.

Young Mr. Tully shrugs at me. I think he's grateful that the plaque, the cops, and, shortly, me, are no longer to be his problem. He busies himself with other matters — shuffling message slips, shifting papers, checking the wall-mounted schedule of upcoming events — and looks a bit startled when he finds me still standing in his office.

"Don't suppose you found a drill press?" I ask him.

"A what?"

"Something to make a hole in that thing."

"No, sir, I did not." A slight note of annoyance in Mr. Tully's voice. I expect he thinks he's free to treat me the way Mooney and Pazzano did.

"It's solid brass isn't it?"

"Bronze, I think." He gives his full attention to next week's responsibilities.

"Hard material."

"I expect," he says. "We didn't supply the award, you understand."

"Was it in your care?"

"Not technically." Now he sounds tired of the entire affair, and especially of me. "The police have already asked these questions."

"I'm sure they did," I say. "I'm just wondering if you recall what happened to the award between the time it was presented to Mr. Alexander, and the time it was found in the speaker's lectern?"

"I'm not sure."

"Okay," I say, and sit down, cross my legs, smile. "What did Leo do with it after he received it?"

He sighs the deep sigh of someone who has much more important things to do. "I believe he put it down on the head table near his plate."

"And then shortly after that, the dancing started and most people moved away from the head table."

"Yes." He isn't going to indulge me much longer.

"And that's when the servers would have started clearing away the plates and cutlery."

"Yes."

"Who was in charge of the cleanup?"

"The event was catered in-house, but there was extra staff taken on for the night."

"All of it coordinated by this office I guess."

"Yes."

"And you're the one who noticed that the plaque had been tampered with because you're the one who came to tell me about it. Which would mean that you were pretty close to the action in the dining room, where the tables were being cleared. And seeing as how you were the coordinator, you probably took a personal interest in the plaque, wanting to make certain it was wrapped up properly, not lost, given to its rightful owner before he left the building."

He's remembered something. "There was a box."

"A box."

"A presentation box, lined with I don't know, velvet probably. After Mr. Alexander and his date left the room I put the plaque in the box …"

"And?"

"And …" Finally, something that will end this annoyance. "I gave it to Mr. Westerby."

"And he is?"

His look suggests that I should know this. "Mr. Westerby is president of the Vancouver Hoteliers Association."

"Thank you very much," I say, getting to my feet, an action which brings noticeable relief. "And where might I locate Mr. Westerby?"

"I would imagine you will find him at *his* hotel, Mr. Grundy. The Orchard Inn."

I head for the door. "That's in …?"

"Park Royal, of course."

"Of course it is. Thank you for your help," I say.

The Orchard Inn was built in the 1950s but if the fire codes allowed it I'm sure the Orchard would have thatched roofs to go with what looks to be a rambling, half-timber, wattle and daub structure dating from the days of Oliver Cromwell. It nestles with a proprietary air beside the Capilano River, which this time of year runs high and wide.

Adrian Westerby wears red suspenders and rolls his sleeves up just below his elbows, the better to show his meaty forearms and reinforce the image of a homespun publican. The gold Rolex on his left wrist suggests otherwise. When I saw him last night he was wearing a tux almost as fine as mine.

"Didn't look anything like him," he says to me. "I told the missus it looked like the profile of Uriah Heep." He pronounces the word *profeel*.

"I'm sure he was touched by the gesture," I say.

"Well," he says, "we independents have to show the flag from time to time. Mine doesn't look much like me either."

He points to a similar plaque behind the check-in counter. His *profeel* is flattering.

"I just wanted to know what you did with it after Mr. Tully gave it to you."

"It hasn't gone missing, has it?"

"No, nothing like that."

"I believe I … yes, I gave it to his chauffeur. At least he said he was Leo's chauffeur."

"Oh. Do you remember if the man had a ponytail?"

"Yes, that's right, swarthy fellow, black moustache, silly little switch down his back. Don't know why men wear their hair inappropriately. Probably a cultural thing, don't you think."

"Possibly," I say. "Thanks for your time."

"My pleasure," he says. He's following me out to the parking lot, looking around to make sure we're alone. "There's a rumour going around that one of the Lord Douglas's maids was killed last night. Is that true?"

No point denying it. "Yes."

"Is the ponytailed man a suspect?"

"I couldn't say, Mr. Westerby. The police are in charge of that investigation. I'm looking into another matter entirely."

"Another matter which involves the driver."

"Not necessarily. It's about the plaque. Someone defaced it between the time the dancing started and we were ready to leave. Not much more than an hour. I'm trying to find out how many people might have handled it."

"Defaced it how?"

"Drilled a hole in it."

"Oh, dear," he says. "So silly. Leo wouldn't have hung it anyway. I've known him a long time. He might have tossed it into a closet, if he didn't throw it out with the trash."

"You do know him," I say.

The man behind the counter isn't old enough to be either Mr. Austin or Mr. Davies. I suppose he might be the great-grandson of one of them. Austin-Davies Tobacconists has been in business for quite a while.

"Hi," I say. "Raquel asked me to pick up a package for her. I have the receipt. It's a birthday present."

"It certainly is," he says. "Twenty-five of each." The cigars have handsome gold bands on them. "The bands are specially made of course. The cigars themselves are Mr. Alexander's personal selection."

Gold and blue bands on one side, gold and pink on the other side. The gold lettering on the blue bands says IT'S A BOY! and on the pink bands, IT'S A GIRL!

"Would you be kind enough to convey our heartfelt congratulations to Mr. Alexander?"

"Certainly."

Young Mr. Austin (or Davies) is so proud of the presentation, I haven't the heart to tell him that it's no longer appropriate. I smile as best I can.

Not content with one death, the murderous bastard, whoever it might be, has compounded the horror. I don't know if Leo can handle it. If I deliver the gift he's going to be devastated. If I don't, he's not going to know. Sticking the box in a drawer and pretending it doesn't exist seems like the kinder choice. Unless he already knows. I don't really have a wide range of options. Besides, Raquel deserves to have her last request honoured.

I'm sitting in a parked car with the engine off, a box of cigars on the passenger seat, watching people walk by; couples, window shopping, holding hands. Most of them look content, perhaps even happy. I don't often procrastinate. My usual approach to a situation is to take care of things as soon as I can so they don't nag at me. Get it over with. Move on. But I'm dragging my feet on this one. Admit it. I don't want to face Leo.

Maurice is a busy man these days, arranging theatre tickets, group tours, special orders. He didn't have a lot of time to devote to my problem.

"I got the runaround from Ultra Limousine Service," Maurice says. "They said any complaints would have to be made to Mr. Goodier who wasn't available. They don't give out information over the phone."

"Even to their best customers?"

"I told them who was calling. They said they'd need some authorization. I told them their attitude was unacceptable. They said I should take it up with Mr. Alexander."

"And you said the complaint was being lodged by Mr. Alexander?"

"Wrong Alexander," says Maurice. "*Theodore* Alexander. His company."

"Sorry, Maurice. I didn't know," I say.

"Theo swung an exclusive contract with the old man a few years back. His name isn't on it. Somebody named Goodier's the manager, but Theo owns it, fleet, licence, garage, the works." He holds his palms up and open, out of options, waiting for orders.

"I'll take it up with Theo, personally," I say. "Thanks, Maurice."

"How's the boss man doing?"

"He'll be okay."

"Yeah, he's a tough old bird," says Maurice.

"I can't talk to you now, Ms. Hiscox," I say. "I've got a job."

I can see Gritch behind his fern giving me an elaborate shrug. Not his fault. She was waiting in the lobby.

"So have I," she says.

"At cross-purposes." I start walking, just to be going somewhere. "Talk to the police."

The mezzanine looks like a possible escape route — displays, boutiques, espresso bar. I seem to recall a Staff Only back door. I head up the wide staircase. The new carpet is striped. Admit it, I'm running for cover.

"I'm not interested in the investigation," she says, matching my stride. She can probably run, too. "I want to know how he's dealing with it."

"I can't help you," I say.

"The last time it happened, he was a suspect, did you know that?"

Halfway up the staircase and nowhere to go. I can feel my shoulders slump. The first words through my brain are, oh Lord, now what?

"The last time *what* happened?" I manage to keep the gloom out of my voice. I think.

"The last time one of his women was killed." She is standing in front of me. She has my complete attention.

Her smile is frosty, almost as cold as her eyes. "You didn't know? Well, not surprising, I suppose. It's not something he advertises."

A party of seven happy travellers descends without a care in the world. I lower my voice. "If you have something to say, why don't you just say it?"

"Why don't you buy me an expensive coffee?" she suggests. This time she leads the way.

Hers is a tall latté. Mine is dark Colombian, double-double. I need the caffeine, and the sugar. We sit in a far corner by the window. Nobody really cares about us anyway. Still, she leans across the table, her voice conspiratorial. She's enjoying this.

"He ever mention his second wife? Lorraine?"

"I heard she passed away," I say.

"He was almost arrested in connection with her 'passing away,'" she says. "Did he tell you that?"

"What was the charge?"

"Oh, he was never charged. He had a good lawyer; the Calgary cops didn't have a case. But he was a suspect. Still is, far as I know. Case was never solved."

"How did she die?"

"Yes, well that's the eerie part, isn't it? She was stabbed. In the back." She has a sip. "And the front." She has a dapper foam moustache. She'll probably twirl it in a minute.

"When was this?"

"Nineteen eighty-two. Spring of '82. Back when he was pretending to be a cattle rancher."

"Ms. Hiscox," I begin.

"Why don't you call me Roselyn?"

"Ms. Hiscox," I reiterate most firmly. "None of this has anything to do with me. I have a hotel to watch over. The police are in charge of the investigation and I've been told to keep my nose out of it."

"You aren't curious?"

"Not even a little," I say. "My general feeling is one of aggravation. Leo was with me when what happened, happened."

"How convenient," she says. "He managed to be somewhere else the other time as well."

"Do you know anything the Calgary cops don't?"

"Not a thing. If he was involved he covered his tracks perfectly."

"And I suppose all of that will be in your book."

"All that, and all *this* as well," she says, taking in the entire hotel with a sweep of her manicured hand. "You've got to admit, Joe, this is going to make a great final chapter."

chapter nine

"The Presbyterians" aren't necessarily Presbyterian or even churchgoers. They are four competent men from Midnight Security that Rachel put on long-term contract shortly after most of my original staff disintegrated a year ago in an unforeseen cluster of calamities that saw two of them dead, and a third hired away by a less dysfunctional organization. The guy who's guarding the door to the Ambassador Suite is named Brian Bester and I know for a fact that he's not Presbyterian because I distinctly overheard him say "Jesus Mary and Joseph!" when he heard about Raquel. Strictly a Catholic expletive.

"He alone?" I ask.

"He's got a roomful, Joe," Brian says. "Lawyers, mostly."

"He eat today?"

"Food came up. I don't know how much of it he ate."

"Okay. You want to take a break for a while? Check in with Rachel?"

"Sure," he says.

"Oh, one thing," I say, reaching into my pocket. "You know your way around a computer, right?"

"I guess," he says modestly.

"Check this out for me, will you?" I untie the medal and hand over the MedicAlert tag.

Brian has a quick look. "Sure," he says, "plugs right into a USB port."

"Hattie has one," I say. "She's diabetic. It'll have all kinds of information inside."

"Anything in particular you want?" he asks.

"Just the name, Brian. I want to return it to its rightful owner."

There are six people in the suite with Leo — four men, two women. I recognize one of them, Leo's lawyer, Winston Mickela. This must be a serious gathering; Winston doesn't cross the street for under five thousand dollars. Leo is sitting at a table covered with documents, surrounded by suits. He looks relieved to see me lurking in the doorway and excuses himself.

"Making any progress, Joseph?" He leads me into the second bedroom, the one he isn't sleeping in.

"This is something Raquel wanted me to pick up." I hand him the package. "For your birthday."

He smiles tightly. "Oh. My birthday."

"A special order."

He opens the lid and stares for a long moment at the special bands, and then suddenly he moans like a wounded animal. I recognize the sound. I once made a noise much like it when a very large man hit me in the kidney and drove me to my knees.

"Oh, God!" he says. He slumps onto the edge of the bed, holding the open cigar box on his lap. Tears are making dark spots on the light candela wrappers. "I told her I was too old." His voice is choked. "It wasn't going to happen. She said she would say a prayer to some saint, the patron saint of impossibility or ... something."

I put my hand on his shoulder. "I'm so sorry."

"Oh, Jesus, Jesus, Jesus, Jesus." It's more a curse than a prayer.

He puts the box carefully on the pillow, excuses himself and goes into the bathroom. I can hear water running, coughing and nose clearing. After a few minutes he opens the door. His face is red as if he's been scrubbing himself with a coarse rag, his shirtfront is damp, his eyes are wide and unfocused.

"I don't want this getting out, Joseph."

"It might be hard to keep it a secret, sir. The police will know. After the autopsy."

"Autopsy? Oh, Christ. Is that necessary?"

"It's standard, with a homicide, exact cause of death, other factors."

"Factors? What factors?"

"I don't know, sir. Factors. Like was she drugged, what exactly caused her ... Factors."

He goes back inside the bathroom and closes the

door again. This time I don't hear any noises. After a minute he opens the door a crack.

"Joseph?"

"Sir?"

"Would you be kind enough to get me a drink?"

"Certainly."

In the sitting room, the six of them are perched uncomfortably, looking at papers, twiddling thumbs. I cross to the bar and pour a stiff shot of Glenlivet into a hotel glass. As I start out, Winston Mikela stands up and reflexively buttons his pinstripes across his belly.

"Is he going to be long?" he asks.

"You'd have to ask him," I say.

"There are still some papers that he needs to sign."

I look around the room at the platoon of legal talent. "I'm sure he'll get to them as soon as he's ready."

"If you could mention that we're waiting?"

"Be happy to," I say. They can spend the afternoon for all I care.

I find Leo sitting in a dark corner holding a corner of the drape aside to give himself a glimpse of overcast sky. He takes the glass with a nod of acknowledgement but doesn't drink right away.

"She made me go to that damn thing," he says. "I said 'who needs it?' She said I needed to get outside, meet some people again. I was … I would have been … happy to stay home. With her. Up there." He drinks half the Scotch in a gulp and inhales deeply through his open mouth. He shakes his head. "She couldn't marry me. Her husband is still alive. She's Catholic. She was Catholic. She wouldn't get a divorce."

"Did you know he was after her for money?" I ask.

"I thought that was taken care of," he says. "I gave the bastard fifty thousand two years ago. Some postal box. Hell, I couldn't even find the son of a bitch. I tried. I hired some people, people in California. He was supposed to be living in Fresno. They couldn't find him. He cashed the damn cheque, I know that much."

"Is it possible he showed up again, looking for more?"

"Oh, Christ," he groans, sits on the bed again. "It started so slowly, Joseph," he says. "Six years ago. I never expected it to grow into anything ... anything meaningful." His voice is low, filled with aching. "I liked the way she folded things. I thought it showed care and respect, not for me, respect for the material. I called the housekeeper, asked who the woman was looking after my place Wednesdays, Thursdays, and Fridays. They thought I was unhappy, thought I wanted her fired. I just wanted her assigned to my personal staff. Full time." He shakes his head. "Vera Dineen thought it set a bad precedent."

I can see tears on his face. "I could send those people away for you," I say.

"No, no," he says wearily. "I'd better finish. They want me to straighten out my will now that ... things have changed. If her damned husband *should* show up they don't want him making messes." He finishes the drink.

"Freshen that up, sir?"

"No, I'm fine. I just needed to pull myself together. Seeing those ... She wanted it so much."

"There's something else, sir. I haven't made a full report what with everything."

"What is it?"

"Someone defaced the award you got last night."

"Throw it in the trash."

"The police have it now."

"What for?"

"To see if there's any connection. It looks like the driver who went missing had it in his possession, for a while anyway."

"Have you tracked him down?"

"No, sir. The police are looking for him. I suppose you know that Ultra Limousine Service is owned by your son."

"It is now," he says. "Used to be owned by a friend of mine." He shakes his head. "Sounds like something Theo might arrange. Hell, pissing on the award sounds like something *I* might arrange."

"So you don't think there could be any connection between that and what happened later?"

Leo stops and turns to me. "I don't think he hates me that much." He has to steady himself for a moment before he can open the door. "If you find out differently you'll let me know."

I leave Leo to sort out details of his estate, or whatever else he's doing, and head up to the penthouse. I deliberately avoided any mention of Roselyn Hiscox, and her story about Leo's late wife — Leo hasn't made it my affair and I'd prefer it to stay that way. My instructions are to do a few chores around the penthouse before the cleaning crew arrives. It's not a job I'm looking forward to but at least it's something I understand. The rest of it looks like a dog's breakfast.

The Crime Scene Unit has departed, and unless I get a look at the police report, which is unlikely, I won't know what pieces of evidence they've taken. To me the place looks the way it did two nights ago. It feels strange to be in here, on my own. My visits to the penthouse always felt like an audience with the Pope. I was welcome enough, invited to watch a baseball game, or have a beer, but no matter how hospitable the atmosphere there was never any doubt that I was a visitor from below decks.

And something else, something I couldn't put my finger on back then but am beginning to understand now, the unspoken, veiled, yet palpable atmosphere of family. This was Leo's home life. When I arrived he'd be settled by the fireplace, or watching a football game, or reading the *Financial Times*, to all appearances a self-sufficient bachelor. And yet, Raquel was always there, somewhere in the background, discreetly out of sight, running his bath, sorting his vitamins and supplements, looking after him.

The formal patio is a squared horseshoe looking west, north, and east.

A wide balcony runs along the west side of the hotel and opens to a broad, north-facing terrace with stone planters and outdoor furniture. When I step outside I can feel a wet wind moving over the top of the city. The sky is darkening. Rain is heading in from Point Grey but it hasn't hit us yet. From up here I can see the mountains and the North Shore and a glimpse of English Bay between the high-rises.

The downward view from terrace to excavation is less appetizing, especially now that I can pinpoint the exact spot where the body landed. Given a few variables — wind, angle of trajectory, desperately flailing arms and legs — he probably began his descent from exactly this spot. There are faint bloodstains on the concrete railing; dirt scattered across the tiles, broken glass from the French doors.

"Who we dealing with here, Ninjas?" Gritch has followed me. He looks over the edge to the street below. "Have to be a human fly to get in this way," he says.

Ledges on the north face of the Lord Douglas are nonexistent, windows are sparse. The old Warburton Building once butted up against the Lord Douglas with barely enough space between for a tight fire lane. Guests regularly complained of being ogled by office staff next door and over time many of the windows were simply bricked up. Which might explain why no one saw a body falling.

"So, what happened?" Gritch wonders. "Two guys climb up, one of them doesn't make it, the other one goes on without him, does a murder and runs down the fire stairs?"

"A bizarre scenario," I admit.

"Have to be nuts," he says.

"Or highly motivated."

"Yeah, well maybe he was hoarding gold bars and bags of diamonds up here. You don't climb fifteen stories to steal furniture."

"I don't think they came in this way."

"I'm with you there, Mr. Moto," he says, "but somebody left from here. And something went on out here. Glass table got knocked over, somebody kicked those flower pots, two panes gone in the French doors ..."

"Kicked from the inside. Probably started in there," I say. "Maybe she tried to run out here, call for help or something, he chased her ..."

"Or *they* chased her," he says. "Officer Chan says more than one."

"Okay, they chased her. And somehow, God bless her, she got one of them, pushed him over, and the other one dragged her back inside."

Inside. There is a clear path of breakage from the terrace to the kitchen to the front hall.

The rain picks a fitting moment to hit. Not the usual Vancouver drizzle, this is a solid cloudburst. I can hear a rumble of thunder in the distance, uncommon in this part of the world.

"Comin' down heavy," says Gritch. "Sky's black. Where'd that come from?"

The question doesn't require an answer.

The kitchen is a mess. Shattered glass and broken china cover the floor. A big platter of assorted canapés strewn countertop to sink, caviar, pâté, fancy cheeses, the air is rich.

"Stinks in here," says Gritch, unnecessarily. "Cops never bother to clean up."

"Not their job."

"Are we supposed to do it, or call Housekeeping?"

"I'll do it," I say. "Go water your fern."

Chaotic or not, the kitchen is well-stocked with garbage bags, cleaning supplies, brooms, dustpans, rags, and mops. I start slowly, picking up the bigger shards one piece at a time, taking a look at each one, not searching for anything in particular and pretty sure I wouldn't recognize a real clue if it cut my finger, which it might do if I handle things in my usual ham-fisted fashion. Take it slow. Broken glass and china into a metal wastebasket, foodstuffs into a plastic bag. Raquel took a lot of care with this buffet — toast points and little spoons, hard-cooked eggs and lemon wedges. All ruined.

The rain hasn't let up and it's getting on to evening by the time I've cleaned up the kitchen. I'm no wiser than I was when I started, merely more informed. There's a knife missing from the wooden knife rack. The carving knife. And by Christ I hope she got to it first, I hope she cut the bastard, I hope that I was washing some of his blood off the tiles.

The rain is pounding the deck, spattering through the battered French doors. I stuff a plastic garbage bag into the biggest gap and get a good scratch on the back of my hand for my trouble. Bound to happen.

Leo's bathroom, like the kitchen, is well-stocked. There's peroxide and Polysporin and I have my choice of Elastoplast or Band-Aid, pretty much anything a wounded klutz might need. As I'm fixing myself up I'm checking the inventory. Looking inside someone's medicine cabinet is akin to reading their mail; not something I'm comfortable doing but under the circumstances not out of line. Mooney and Pazzano probably handled these pill bottles. It appears that Leo has his choice of Viagra or Cialis, as well as a Chinese male potency booster called Hua Fo. He also has prescriptions for various age-related medications, none of which I'm familiar with. They don't have any bearing on what I'm supposed to be up here doing anyway, which definitely isn't standing in Leo's bathroom looking at his privacy. I already know a lot more than I want to about my boss.

And how much do I really know? Not that much. I may be a "house dick" by occupation, but I'm no detective. I don't have a snooper's curiosity. Private lives? None of my business. Back when I earned a living doing physical labour I took comfort in the precise outlines of the job. I knew what was expected of me, what I would be required to pay in pain and effort, the exact proportions of my roped-off territory. No confusion. The Lord Douglas is a bigger ring, but it's measurable, in size and requirements. At least that's how it's supposed to be.

Most of Raquel's personal things are in her own suite at the southernmost corner of the penthouse; self-contained chambers — kitchen, sitting room, bedroom — through a door at the end of the hall. According to Leo, I'll find suitcases there. Packing up that apartment will be a job for another day; right now Leo would like me to remove her things from his bedroom closets. He doubts he'll be able to sleep in there anyway. He says he may use one of the guestrooms. If he doesn't move out permanently.

It looks like Raquel had her sitting room organized for sewing. Two machines, bolts of cloth, a dress form, work tables, threads, ribbons, scissors, all neatly arranged. The half-finished dress on the mannequin is white. There is lace around the neckline. To my untaught eye it looks a lot like a wedding gown. Heartbreak upon heartbreak.

Back in Leo's bedroom, once very much *their* bedroom, obviously arranged for two people to watch television, read, sleep, side by side. I pack up Raquel's things as neatly as I can. Dresser drawers filled with underclothing, slips and stockings, jewellery box, makeup. Everything I touch reminds me of the woman who wore them. I'm clumsy with delicate things.

She had her own bathroom. Her pink robe is hanging on the back of the door, her moisturizers and creams and conditioners lined up on an open shelf. Near the tub is a wall rack holding a sheaf of magazines: *Prevention*, *Cigar Aficionado*, *Men's Health*, *Conceive*, and a glossy Spanish language magazine called *Agenda Para Mama*.

It's that last one that does it. My eyes are blurring and my face is getting hot and I have an urgent primitive need to punch something, punish someone, almost anyone. And I didn't love her; I just liked her, liked trying out my meagre Spanish on her, seeing her smile when I got it right.

Fresh air. Clear my head, cool my face. The sky is clearing in the west when I get outside, the rain has moved on. The trailing end of the storm has diminished to a steady breeze across the roof garden. The moon is breaking through the clouds. I can almost see stars.

I walk to the railing and look down at the street. At fifteen stories, plus the penthouse structure, the Lord Douglas is dwarfed by most of the buildings around it. When it was built it was a monument, now it's merely a mesa. Still, it plants a massive footprint, almost a full city block, hugging the sidewalk on three sides, flanked to the north by the empty pit.

Whoever originally designed what became Leo's penthouse fortress must have had a whimsical streak. The penthouse roof is cantilevered, dormered, cupolaed, and chimneyed. The cops have probably been up there. Not sure how they made the climb. Probably brought a ladder. Or stood on a planter. Or knocked one over.

Not as easy as I thought it would be. The planter isn't tall enough. There's a table that gives me another step. After that it's a matter of arm strength. I always hated chin-ups; they weren't part of my regular workout. Biceps aren't the most important arm muscles to a boxer and you definitely don't want them bulging and slowing punches down. Morely Kline considered weight-lifting to be one of the Seven Deadly Sins for a fighter.

Nevertheless, it looks like I still have enough residual curling strength to haul my bulk over the eaves and onto the penthouse roof.

No crime scene tape up here, nothing marked off, no sign that the police have crossed these peaks and valleys, hiked this expanse of slate, skirted these copper-sheathed cupolas. All the evidence said the crime happened inside Leo's domicile, and then I was helpful enough to focus things elsewhere by chasing footsteps down the fire stairs. They might not have checked up here at all.

Not enough moonlight to make searching worthwhile. I'm just happy I make it to the south end without breaking my neck. It turns out that Leo's aerie is a citadel taking up less than a quarter of the hotel. I stand at the roof's edge looking down on a wide expanse of tar and gravel occupied by massive air-conditioner and elevator housings, vents and pipes, aerials and satellite dishes. That much equipment needs regular maintenance.

There will be a service access somewhere.

It's a long drop to the roof of the fifteenth floor but, hey, damned if there isn't a handy iron ladder bolted to the wall to make for a smooth climb. Who needs special keys and security codes? Simple, if you know where you're going.

People have spent time up here. Impossible to tell who and when but it looks like a popular gathering place. Cigarette butts, Styrofoam cups, discarded rags, a rank of dubious plastic lounge chairs aimed to catch the afternoon sun, a gas barbecue, a picnic table, an awning swollen with collected rainwater. I recall Gritch mentioning the summer lunch breaks on the roof, maintenance staff cooking burgers and steaks in the afternoons. He suggested that it was a tradition. I'd never been invited.

Housings for the six passenger and two service elevators are barnlike, padlocked from the outside. So? So, no one came or left through them. What does that leave? The other fire stairs. That door has a lock as well. It is conveniently broken. Light switch inside the door. This stairwell descends to the fifteenth floor and opens near the service elevators.

And Gritch is climbing the stairs.

"Thought crossed my mind, too," he says.

"Did you know there was a ladder up the back of Leo's castle?"

"That's what crossed my mind," he says.

"I don't think Pazzano and Mooney have been up here," I say.

"Probably right. Otherwise they might have noticed the pair of gloves at the bottom of the stairs."

"You've got to be kidding," I say.

"Check it out," he says.

Sure enough. A pair of black gloves, one lying on the bottom step, the other a level higher.

"Okay," I say. "Let's get Maintenance to padlock this door until the police are inclined to do a thorough search of the premises."

"They're going to just lo-ve you to death," he says.

Brian Bester is looking for me when we get to the lobby. "I'm clocking off, Joe," he says, "but I thought you might want this stuff." He hands me a printout. "I left the medical tag on your desk."

"Thanks Bri, I appreciate it."

"My pleasure," he says. "Good night. Good night, Mr. Gritchfield."

"Yeah, right," Gritch says. He watches Brian leave. "Probably running off to get a shoeshine and a trim. They always have fresh haircuts, you notice?"

I'm looking at the printout.

"What'cha got?" he asks.

"I found a thing at the construction site. Computer thing. Medical alert tag. He's got allergies."

"Who has?"

"Jesus Santiago."

Gritch says. "Jesus was camped out next door?

"He's from Fresno, California. He's in the Army."

"Our army?"

"American," I say. I take the Bronze Star out of my pocket. "Maybe a hero."

"Maybe just a thief," Gritch says.

chapter ten

Midnight. I've made the late walkabout. I usually have a beer around this time. Once or twice a week lately I've had company. Sometimes I find her waiting for me at the foot of the handsome new staircase leading down from the lobby. That's where she is tonight, watching me descend, her curly head cocked to one side and her bright eyes squinting.

"You're all backlit," she says. "Can't see your face. Are you smiling?"

"Always, when you show up."

"You don't look very smiley."

She puts her arms around me. It feels good and I wrap her close. Her tousled head is under my chin and I inhale the scent of her hair.

"This helps," I say.

"That was a big sigh," she says. She looks up.

"More groan-like."

"It's been a dreary day. You?"

"Not so bad," she says. "Come on. Let me buy you a beer."

"Not so bad? Is that akin to good?"

She takes me by the hand and leads me into Olive's. Olive herself is sitting in her private corner with her bassist and long-time friend, Jimmy Hinds. They must be reminiscing; they both have faraway smiles. Olive looks up and blows me a kiss as we pass.

"I hesitate to be overly cheery," Connie says. "Seeing as how you are swathed in melancholy."

"Maybe some cheery news will unswath me."

"Maybe not," she says. She parks herself on a barstool, pats the vacant one next to her, grins at me as I sit. "I'm going to China," she says.

Barney shows up with a beer for me and a red wine for her.

"Hi, Champ," he says. "Hi, TV-star."

Perfect time for an interruption. Gives me time to digest, or at least swallow. I spot a distraction at the far end of the bar.

"How long has Weed been here?" I ask him.

"Just showed up," Barney says.

"He ask for me?"

"Wanted to know if Olive was doing another set."

"Is she?"

Barney looks around the room. It's not crowded.

"I doubt it," says Barney. "But you never know."

Barney departs to pour beer for someone else and I turn to look at Connie. She is sitting somewhat primly with her lips pursed and an innocent pussycat smile that says *What* canary?

"China," she says again.

"Good," I say finally, with conviction. "That's good because I was worried to distraction you were being sent to Afghanistan."

"I'm still angling for that."

"Fills my heart with dread," I say.

"I've been on the list for a year," she says. "I've had my familiarization course. I know how to make a splint out of a *Hustler* magazine. It's only a matter of time, big boy. Better get used to it."

"China is the thin edge of the wedge."

"This one is easy-peasy," she says. "Big trade delegation, governor general's coming along, press corps, hotels, buffets."

"Somebody drop a camera on Anchor Girl, what's her name, the Number One?"

"She's having a baby."

"Oh."

"What did I say? Your face went all sour again."

"It's all right."

"You want to stay here or go somewhere else?"

"No. No, this is good."

"I meant back to your room."

"I know what you meant," I say. I squeeze her hand. "There's a cop at the end of the bar I need to chat with for a minute."

"He looks a bit swathed himself. Maybe I should buy him a beer, too."

"Rum and Coke," I say.

Weed looks up as I grab the stool beside him.

"You behaving yourself?" he says.

"Oh, yeah."

"I heard you were poking around the crime scene."

"Wasn't a crime scene anymore."

"Find anything interesting?"

"Pazzano didn't mention?" I say. "Mooney?"

"I heard something."

"Nobody thanked me."

"Yeah, well, you didn't do them any favours. List of suspects went from who had a key to who knew the Lord Douglas had a roof."

"News to me, too," I say.

"You didn't have to rub it in."

I shrug. "The gloves were a bonus."

A rum and Coke is placed before him. He looks up. Connie has been invited to join Olive and Jimmy. She waves the length of the bar before she turns her back on us. Weed eats a few peanuts. I sip my beer.

"There was a knife missing," I say.

"Oh?"

"Was it the murder weapon?"

"Still waiting on the Medical Examiner," he says.

"Sure you are. Well, maybe you could let it slip if she was stabbed or shot or strangled."

He looks around the room like he's about to betray his government. "She wasn't shot or strangled."

"So, then Mooney and Pazzano might be thinking that it was a confrontation that got out of hand," I say.

He adds more Coke to his rum and looks wistfully at the bare stage and the vacant piano stool. "Who knows what they're thinking?"

"They might be thinking that if the murder weapon came from the kitchen, whoever did it didn't bring a weapon of their own, and that the murder wasn't premeditated."

He concedes the point, grudgingly. "They're probably considering that. Along with everything else."

"And they're probably checking to see if there was anyone else's blood around."

"That'd be lab stuff. Sometimes it takes awhile."

"How about a time of death?"

"Lab stuff."

"Right," I say. "How about the fallen man? You got an ID yet?"

"You'll have to check with the guys running the case. I'm here for the music."

"When did we stop being on the same side?" I ask him.

"You withheld evidence, you big palooka."

"Speaking of which," I start. "Here's something your search party at the construction site didn't find." I hand him the MedicAlert fob along with the printout.

He has to put on his reading glasses. "Who's this Jesus guy?"

"He's the one with the motorcycle. Army, or ex-Army, or AWOL, or deserter. Used to get a lot of them up here at one time."

"Those were draft dodgers," he says. He takes off his glasses and rubs his eyes with both hands. "If this wasn't the best piano bar in the city," he starts, "and if Barney wasn't the best bartender, and if Olive didn't occasionally do a late set, just for me, I might consider taking my custom elsewhere."

"Just doing my part," I say. "Wouldn't want anyone accusing me of withholding."

He blots a few rum and Coke droplets from his orange and yellow tie. "Bugger off now," he says. "Olive's going to sing."

"You're welcome," I say.

"I guess the renovations didn't extend to your end of the building," Connie says.

We've had this discussion before. She hates the wallpaper, dislikes the hand-me-down art on the wall. "I get fresh bed linen every day," I say.

She concedes the point. "Yes, you do," she says.

"And you will notice they supply me with *two* robes these days."

"Those maids are so canny," she says as she wraps white terrycloth around herself.

"You think if they send you to Afghanistan you'll get clean towels every day, and scented soap?"

"When did you start getting scented soap?"

"I could get scented soap if I asked for it. I just happen to like that other stuff."

"Which is why I bring my own."

"How long will you be gone?"

"Six days." She drops the robe and climbs back into bed. "Relax, big guy. This is a joyride. I'll attend a few briefings; get my face in front of the camera."

"I'm happy for you, Connie, really. You want this."

"Okay," she says. "Your general aura of gloom notwithstanding."

I put an arm around her, pull her close to my chest.

"Raquel was pregnant," I say. "Raquel and Leo were going to have a baby."

"Oh, dear," she says. "That makes it so much sadder."

Connie Gagliardi rises in the dark these days, even when she sleeps over. A quick kiss on the forehead and she's out the door, heading for Channel 20 to tell the world what's happened overnight. Her new job on the morning news desk is a promotion she tells me, and a definite step toward prime time, but it's a relentless schedule and doesn't leave much room for cuddling. She's hoping she'll get to sleep in during the China junket. A lot of good that'll do me. After I hear the door close, the bed feels empty, her scent lingers, I worry about traffic, and I can't get back to sleep. I'll be a basket case if she ever makes it to Afghanistan.

Having Connie in my life this past year has been a big change for me. A good one. I'm eating more vegetables. But she's younger than I am, has ambition, and a definite plan for where she wants to be in ten years. If she winds up with a big network back east, or even south of the border where she'd like to be, I won't be part of her life. Gritch tells me to enjoy it while I can. Rachel says I should put a ring on her finger, buy her a house, and get her pregnant. Mostly I just try to count my blessings, cheer her on as she makes her run for the roses, and avoid thinking about Afghanistan.

chapter eleven

The Lobby Café doesn't open until eight o'clock but Hattie spots me lurking by the newsstand and lets me in through the kitchen.

"It'll take a minute for the coffee, Joe," she says. "You want some juice?"

"No, thanks. Wait. Yeah, juice is a good idea."

"Orange, grapefruit, V8?"

"What's best for a man of my years? Nutritionally?"

"Grapefruit," she says. "Connie spent the night?"

"Yes."

"So you'll be wanting whole-grain toast this morning."

"I suppose."

"She's good for you, Joe. Got you running again, taking better care of yourself." She puts a large glass of juice in front of me. "Actually, *eating* a grapefruit is better than just drinking the juice."

"I'll remember that for next time." I take a gulp of juice. It's sour, bracing, probably good for me. "She's going to China," I say.

"For good?"

"Six days."

"You'll survive."

The *Emblem* has the story on page three. HOTEL MAID STABBED. No mention of Raquel's connection to Leo. The discovery of a dead body in the Warburton site has been treated as a separate item. That won't last long.

Hattie puts a cup of coffee in front of me and nods toward the door. "Should I let him in?" she asks.

As if on cue, Larry Gormé, crime beat reporter for the very paper I'm dripping coffee on, is looking in through the glass. I check the wall clock: 7:53.

"Don't do it on my account," I say.

"Oh, well," she says "The coffee's ready."

Hattie unlocks the door and Larry bustles in, tipping his fedora like a gentleman, grabbing the stool two down from me, craning his head to see which page I'm on.

"See that?" he says. "Circumspection. Restraint. Nothing about how she may or may not have had a romantic relationship with the head honcho."

"You're a credit to your trade," I say.

"A shining example. Thanks darlin'," he says as Hattie gives him a coffee at the same time she brings my toast.

"You having breakfast?" she asks.

"In the morning?" He looks horrified. "I'll take a couple of aspirin if you've got 'em."

"I'll see what I can do," she says.

"I tried to track you down yesterday," he says.

"I was out."

"Working this case?"

"Nope." The toast is full of whole-grain goodness. All I need now is yogurt and I'll be too healthy. "You know Mooney and his partner?"

"Pizzaria? Sure."

"I don't think that's his name."

"What we call him in the city room," he says. "He's broken a few noses. Not mine o'course. My nose is clean."

"And your heart is pure."

"Here's your aspirin," says Hattie.

"Life saver. How's the little bingo-caller?" he asks.

"Packing."

"You two taking a trip?"

"She is. Going to China with the governor general and a trade delegation."

"Hey. Next stop, *Canada AM*."

"Wouldn't surprise me," I say. "She's good enough."

"Good-looking enough, too." Larry washes the aspirin down with his coffee. "Networks have a strict no-mutts policy. It's what's kept me out of the big time."

"I can't give you anything you can publish, Larry."

"Sure, sure, I know that. I don't want an interview, but I know you, you'll be poking around even when you say you're not poking around."

"I have been warned, in no uncertain terms, that if I ask too many questions the cops will make my life semi-miserable."

"That's you. They can't tell me to keep my nose out of it; asking questions is what I do for a living. What do you want me to ask?"

Good question. A better one might be *Do I really want answers?* He pulls a notepad out of his inside pocket. I munch toast for a minute, consult a mental checklist: Don't broach the subject of Leo's dead wife, oath of vengeance, definitely nope, and stay away from the fact that Raquel was in all likelihood pregnant at the time of her death. However …

"I'd like to find out who defaced Leo's award at the fancy-dress bunfight Monday night," I say.

"Defaced, how?"

"Somebody bored a hole through his eye. Took some gear, timing, and somebody to do the job."

"That's new stuff," he says. His pen is moving but he doesn't look down. "You figure it's connected?"

"Somehow. And the dead body, as yet unidentified, that they found in the construction hole, most likely fell from the penthouse."

"Aha!" he says. "This is *not* information that's readily available."

"Something else," I say.

"Lay it on me."

"Okay, the limo company switched drivers between the time we got there and the time we left."

"So?"

"So. The driver was the last one who had the award, and he's gone missing."

"Better and better," says Larry. "Cops looking for him I suppose?"

"I suppose."

"Which company is it?"

"Ultra."

"Oh, yeah?" He laughs. "I know that outfit. They chauffeured Ben Affleck last time he was in town. The entertainment mob was following them around for a week. Who's the driver?"

"Guy named Starr. Dimitar Starr." I spell it for him.

He writes it down carefully. "Never heard of him," says Larry.

"There's a kicker," I say.

"Hey, don't stop now."

"Ultra is owned by Theo Alexander."

Hattie's holding the phone out to me. "Joe? It's him."

Leo's in the penthouse with Mooney and Pazzano. When I get there the three of them are outside. Gulls are wheeling overhead, yelling at the humans below to throw them something. Rain clouds are being pushed up the valley by a west wind and shafts of sunlight are bouncing off the puddles on the terrace. Leo and Mooney are engaged in an intense discussion that doesn't look amicable. Pazzano is off to the side, edgy, like Cujo on a chain. His eyes light up when he spots me and he dances across the patio to block the French doors.

"They're busy," he says.

"Fine by me," I say.

"What were you doing up on the roof?"

"My job, Detective," I say.

"Told you to keep your nose out of it."

"Didn't think it was off-limits since you fellows had released the Crime Scene," I say. "Prematurely as it turns out."

Pazzano's hands are curled, almost fists, and he can barely keep from bouncing.

"You gonna drop by for a workout one of these days?" he asks.

"Detective, my fighting days are history," I say. "Lately I've been thinking a lot about miniature golf."

"Sorry to hear that." He doesn't bother to take the sneer out of his tone. "I was looking forward to working on a few things."

I move two steps sideways to look at the big oil painting over the fireplace; an America's Cup race from the 30s, J-Boats, majestic sloops heeled over in a brisk Newport breeze. The brass plaque on the frame identifies them as *Enterprise* and *Shamrock V.*

Pazzano follows me. "Guy in your line of work needs to stay sharp," he says. "Don't you think?"

"I've been kicked up to management," I say. "Got some fresh faces looking after the day-to-day."

There's another marine painting on the wall to my left. Tyrannous, off Cape Flattery reads the inscription. The lee rail is awash, the crew hanging over the high side, the man at the helm, bareheaded, windblown, bears a striking resemblance to Leo.

"There's a safe behind this painting," Pazzano says. "You know what's in it?"

"None of my business, Detective," I say. "Was it touched?"

He doesn't bother to answer.

On a shelf is a model of the boat in the painting. A racing sloop, navy blue with a thin red stripe the length of the hull.

"You like boats?"

"Don't know a thing about them, Detective," I say.

"She was knocked up. Did you know that?"

"I do now," I say.

He makes a tour of the room, touching things, lifting things and putting them back in the wrong places, cigar box, porcelain figurine, a first edition Jack London *Call of the Wild*. He's trying to irk me.

"Yep. His little Senorita got herself knocked up. The lab hasn't quite determined if *he* was the father, or if she had something going on the side, but we'll find out sooner or later."

Mooney comes in from the patio. Leo is still outside, smoking a cigar, his eyes on mountains.

"You ever heard of this Jesus Santiago before?" Mooney asks.

"No, Detective," I say. "Located him yet?"

"He's on everybody's 'Bust His Ass' list," he says.

"Glad to be of help," I say.

"Some help," he says.

Leo glares in my direction when I step onto the terrace. The muscles in his jaw are clenched, the end of his cigar is ragged. Mooney's interrogation has left him bruised and bitter.

"Offensive and incompetent," he growls. "They're no closer than they were two days ago. They haven't found the limo driver, they don't have any witnesses, so now they're coming at me."

"It's what cops do," I say. "Start over, re-interview everyone. Next they'll be bothering Connie, Gritch, Ms. Saunders."

"Those people aren't suspects."

"And you are?"

"Not in so many words, but the implication was clear. Rich older man, hotel maid, pregnant, in the will for who knows how much, history of …"

"Of?"

"Old scars, Joseph. Old scars."

If he doesn't want to tell me, fine. I'm happy to stay out of it.

He wanders away from me toward a far railing, stands looking out at his city, hands clasped behind his back, cigar in his teeth. For a moment I can see him on the bridge of a clipper heading for Rangoon.

"I once was a man, Joseph. I rode the range, I sailed the seas, I wasn't locked up like fucking Rapunzel."

"If you want to go out somewhere, sir, I'll be happy to come along."

"That's just the point, Joseph! I have nowhere *to* go, or *want* to go, or *need* to go. I've cut myself off."

"Takes a little time."

His hands are gripping the railing and he's leaning out, looking down. He takes a step back and jerks his head sharply as if banishing a fleeting impulse. "Find the son of a bitch, Joseph!" Leo mashes his cigar into the wet soil of a planter and heads back inside. "I need the books closed!"

chapter twelve

The Champagne Baths Spa and Fitness Centre has a full complement of Nautilus machines, treadmills, and free weights, none of which interest me much. However, on Leo's instructions, a private corner has been set aside for my use, and for the convenience of anyone else who might feel the need to beat the living crap out of a heavy bag from time to time. I don't do it every day, maybe three times a week, or on those occasions when there really isn't any other way to relieve pressure. I'm making the big bag talk, snapping off left jabs, straight rights, left hooks, body shots, combinations, doubling up on the jabs, hooking to the body, back to the head, all the while indulging myself with mental glimpses of Pazzano's smug kisser, Theo Alexander's walrus belly, Lenny Alexander's pugnacious nose, a half-remembered face with a moustache and a twitchy ponytail, and the heaviest shots reserved for a shadowman, a murderer, an evil sonofabitch, who robbed Leo, robbed the whole, damn, world, of a sweet, pretty, gentle, loving, woman, and who deserves each, and, every, bone-breaking, jaw-crushing, kidney-bruising, spleen-rupturing ...

Sweat is pouring off me, my arms are sore and my hands are hanging down like sacks of lead.

"I hear regular light workouts are good for one's general outlook," says Gritch.

I haul in some ragged breaths and turn to see him perched on a padded bench chewing an unlit cigar stub.

"How long have you been sitting there?"

"Long enough to watch you trash five-hundred-dollars-worth of Everlast."

A brief wave of dizziness washes over me as I grab a towel and a water bottle off the floor. "A heavy bag's not earning its keep if it hasn't picked up some duct tape along the way," I grunt.

"Sucker's going to need a big roll," he says.

"He had it coming." I pour some water over my head and towel my face. "I'm going to grab a shower."

"How about a steam after that?"

"I don't do steam," I say. "Morley never let me steam. Said it sapped the body."

"You're already sapped, pal," he says. "Make it the sauna. I could use one myself."

Three ladies in the shallow end of the pool watch me warily as I trudge toward the men's locker room. I'm pretty sure my cursing was all internal, I don't think any of the words were audible, maybe the grunts alone were enough to make them huddle up. I force a smile as I pass by. It seems to terrify them even more.

When I enter the sauna, Gritch is already there, sitting on the lowest tier, wearing a towel tied high under his armpits, his face ruddy as an apple.

"Your hand's bleeding."

"I scratched it up in the penthouse. Broken window. It's not deep."

I sit one level higher with my elbows on my knees, hands dangling, head hanging, sweat dripping like a steady downpour. I can feel the toxins flushing out of me.

"You've been down here almost two hours," he says. "I thought you might've drowned in the new pool."

"Don't swim either," I say. "Another thing Morley Kline frowned upon."

"Chlorine's bad for fighters?"

"Everything was bad unless Morley said it was good. No swimming, no steam. Roadwork, protein, and lots of sleep. I never saw midnight except on New Year's Eve."

We sit in silence for a while, listening to droplets tapping on cedar. My heartbeat is returning to a normal cadence, my breathing is slowing, the ache in my muscles receding, my murderous impulses returning to their locked compartment at the rear of my skull.

"You thinking deep thoughts?"

"Thinking about quitting my job," I say.

"And doing what?"

"Always wanted to visit China."

"Sure you did."

"Well I could use a damn vacation," I say. I sound grouchy. "They're starting to look at Leo for this."

"Makes sense."

"The perfect suspect. Even he thinks so."

"What do you think?"

"I don't have a clue, damn it."

"Only two choices, pal," says Gritch. "Choice One, Leo did a bad thing, in which case the pucky hits the fan and the world as we know it dims and dies. Or, Choice Two, Leo is innocent of any wrongdoing, and someone murdered his true love." He smiles encouragingly. "So? Which one do you buy into?"

A workout like that pretty much demands a beer. In the old days Morley would have the beer on my behalf. It always seemed to do him good. Besides, at this time of day Olive's is a calm and quiet place where a man can mull over his limited options.

Kyra handles the bar in the afternoons. "Hi, Joe," she says. "Coffee?"

"A cold Beck's in a cold glass."

"You're glowing. Steam room?"

"Sauna."

"This'll fix you up," she says.

The glass is frosted, the beer is glacial. I inhale half of it, like a man coming out of the desert. Kyra lets me be, goes off to change the CD. She knows what I like, something to warm a gloomy afternoon. I sit at the end of the bar and listen to Ibrahim Ferrer. The

Havana rhythms remind me of Raquel and I long for a day when I can remember her as she was, cheerful, competent, alive. Instead, I keep getting flashes of her body on the kitchen floor. White apron, soaked in blood. A maid's apron. Was it important for her to maintain the fiction that she was just his personal maid? It was her decision most likely; she was the married woman sharing quarters with a man not her husband. Leo says he wanted to marry her, and yet there he was, evidently at her urging, squiring a fashionable divorcée to a formal dinner while she stayed behind, in her maid's uniform, arranging platters of snacks. No point trying to fathom other people's relationships. No doubt they'd worked something out that suited them, or at least protected them from the outside world. But, despite all the insulation, the world barged in and now their relationship, their unborn child, the missing husband, and, if some reporter really wants to dig, the eerily similar murder of Leo's first wife, will all come out. There isn't much I can do about that. And I can't shake the feeling that there's a connection with what happened eight years ago. The police never solved that one. But then Leo didn't give them much to go on.

"Track you down sooner or later," says Larry Gormé.

"Who ratted me out?"

"Gritch. He says you're currently clueless."

"Accurate," I say. "Beer?"

"Definitely," he says, grabbing the barstool around the corner from mine so that we can face each other. "Kyra, darling, one of those imported things. He's buying."

"For you, Joe?"

"Oh, why not?" I ask no one in particular.

"My, my," says Larry.

"I'm being sociable," I say.

"I can see that," he says. "Got a name for you."

"Whose name?"

"The guy who got skewered. Name's Newton."

"That a first or last name?"

"Haven't a clue. That's all I could get from my friend in the Medical Examiner's office. Newton."

"Never heard of him." I roll the cold bottle across my forehead. There's a headache lurking in there.

"That guy Goodier at Ultra Limos is making himself hard to reach."

"Another dead end."

"Not quite," he says. "Turns out you know one of the mechanics down there."

"I do?"

"Mo Feivel. Used to fight out of Bellingham."

"Heavyweight?"

"Yeah, you took his head off back in '87, '88, somewhere in there. Third Round, TKO, 'referee stops contest.'"

"He's a mechanic?"

"I'm nosing around the garage, figuring I'll get the bum's rush any minute, and up comes this face from the past. Recognized him right away. I covered that fight. Hey Mo, I say, how you doin'? He says, 'Who the fuck're you?' Pardon my specificity, Kyra dear. Thank you. Have you trimmed your hair? It barely reaches your coccyx." Larry eschews a glass, tips the green bottle and refreshes his larynx. "Anyway, before he can brain me with a tire iron I establish my *bona fides* and tell him what a great fighter he was in his day, which mollifies him somewhat. At least he let me walk. So I figure you two, belonging to the same fraternity as it were, might be able to establish some rapport, find common ground."

"We weren't exactly best buds," I say.

"Don't you guys have a secret handshake?"

"If I have to drive, you'd better have this other beer," I say.

"Don't mind if I do," says Larry.

chapter thirteen

"Listen, Joe," Larry says. "I'm not writing this up. Not for reasons of taste or anything alien to my nature, I'd just rather stay on your good side for a while."

"Do up your seat belt," I say. "Not writing what up?"

"I just want you to know that it'll be common knowledge by tomorrow morning that Raquel Mendez was pregnant at the time of her murder, and that Leo is the presumed father, although the cops haven't confirmed their findings."

"They'd been trying for a while," I say.

We travel for a time in silence, straight up Granville, heading toward the airport.

"So why aren't you writing it?" I ask.

"I don't think it's the big story," he says. "I'd rather see where you're going."

"Appreciate it."

He stretches his seat belt over his shoulder. "Besides, Gloria will have it in the morning edition."

"Beat you to it, did she?"

"The young ones are so ambitious."

"Reminds me. I need to buy some Kevlar."

"At least you get to cuddle with yours."

"Not since she switched to mornings."

"Hate these seat belts," he says. "Always feel like I'm being garroted."

"What kind of a name is Starr?" I ask. "Dimitar Starr, what is that?"

"Bulgarian. I think. Bulgarian or Russian maybe. Same part of the world anyway. He speak with an accent?"

"Didn't say anything."

"He look Russian?"

"He looked, I don't know, Mediterranean, I guess. Black hair, black moustache."

"What'd the replacement driver look like?"

"Same. Sort of. Without the pony tail."

Ultra Limousine Service doesn't present an ultra upmarket facade and were it not for the line of extremely expensive German transportation parked outside, it would look like any used car lot in the city.

"Hey, hey, we're in luck," Larry says as I pull up to the curb.

"How so?"

"Parking space near the front door," he says. "Reserved for B. Goodier. That's the manager."

The obese man prying himself out of a Lexus has a

neatly trimmed beard and wears a snap-brim hat of fuzzy green felt. He grabs a briefcase and a stack of files from the passenger seat and waddles toward the main entrance where he stops, perhaps wondering how to open it with both hands full.

"Let me get that for you," I say.

He turns to give me a once-over. "Thanks," he says. I don't think he means it.

"Mr. Goodier?"

He doesn't bother to answer. Larry and I follow him inside where he dumps his impedimenta on the reception counter with evident relief and takes a deep breath. The trek from car to lobby was about as much as he could handle.

"Mr. Goodier, my name's Grundy, I work for Leo Alexander at the Lord Douglas Hotel. This gentleman is Larry Gormé; he's a reporter for the *Emblem*."

He looks us up and down, doesn't like what he sees, shakes his head in annoyance and starts bustling toward his office. "Already talked to the police," he growls. "Said I shouldn't speak to you."

"Seems harsh."

"Said the whereabouts of Mr. Starr was part of an ongoing investigation and you were told to stay away from it."

"What if I want to talk about something else?"

"Such as?"

"Let's start with Theodore Alexander."

He enters his office and tries to slam the door in my face but I'm too close behind for that to work. Goodier does the next best thing, positions himself behind his executive-size desk and adopts what he probably figures is the air of a man far to busy to deal with inconsequentials. Larry follows me in and closes the door softly behind him.

"I rarely see the man," he says. "He doesn't involve himself in the day-to-day operation."

"So, he wouldn't have been the one who hired Mr. Starr."

"Now you see, Mr. Grundy, there you've strayed into that police matter."

"And you wouldn't know if Mr. Starr and Mr. Alexander had met before."

"Once again …"

"And I presume the police have had a careful look at the limousine he was driving?"

"Look, if you don't have a warrant, or a police badge, we've got nothing further to discuss."

"We could talk about the ten million dollars."

Mention of money usually gets people's attention. "What ten million dollars?" he wants to know.

"The ten million dollar lawsuit that Leo Alexander's lawyer, Winston Mickela, of whom you may have heard, is about to file against Ultra."

"On what grounds?"

"Hotelier of the Year is a prestigious award which Mr. Alexander was deeply honoured to receive. To have it destroyed by one of your drivers, either as a personal attack, or under orders from someone higher up, has caused him great emotional distress and well as immense professional embarrassment." I'm making this up as I go along but it seems to be having the desired effect. I give him another push. "I can assure you that the suit will be pressed with all due diligence."

"I had nothing to do with that!"

"That will be for the courts to decide. I'm certain your lawyers will advise you on potential liability. You should also be aware that Mr. Gormé's newspaper is very interested in the story. That's not likely to be good for business."

"I get it. This is some sort of squeeze play."

"Are you feeling squeezed, Mr. Goodier?"

"Wasn't that the whole idea? First the police turn the place inside out, then you barge in threatening me with a lawsuit, dragging the newspapers in ..."

Larry takes umbrage at that. "No one has to drag a newspaper," he says. "A story's either a story or it isn't."

"What the hell is it you want?"

"Hey, I just want to talk to Dimitar Starr."

"Well, good luck with that! No one has seen or heard from him since the night in question."

"What about the other driver?"

"What other driver?"

"The one who took over for Mr. Starr when he disappeared. Someone must have notified the dispatcher that another driver was needed."

"I guess, I don't know, you'd have to ask the dispatcher."

"Do I have your permission to do that?"

"Oh, for Chrissake! Do what you want."

"Who's the dispatcher?"

"Amina. The woman in the office."

"Hi, Amina? My name's Joe Grundy. Mr. Goodier said you might be able to help me."

"How can I do that?" Her lips are pursed and she is shaking her head as she sorts the stack of files dumped on the counter.

"Monday night one of your drivers, a Mr. Starr, drove my boss to a function, but when we were ready to leave we noticed that we had a new driver. Do you remember the occasion?"

"Tuesday. Eight p.m., Lord Douglas Hotel for Mr. Alexander and party. The police needed the same information."

"That's the one. Does it mention what happened after he drove us there?"

"There was a call that the car had developed a problem. We sent a different car to replace it."

"And who was that driven by?"

"Also Mr. Starr."

"No, the driver was a different man."

"I think you are mistaken. A mechanic delivered the new vehicle, and then most likely brought the other one back here. Mr. Starr stayed with the new vehicle."

"The second driver looked like Mr. Starr, superficially at least, but it was a different man."

"Did you really look at Mr. Starr? Sometimes people don't really notice the driver, if they're on the way to a party, you know."

"I suppose that's possible. Thank you for your time."

"No problem."

"One other thing. What was wrong with the car? The first car?"

"You'd have to talk to one of the mechanics."

"Thank you, I will."

"You won't need a ref this time, will you?" Larry asks.

"We do have a secret handshake," I say. "You're just not allowed to see it. Wait in the car."

There are two Mercedes in the garage, one of them large enough to house a travelling carnival, the other one slightly bigger. I recognize Mo Feivel immediately; he looks like the front end of a Mack truck. His shape is similar to Looch Pazzano's but I can pretty much guarantee that Mo hits harder. He still has that sailor's walk, legs apart, shoulders swaying. I remember that I nearly broke a knuckle on his boulder of a head.

"Hey Mo, how're you doing?"

He squints across the hood of the Mercedes. "Who's that?" I can see the scar tissue over his eyes.

"It's Joe Grundy. Eight-round prelim. What was it, '88, '89?"

"What? Oh, shit! Hammer Joe. Sure! February, '89. Ref stops it in the third." He comes around the front of the car, wipes his hands on a rag and sticks one out. "The ref held up two fingers, I counted four. Game over."

"You hurt me in the second," I say.

"Yeah, I thought so," he says. "Body shot, right?"

"Bruised my liver."

"Those were the days," he says.

"I don't miss them either," I say. "So, how's it going?"

"This is a good gig. Steady pay, nice clean machinery. What are you doing these days?"

"Security. At the Lord Douglas Hotel."

"Oh, yeah?" He gives me a careful look. "So what is this, you looking for a rematch?"

"Trying to find one of your drivers. Starr? Dimitar Starr?"

"Lorne? I'm taking a smoke break."

"Have one for me," says a man vacuuming the back seat of the stretch.

We step outside, he offers me a Players, which I decline, with thanks, and we walk around the side of the building where the parked vehicles are clearly not part of the fleet.

"Can I have a look at the car he was driving Tuesday night?"

"He never brought it back," Mo says. "I told the cops."

"Dispatcher says a mechanic delivered a replacement and brought the first car back here."

"Never happened," Mo says, lighting up.

"You sure of that?"

"All you've got to do is count 'em. "Supposed to be nine. Eight now. Two stretch — one of them is armoured, couple of Lincoln Town Cars. S320 Mercs, a 560, also bulletproof."

"And one of them is missing."

"Yeah, one of the 320s."

"Any idea who the other driver was?"

"What other driver?"

"There was a second driver. If the first car went missing, and there was a second car delivered, there had to be a second driver. Did the second limo come back?"

"Yeah. It's here."

"So, who was driving that one?"

Mo delicately taps ash onto the asphalt and shakes his head. "That would most likely have been Dimi's asshole buddy, Farrel."

"Who's Farrel?"

"Farrel Newton. Don't know what he's doing here. Not qualified to work on these machines." He stops, leans against a Honda Accord. "Goodier keeps him on the payroll as janitor, handyman, carwasher, who knows? About once a month he goes off his meds and starts foaming at the mouth. Guy's a nutbar."

"And he's most likely dead," I say.

"Yeah? How?"

"Unless there's more than one Newton connected with this case. He either fell or was pushed off the roof of the hotel."

"Holy shit!" He turns his head to blow the smoke in another direction. "This is all about the murder, right?"

"It was my boss's girlfriend who was killed. Maybe by mistake."

"That's a little out of their league. Ripping off the company's more Dimi's speed."

"Homicide would like to talk to him."

"They'll have to get in line," he says. "Dimi's a wanted man."

"Who else wants him?"

"Fraud squad was around last month, two different insurance investigators." He looks around, motions me to keep in step and walks further down the side of the building. "We've had two limos stolen in the past year. Maybe three, if that other one doesn't turn up. All the units were signed out to either Starr or Newton."

"They're stealing cars?"

"They're doing something." Mo looks around. "Two limos. Insurance company detectives. We're talking easy two hundred, closer to three hundred thousand insurance, plus whatever a stolen Mercedes is worth outside the country."

"And the Fraud Squad thinks something's fishy."

"Hey, they *know* something's fishy, they just don't have anything they can prove."

"What do you think's going on?"

"Those guys lost two, maybe three expensive machines and they're still working here? You'd have fired them, wouldn't you? Like after the second time it happened?" Mo butts his smoke on the underside of his boot. "Tell you one thing the cops might not know, Dimi's name isn't Starr. It's Starjac, or Stazruk, some Bulgarian name. Used to work some car lot down on Broadway."

chapter fourteen

"Wanted to bill himself as 'The Battling Jewboy,' remember that? The promoters wouldn't let him."

"He was a wrecking ball," I say.

"Yeah, but his arms were too short," says Larry.

"Newton," I say.

"What about him?"

"It's a last name. First name, Farrel. He used to work at Ultra."

"All *right*!" Larry chortles, hauling out his ballpoint. "Better and better." He scribbles. "Farrel with two ars or two els?"

"Haven't a clue."

"I can find out. Where're we going again?"

"Used car lot," I say. "Do up your seat belt."

"What's at the used car lot?"

"Besides the obvious?"

"You figure they're selling stolen limos out the back door?"

"Somebody's stealing limos, we know that much. Mo figures they're leaving the country."

"Looks pretty good for his age, don't you think?" says Larry.

"Who?"

"Mo Feivel. I'm just saying, looks pretty good."

"What do you mean *for his age*? We're the same age, more or less."

"Maybe it's working with his hands," he says. "Or maybe there's less confusion in his life. He doesn't have that worried crease between his eyes."

"I have a worried crease between my eyes?"

Dysart Motors. The banner reads LOWEST PRICES! HIGH-EST VALUE! Plastic pennants hang limply over a dubious fleet. The prices on most of the windshields wouldn't replace a bumper on one of Ultra's vehicles. I'm barely out of the front seat before a hopeful looking man sidles up. He gives the hotel's utility sedan a once-over, no doubt calculating to a penny how much it might be worth as a trade-in.

"Hey there, my friend," he says as if he's known me all his life. "Looks like you're ready to move into something a bit more your style."

"What style would that be?" I want to know.

"Let's see now," he says. "Big man like yourself might want a little headroom, legroom. Got a fine Cherokee over here, A-1 condish, four-wheel drive, just sit yourself in the front seat there and tell me if that doesn't fit you like a glove."

"Handsome ride," I say. "But I don't want to waste your time ..."

"You let me worry about that," he says. "Nothing makes me happier than finding the right match of man and machine."

"I'm really here to talk to Mr. Dysart."

His hopeful smile disappears. "Outta luck there, pal. Old Dysart checked out five years ago."

"Oh? Who runs the place these days?"

"Mr. Starryk."

"Is he here?"

"George? Sure. He's inside."

"Thanks," I say, heading for the showroom.

"Sure you wouldn't like to just sit behind the wheel for a minute? It's a great feeling."

"I'm sure it is," I say. "Why don't you show it to my friend? He's always interested in new experiences."

Inside, a young man and woman are hotly debating the merits and possible drawbacks of owning the canary yellow Mustang on the showroom floor. The man mediating the discussion could be Dimi's twin, blood relation at least. He recognizes me immediately and takes off toward the far end, past a silver Focus and through a wooden door marked STAFF ONLY.

"Mr. Starryk?" I call after him. "Could I talk to you for a minute?"

Just before the door slams I distinctly hear the words, "Piss off!"

That's not going to happen. I disobey the door's

injunction and follow him into a windowless sector of tight office cubicles. The lone employee visible is a woman on her knees in the narrow corridor picking up scattered papers with an aggrieved look on her face. She looks angry even as I'm helping her.

"Did he say sorry?" she asks me. "Hell, no. Goddamn rhinoceros."

"Did you see where he went, Ma'am?" I ask politely.

"Nobody has to pee that bad," she says.

The door to the Gents is locked. I knock. No answer.

"Mr. Starryk? I have to talk to you."

The voice from inside sounds preoccupied, perhaps wrestling with a stuck zipper. "Piss off!"

"I need to ask you a few questions."

"Go away! I got nothing to say to you!"

"I'm looking for Dimitar. You're related, aren't you?"

"Piss off, I'm calling the police."

The sounds from inside aren't generally associated with calls of nature. "Good. You do that," I say. Something is being dragged across the floor. It occurs to the quick-witted sleuth that there may be at least one window in this part of the building. "That will work out fine." I can't spot a rear exit. "I'll wait right here until they show up. I'm sure they'd like to talk to you as well."

I lied. I have no intention of waiting outside the men's room. I retrace my path through the showroom and onto the lot. The Cherokee is missing, presumably with Larry Gormé at the wheel. I head for the rear of the building and arrive in time to see George Starryk extricating himself from a bathroom window. There's a wall at the far end of the lane and nowhere to run.

"What do you want?" he says. "I don't know you. I've got nothing to do with you."

"You filled in for Dimi on Monday night."

"So? I was doing a favour. One brother for another. That's no crime."

"You are going to have to tell that story to the police, sir. Better just sit tight until they get here. They hate having to look for people."

He doesn't much care for that option. He picks up a handy length of two-by-four.

"Take it easy, Mr. Starryk," I say. "We need to sort this thing out."

"Why don't I sort you out? You're an intruder."

He takes a swing at my head, which wasn't his best move; I'd have gone for the wonky knee. I duck the bat and get too close for him to try it again. I don't want to hit him. He's right about one thing, I am an intruder. I tie him up, force him back against the wall and take the stick away from him.

"You don't want to make this worse than it is, Mr. Starryk. Seriously. Calm down. I need to find your brother."

"I drove a car. That's all."

"Did you see your brother that night?"

"Him and the little guy drove away. I put on the hat and jacket, you guys come out, you grab a cab. None of my business. I wait around until some guy says move the car, then I bring it back to the shop and come home."

"That first limo is still missing. Were you aware of that?"

"Nothing to do with me."

"And I just heard that two other limos have gone

missing from Ultra this year. Were you aware of that?"

He pulls away from me, brushes off his jacket and straightens his tie.

"I've got nothing to do with what he does."

"So none of those vehicles have shown up here at any time?"

"Look around. I got nothing to hide."

"Well, they'd be in South America or somewhere by now, wouldn't they?"

Larry Gormé and the Jeep Cherokee are still missing when I get to the car. I sit in the front seat of the hotel's sedan, which does look in need of a fresh set of tires, and at very least a visit to the carwash. I manage to make the cellphone work and punch in Gritch's number.

"Hey, Gritch? Call Mooney and Pazzano will you? Tell them to check out Dysart Motors. The manager is a guy named Starryk, S-T-A-R-R-Y-K. Dimi's brother. He was the replacement driver Monday night."

"Oh, yeah?" he says. "You want me to tell them about the limo we found in the parking garage first?"

"Mercedes?"

"Oh, it's the right one," he says. "Got the Ultra sticker and everything."

"Where was it?"

"Top level. Far side of the elevator where they usually keep the dumpster," he says. "Garbage guys were pissed, phoned down. One of the Presbyterians went up and found it ten minutes ago."

"Stick with it. I'm on my way back."

"You going to call them or should I?"

"I'll call them."

Much as I dislike making Pazzano's day ... "Hello? Detective Pazzano, please. Okay. How about Mooney? Okay, well could you reach out for them? Tell them it's Joe Grundy. Tell them one of our security guys found that limo they've been looking for."

I start the car, count to ten, about ready to maroon Larry when he squeals into the lot and shudders to a stop a few inches from the rear of a Pontiac Firebird. He bounces out of the Jeep and swaggers over with a big grin on his face. I can see the salesman dismounting gingerly.

Larry climbs in beside me and slams the door.

"Have fun?" I ask.

"It was a blast," he says. "I drive like one of the Andretti boys. Don't know why they pulled my licence."

Gritch is waiting on the open roof of the parking garage, puffing happily on an El Producto as we pull up. Larry is still pumped after his test drive, or maybe it's because he's about to steal a story from an ambitious young reporter who's been beating him to the punch. Whatever the reason, he's cheerful as a songbird, snapping pictures with his cellphone. Mine doesn't have that function. At least I don't think it does.

"Right on your doorstep," he says. "With any luck there's a dead body in the trunk."

"Be careful what you wish for," says Gritch. "The trunk lid isn't latched all the way. Something's sticking out. Could be a coat."

Larry wants a closer look but I grab his arm. "Let's wait for the authorities," I tell him.

"Aren't you prudent all of a sudden," he says. He grabs another shot.

"Security camera up here?" I ask Gritch.

"Yeah, there's one over there and one on the ramp. And they should have picked it up driving in from the street, too. Rachel's getting that organized."

A cruiser pulls onto the roof. Melody Chan gets out. She looks happy to see Gritch. He's definitely happy to see her. They don't have any chance to swap war stories because Pazzano and Mooney are right behind them. I can't tell whether they're pleased or pissed, they have their cop faces on — we've heard 'em all, we believe no one, and where were you on the night in question?

"Anybody touch it?" Pazzano.

"Not from our staff," Gritch says. "Can't speak for the rest of the world."

"Goddamn tinted windows," says Mooney. The limo is parked nose out. He walks around to the rear, crouches. "Trunk isn't closed all the way."

"Pop it," says Pazzano.

Mooney puts on a glove and pops the lid. No body. Larry looks disappointed.

"Got a cordless drill," Mooney says.

"Rachel Golden's getting the security tapes for you," Gritch says.

"Okay," Mooney says, taking control of the situation, moving Pazzano and me a few steps apart. "You uniforms bag this area. Civilians out. You!"

"Have you guys talked to Dimi's brother yet?" I ask.

"Who?" says Pazzano.

"Dimi Starr's real name is Starryk. His brother George, also named Starryk, is currently managing Dysart Motors on Broadway."

"I thought we told you to keep your nose out of this," Pazzano says.

"Oh, Lord!" I say, thoroughly fed up. "If you two were half as good as you think you are, you'd know all this."

Pazzano muscles up to my chest, getting his feet set. He'd like to make this physical, provoke me into shoving back. Stupid as that might be, I'm getting perilously close to obliging him. I can feel Gritch's hand on my wrist.

"Oh, I'm sure they would have found all this out in a few more days," Gritch says.

"While you're at it," I say, "you might want to check with the fraud guys. This is the third limo's gone missing at Ultra."

"Get away from the car or I'll break your little camera," Pazzano says.

Larry turns. "Me?"

"Not a lot of gratitude around here," Gritch says.

"Hey, I appreciate," says Melody Chan. "I was on my way to guard a dead horse."

chapter fifteen

"You wouldn't believe the checklist," Connie says. "It's a masterpiece of bafflegab — what to say, what *not* to say, to our hosts, to our guides, to the governor general, questions you can ask, questions you must never ask. Not to mention the security clearance, medical checkup, shots …"

"You likely to pick up an exotic disease over there?"

"Don't want me spreading any. I'm going to be cooped up in a plane with the G.G. for ten hours — can't have me incubating microbes all the way. She has to disembark looking bright-eyed and ready for business."

"How long before you take off?"

"Four hours. Finish your lamb chop, big guy, I haven't got all night."

The Palm Court is beginning to fill up with the pre-theatre dining crowd. Rolf Kalman, the maître d', has given us one of his premium tables, secluded, by the potted trees for which the place is named. I promised him we wouldn't occupy it all night, it's worth at least a hundred-dollar gratuity from the right couple seeking public privacy. Connie is dressed for travelling — a soft, tailored jacket over a very fetching silk blouse. She looks chic, alert, filled with anticipation, fully capable of handling anything that comes her way. I must stop fretting about her. I try not to hover but it's in my nature. Inside my jacket is the little black box I've been carrying for two days.

"Safe trip," I say.

"Awww," she says, pulling out the thin gold chain and medallion. "A Saint Christopher medal. You cashiered altar boys sure know the way to a gal's heart."

"I wanted to get you a flak jacket but they didn't have one in your colour."

"I thought the Pope had this guy decommissioned," she says, deftly fastening the almost invisible catch. She knows better than to ask me to handle it.

"Don't tell my Uncle Victor," I say. "He flew twenty missions in Korea wearing one just like that."

"Uncle Victor still around?"

"Oh, yeah. Eighty-four, never had a fender-bender. Doesn't matter what Rome says, Saint Christopher looms large where I come from."

She tucks the medal inside her blouse and jiggles sweetly to settle the erstwhile saint. "He'll be happy there," she says with a smirk.

"Who could blame him?"

"You want dessert?" she wants to know.

"I haven't looked at the menu."

"It wouldn't be on the regular menu," she says.

We can't linger over dessert nearly as long as I'd like. The airport beckons, China beckons.

"I'll drive you."

"You don't have to do that," she says. "I'll grab a cab."

"I'd get another hour out of the deal."

"Well, get a move on then. Miss that plane, you'll never get lamb chops again. Don't look at me like that."

"Like what?"

"All gooshy."

"I'll miss you."

"I'll be back."

"While you're away I'll miss you."

"Don't fret." She touches Saint Christopher. "I'm in good hands."

"Button your shirt," I say. "The governor general's waiting."

I stick around the airport until takeoff. One brief wave passing through security and she's out of sight. Still, I stay until the plane is safely airborne, and longer than that, sitting in the cafeteria, drinking poor coffee, looking out at arrivals and departures, aware of being alone. I've never minded being alone all that much, not for some time anyway, but tonight it's getting to me, just a little.

I stash the car in the parking garage and descend to street level. My mind is occupied with vague concerns about trans-Pacific air travel and hijackers masquerading as flight attendants. I need sleep. The wall clock in Connor's darkened diner says it's 3:38 a.m., the one in the brightly-lit Scientology reading room disagrees by two minutes. The street is empty. I barely notice the wasp whine of the approaching motorcycle until it's nearly on me. The rider isn't wearing a helmet. The bike disappears around the corner by the construction site and the noise quits. He's parked it. It's possible he's come back for his copy of *Conan the Barbarian*, but I wonder how he plans on getting in with his hacksaw still at the bottom of the excavation, or tagged in a police evidence locker.

I stay on the opposite sidewalk and make an effort to walk like an unconcerned pedestrian. I can see the bike stashed around the corner in the shadows but no sign of the man who rode in on it. No sign of anyone working on the padlocked gate. Then I spot him. He's on the roof of the walkway, taking the long way down. Agile, too, no wasted motion, no fumbling, a skilled porch-climber.

My choices are limited. I could follow him into the pit, but taking into account my dubious left knee and the possibility that he could be waiting in the dark with something more lethal than a pocketknife, it seems that the best plan is to wait near his Suzuki.

I don't have to wait long. I can hear him clambering across the roof directly overhead. He swings down like a trapeze artist, duffel bag slung across his back, spots me instantly and freezes, like a cat. A young man, in his twenties probably, close-cropped hair, black moustache and beard. A streetlight catches his dark eyes when he spins around to make sure we're alone. He sets his feet like a man who's fought before.

"Excuse me, you're Mr. Santiago, Jesus, is that right?" I begin politely. "I have something of yours. I think it's a Bronze Star."

"Ten bucks and it's yours."

"Someone was murdered Monday night, and you were close by. You need to answer some questions."

"How about you answer one. Who the fuck are you?"

"Joe Grundy. I work at the hotel. I'm helping with the investigation."

"Good. You do that. I've got other plans."

"The police want a word with you as well."

"I won't be around that long."

I can see that he isn't going to cooperate and I'm too tired to spend the night arguing. I fumble in my pocket for the cellphone, pop it open and try to remember where 911 is on the miniscule keypad. "Hello, this is Joe Grundy at the Lord Douglas, corner of ..."

Without actually seeing where it came from, I find myself looking at a very shiny blade, some kind of combat knife with brass knuckle accessories. The thing probably has a compass in the handle, too. He slashes the air a foot from my face. "You can fuck off or get cut, your call," he says.

A person takes extra care when cold steel is waved in their face. I know I do. I drag off my jacket and start wrapping it around my left forearm.

"Wish I could," I say, "but I really need some answers."

"Yeah, life is just full of disappointments, isn't it?"

He knows how to use a knife, I can tell that much in a hurry. He slashes and darts and never stays in one spot for long. He's whipping slices at my face and lunges at my midsection. The only thing hampering him is how narrow the walkway is. The wooden fence and the sidewalk railing are keeping him from circling me and it's pretty much straight back and forth. In my case, mostly back.

"Leave me the fuck alone!" he yells.

I can hear desperation in his voice. Desperate men are dangerous. His next slash cuts through my jacket and I can feel hot wetness well up on my arm. Another article of clothing ruined. I duck as he makes a lunge at my eyes and bump backward into the Suzuki, barely managing to stumble around to the other side without landing on my butt. The bike tips over, whacking me on my bad knee. Well, he's got steel to work with; I might as well have some too. Good thing it's not a Harley, although with my adrenaline pumping the way it is I could probably lift that as well. I grab the bike by the front forks and the seat and charge straight at him. Now he's backing up, tripping, stabbing wildly, the blade catches somewhere in the motor mount and when he tries to wrench it free he goes down hard. The Suzuki crashes onto his chest. I club him twice on the side of his jaw with my good right fist. He's out cold. I'm bleeding, my knee hurts, but I'm very much alive. I resist the urge to bellow. I can hear a siren getting closer. A welcome sound. I could use some backup. I'm tired.

A very nice, very kind Korean doctor sews up my forearm, clucking disapprovingly with every stitch. There are thirty-six of them.

"Very deep cut," she says. "Clean edges."

"It was a sharp knife."

"Tsk tsk." She shakes her head.

"It's starting to hurt."

"You gashed a muscle. It's supposed to hurt."

"That's a comfort."

She looks over her shoulder at the man in the doorway. "Last one," she says.

"Take your time," says Norman Quincy Weed. He yawns. "I'm not awake yet."

"All done." She snips the last knot. "Sit tight. A nurse will come in and dress it."

"Thank you, doctor," I say. "You sew a fine seam."

"Watch out for infection," she says. I can hear a few clucks as she heads for her next emergency.

Norman has a close look at the stitching. "Nice one," he says. "I just love visiting you in the hospital. Gets my day off to a sunny start."

"Is he locked up?"

"More or less," he says. "In the Infirmary, under guard. Someone hit him over the head with a motorcycle."

"Just a small one." Small or not, my shoulder muscles are sore, my hands are torn up and I've got grease on my shirt. "Is he conscious?"

"He's moaning a lot. You broke a few ribs."

"He started it."

"Yeah, well, be careful he doesn't sue you," Weed says. "You bent his bike."

I lift my arm gingerly off the table and rest it against my chest. It feels heavy. And useless.

"I don't think this can be repaired," he says, holding up my jacket. The left sleeve is much darker than the right one. Weed sits in the vacated doctor's chair and looks at me for a long moment. I can see in his eyes that'd really like to smack me upside the head. "If I really felt like it, you know," he says, "I'm pretty sure I could get you ninety days for being an all-round pain in the ass, but then we'd have to nurse you through your convalescence."

"You talked to the Americans yet?" I ask.

"Time you took a vacation, Joe, my boy," he says pointedly. "Before my detectives bust your ass, or before you get yourself killed."

"Say what he was doing here?"

"I plan on asking him that very question when he stops bellyaching about his ribs." He steps aside as a nurse comes in carrying a tray of bandages and tape. "And after I've had breakfast," he says.

Almost noon. I'm outside now, and I have new visitors. Mooney's wandered off to watch ambulances arrive and depart while he talks to Weed on his cellphone. The questioning began inside some time ago — how do you know this guy? What were you doing there that time of night? — all of which I manage to deal with — Leo owns the property, I work for Leo, Santiago was trespassing. Just doing my job.

Pazzano watches me fumbling to adjust the sling. My left arm feels like a half-cooked leg of lamb.

"That's gonna mess up your jab for a while," Pazzano says.

"Making a fist is not an option right now," I say.

"Got stuck in the leg a few years back," Pazzano says. "Infection, antibiotics, swollen up. Hate knives." He looks at me with something akin to tolerance. "Better hope he kept his blade clean," he says.

"He kept it sharp," I say.

"I hear you."

It seems we're blood brothers. Temporarily, at least.

Mooney rejoins us. "He's awake," he says, "pissing and moaning."

"Let's go brighten his day," Pazzano says. "Give him something substantial to moan about."

As much as I hate to admit it, the arm is less painful when I leave it in the sling but it does tend to give the game away.

Gritch says, "What the hell happened to you?"

Rachel's reaction is somewhat more motherly. "Oh, Christ, Joe, now what have you done?"

"I was hoping for a 'there-there, poor thing,'" I say. "Is there any coffee?"

"I'll get it," she says. "Is it broken?"

"No, no, just a few stitches?"

"How few?" She hands me a mug.

"I forget."

"Bullshit," she says. "What happened?"

"I bumped into that guy Santiago, the one who's been camped out next door. He had a knife."

"He get away?" asks Gritch.

"In the hospital. Under guard." The coffee has extra sugar. Rachel probably thinks I'm in shock.

"So?" Rachel is insistent. "When did this happen?"

"About four a.m.," I say. "He was climbing out of the gravel pit. We had a scuffle, that's all. He nicked me. I knocked him down and called the cops."

"Did he do it?" Rachel asks. "Raquel?

"That I don't know," I tell her. I need to sit down. I'm spilling coffee. My hand is shaking. "I don't know. Truly. He had a knife. He was here that night. He's certainly capable ..." Rachel takes the cup from my hand and helps me into her chair. It feels solid and supportive; there's an ObusForm insert to cradle my lower back. My hand is still shaking.

"You in pain?" she asks.

"Temporarily," I say. "I've got some pills."

"Have you taken them?"

"Not yet."

"Gimme."

"In my jacket."

Gritch picks my jacket off the floor and locates the pharmacy package. He dangles the bloody rag. "Holy shit!" he says.

"Oh, God," Rachel says. "Let me see."

She gently pulls the sling aside. The bandage runs from my wrist to my elbow. It's somewhat stained with this and that.

"A few stitches," she says. "How much blood did you lose?"

"Not that much. Didn't nick a vein."

"Lucky bastard," says Gritch.

"*Crazy* bastard, more like," Rachel says. "Why didn't you just phone the police?"

"I did."

"I mean *before* he cut your arm off." She checks the label on the pill bottle and shakes out a pair. "Take these. Now."

"I need to talk to Leo."

"You need your head examined," she says. "Take."

I wash the pills down with lukewarm coffee and lean back in the chair. "This is a nice chair," I say. "I should get one of these."

I didn't finish the coffee. Rachel gave me orange juice instead and put me to bed, clucking like a Korean doctor. I must have slept a long time because when I wake up it's almost midnight, and the pills have worn off. My left arm is throbbing. My cellphone is ringing.

I'm still not used to getting calls on a device the size of a chocolate bar. That the caller is on the other side of the world, speaking from the future, is an aspect I wish I could exploit.

"So you can't actually tell me what happens tomorrow?"

"'Fraid not, big guy."

"This international dateline nonsense is no use whatsoever."

"You heading down to Olive's for your nightly brew?"

"I guess." First I'd have to locate my pants.

"You sound a trifle groggy."

"I just woke up."

"Did I wake you?"

"No, no, I was stirring." My arm woke me up but she doesn't need to know that.

"Just wanted you to know that Saint Chris and I made it in one piece."

"Tell him he's still on the clock."

"How about you? Get anywhere today?"

"Truth is, I slept much of it," I say.

"Tomorrow is another day."

"From where you are it's already yesterday."

"I'll call again yesterday," she says. "Go have your beer."

After she hangs up I give some thought to making my late tour, but the idea of getting dressed defeats me. My arm feels hot. I give in and take two more painkillers and walk around my bedroom until I can feel them kick in.

This time the bedside clock reads 08:09. I'm stiff and sore and wouldn't stir except for the basic biological imperatives. I wash up as best I can without risking a shower. Wearing a clean shirt and a jacket with two intact sleeves makes me look semi-presentable. I leave off the sling and take two more painkillers.

The office is crowded; Gritch, Rachel, Roland, Brian, Margo, Maurice, voices hushed as a funeral home viewing. I certainly don't think my wound rates that kind of observance.

"It's not that bad," I say.

"They've arrested Leo," says Margo.

chapter sixteen

Leo is being held. Somewhere. I can't get in to see him but I'm assured that Winston Mikela has met with him, or will soon meet with him, or has been contacted, or is on the way.

On the way to where? I'd like to know.

Sorry, sir. You should check with Detective Mooney. You should check with Detective Pazzano. You should bugger off and stop bothering people.

Finally, after annoying about twenty hard-working cops — never a good plan — I manage to irritate my way to Norman Weed's office door.

"Shouldn't you be in bed?" he says pleasantly.

He's wearing tweed today. It's stylish, for him, various shades of heather and blue. "New jacket?" I ask politely.

"My wife," he says. "She's got me on a diet. Says my old suits don't fit me any more."

"I hadn't noticed."

"Oh, yeah? Observational skills are rumoured to be a prerequisite in your line of work, aren't they?"

"I usually let Gritch do the serious looking," I say. I give the overture a chance to die out before spreading my good arm, palm up. "So?"

"He's being interviewed. He's got a lawyer, hell, ten lawyers far as I can tell."

"What's the charge?"

"He hasn't been charged. Yet."

"He was arrested."

"He's a person-of-interest and they want to have a long talk with him."

"They don't make an arrest, especially one involving such a high-profile citizen, without running it by you first."

"Your point?"

"You gave them the green light."

"They used their own initiative."

"What did you get from Jesus? What's he saying?"

Weed stands up, settles his shoulders inside his new jacket, buttons it, comes around the desk with one arm out like an usher. I'm being given a polite bum's rush. "Gosh-almighty, Joe," he says, "I sure would like to help you but I don't think I will. I let my detectives run their own cases as much as possible. That includes deciding who gets to know what, and when."

"Come on, Norman." There's an unfortunate note of pleading in my voice; he probably caught it, too. "I've been a big help," I finish lamely.

"Oh, yeah," he says graciously, "and don't think we're not grateful."

"I need to see Leo."

"And as soon as that can be arranged, you'll have a chance to talk about old times. But right now ..." I see that he's ushered me as far as the exit. "I have work that doesn't involve you, or your boss, or your hotel. This is a big town and other bad things are demanding my attention, so why don't you go home, change your bandages, and let me do my job?"

And, of course, Winston Mikela is away from the office and, yes, we'll make sure he has your cellphone number, sir. What was the name again?

There's a birthday card in my office mailbox. I get a Christmas card every year, usually accompanied by a pair of warm socks. And every year on Leo's birthday I get another card, because, according to Madge Killian, Leo wouldn't be having a birthday were it not for how big a target I was. This year's card says, "God bless our Guardian Angel." Yeah, getting shot at, those were the days. I toss the card on my desk.

"My Granny always put a two-dollar bill in my birthday card," Gritch says.

"Made the front page again," says Rachel. "All we need now is a bomb scare and we can close up shop."

I've already seen it. Larry Gormé's byline is under the headline HOTEL HIGH DIVE! Trust the *Emblem* to use red ink.

"Tomorrow's should be even better," says Gritch. "Hotelier of the Year — Busted!"

"How's that arm?" Rachel wants to know.

"Sore, unserviceable, but otherwise okay," I say.

"Why aren't you wearing the sling?"

"Makes me feel like an invalid."

"You are an invalid," she says.

"Get to see the old man?" Gritch asks.

"He's being held at an undisclosed location," I say. "You got Theo's office number?" I ask Gritch.

"What are you asking him for?" Rachel wants to know. "I'll dial it for you."

"T. Alexander, may I help you?" asks a receptionist without enthusiasm.

"Yes," I say. "I'd like to speak to Theo Alexander. Tell him it's Joe Grundy at the Lord Douglas Hotel."

"Mr. Alexander is out of town. May I take a message?"

"Could you tell me when he'll be back?"

"He was expected back on Wednesday but he called to say he'd be a while longer. He didn't give a definite return date."

"I see. Is there any way I can contact him?"

"I'm afraid not. He was in Las Vegas, but I think he may have gone to Los Angeles on business."

"Would you tell him that I called, please? Joe Grundy. He knows how to reach me."

"Certainly, Mr. Grundy, I'll leave him that message,"

"Thank you." I hang up. "Still out of town," I say. "Was in Las Vegas, now in L.A. Maybe."

"Making himself conspicuously scarce," says Rachel.

"Thing is, he was due back Wednesday."

"No mention of his travelling companion?" Gritch throws in.

"Nope."

"Who would that be?" asks Rachel.

"Why don't I just find out for you guys?" Gritch picks up the phone and redials. "Hi there," he says, "my name's Ray Brando. Wanna talk to Theo. Yeah, where is he? Lissen up, don't give me the runaround here, he's got my little sister with him. Julia Brando. I got news for him, if he's messing ... baloney!" He has a wicked grin on his face. "Look lady, I'm a police officer and I know he's got a woman with him down in Vegas and it's my sister. Oh, yeah? He's got a woman with him, right? What's she calling herself these days? Marcia? *Marcia*!? Yeah, sure. She got a last name? I'll have the cops pick him up. My sister's underage. What? Duhamel? Marcia Duhamel? Sounds made-up to me. Yeah, well, I'm sure that's the information you have but I bet that asshole doesn't tell you everything!" He hangs up, beams at the two of us, pleased with himself. "Marcia Duhamel."

Rachel shakes her head. "I think impersonating a cop is against the law."

"I just threw that in," he says. "Besides, it's against the law if you flash a phony badge for a free lunch. You can do practically anything over the phone." He's leafing through the phone book. "Marcia Duhamel. Here she is. False Creek. Nice neighbourhood." He punches in the numbers, hands me the phone.

"Hi, it's Marcia. I'm not in. Leave me a number, or call my cell."

I have to listen to the message three times before I can write down the cellphone number she's rattling off.

"Hi, it's Marcia. I'm not answering my cell right now. If this is Brandi, we'll be back Sunday. Love you, bye."

"Message says she'll, no, *they'll* be back on Sunday," I tell Gritch.

"Bet they're having more laughs than we are."

"Gotta take off," I say. "I'm meeting Leo's lawyer in …" It hurts to pronate my forearm. My watch isn't on my left wrist and I can't remember where it wound up. That's annoying. It's a good watch. "Did you throw out my jacket?"

"I was going to have it framed with the rest of your mangled wardrobe."

"Was my watch in the pocket?"

"I've got your watch," Rachel says. She opens her desk drawer, looks at me. "You don't think Leo did it, do you Joe?" she asks.

"I think he really loved her," I say.

She buckles the watch on my good wrist. It feels odd there. "That's not exactly an answer," she says.

The watch crystal has a scratch from the 3 to the 7. "I don't have any answers," I say.

But I do have a fresh thought, possibly my first of the day. "See if Bri can run a check on that Hiscox woman. Roselyn Hiscox. She says she's writing a book but I have yet to see her make a note."

Winston Mikela doesn't handle criminal cases. He has invited the justly famous Arnold Köenigsberg to look after things, for which phone call Winston will no doubt charge Leo a substantial fee. Arnold is what Louis Schurr would have called a "shlub," an observation based on the man's inability to knot his tie properly or deal with his unruly eyebrows. But notwithstanding his somewhat casual aspect, Arnold Köenigsberg is the man I'd want representing me in a capital case. Arnold's command of a courtroom is the stuff of legend.

Arnold says we can talk for a few minutes if I show up at Connor's at 12:45. As I cross the intersection I can see him standing at the window counter, arms spread like a condor, two open newspapers, his bulging briefcase, and a legal pad arrayed before him. He is eating a tuna salad sandwich and drinking 2 percent milk from a carton. His tie is askew. His eyes are sweeping like radar, scanning both papers, consulting files, and scribbling notes. I'm impressed that he can spare a blip to acknowledge my arrival while turning pages of both the *Emblem* and the *Globe and Mail*.

"Is he okay?" I ask him. "Is he locked up?"

"Private room. They take good care of high-profile murder suspects."

"Can I get in to see him?"

"Why bother?" he says with his mouth full. "I should have him out before supper."

"How bad is it?"

"Feh," he says. He has a big drink of milk, wipes his face with a wad of napkins, and uses it to brush some tuna flakes off the legal pad. "The Crown won't go in front of a judge with what they have."

"What do they have?"

"Nothing substantive. Circumstantial at best. Rumours, theories. I think they jumped the gun."

"What?" I'm pressing him more than he'd like. "This isn't privileged information."

Arnold has a lawyer's natural disinclination to hand a third party anything other than a subpoena but he seems willing to accept, at least for the time being, that we're on the same team.

He lowers his voice. "They've got one of Leo's business cards. It was in the pocket of the dead man. It has the security code for the fire door at the top of the stairs."

"So?"

"In Leo's handwriting."

"They can prove that?"

"I doubt it," he says, "but they have it."

"What about the driver?"

"Dimi Starr, AKA Dimitar Starryk, is still among the missing."

"What else?"

"Theory. Far as I can see. Raquel was pregnant, she was talking to a lawyer, Leo changed his will immediately after she was killed, Leo's past relationship with Vivienne Griese, *née* Saunders ..."

"Past relationship?"

"According to Leo they had a brief affair some years ago."

"Ri-ight," I say. I can hear the weariness in my voice. Of course he'd had an affair with Vivienne. One more fact I didn't want to know. "They think it was a love triangle?"

"That looks like the way they're going at it. Leo was in a bind with Ms. Mendez getting pregnant, possibly entitled to a large sum of money, perhaps pressing him to get married."

"Idiots."

"Well," he says, starting to collect his trash, "the Crown won't let it go any further. At least not yet. They'd need a lot more than they have now. I think they were shaking the tree to see if anything would fall out."

"Like the business with his first wife?"

"Second wife," Arnold says. "Can't drag that in." He tosses the newspapers in a recycle box and the rest in the garbage. "Leo was never charged with anything."

"But it won't help him."

"It has no bearing." His opens his briefcase to pack for the afternoon.

"We'd better hope not," I say.

They haven't let him shave yet. I can see silver stubble on his jaw and there are dark smudges under his eyes. I've been granted a grudging fifteen-minute visit and I have no doubt the guard has his eye on the clock.

"I'm fine," he says. "Don't fret, Joseph. I've been waiting for the other shoe to drop. They made their move, now we can fight back." He shakes his head. "Timed it nicely," he says. "Can't get in front of a judge until Monday. I'm stuck for the weekend. Gives them two free days to dig."

"How do they come up with second-degree murder?" I want to know.

"Probably sounds better than, 'We've-got-bugger-all-but-let's-charge-him-anyway.'" He makes a noise that might be a laugh. "They can amend it, up or down, depending."

"On what?"

"On what they think they can prove."

My frustration is building, or maybe my arm is putting me in a bad mood. "Mr. Alexander," I begin, trying to maintain an even tone below the guard's earshot but aware that my voice is pulled tight and ready to snap. "I don't think I can be of any further help to you with this matter."

"What do you mean?"

"I mean, I can't operate in the dark. I've been fed information, and not by you, about your wife's murder in Alberta, the fact that you were, for a time at least, the prime suspect, that the case is still open." I take a deep breath. Leo doesn't interrupt. "Assuming your hands are clean, and damn it, that's the only way I've been able to go this far, you'd better start being straight with me or I'll walk. I mean it."

"What do you want to know?"

"I don't *want* to know anything about this. It wasn't part of the job description, poking around in people's private lives gives me a headache."

"You're an honourable man, Joseph. You won't make it worse than it is."

"Just how bad is it?"

"Ask."

"You took Ms. Saunders to the awards dinner. Was it starting up again?" I need to know.

"No. That was Raquel's idea. Vivienne had been suggesting that we should ... see each other again ... now that she was getting a divorce. Raquel thought I should explain to her that I was taking myself off the market, so to speak." There's a sad little smile tugging the corner of his mouth. "I never kept secrets from Raquel. I told her everything."

I wonder what time it is in Beijing.

My frustration is surfacing. "Find the damn driver!" I say. "Am I missing something? They've got a dead body, they've got a limo with prints over everything, including a cordless drill. What the hell more do they need?"

"I am assured there is a massive manhunt underway," he says.

"All right then," I say. "Track him down, sort things out. Good." I can hear the false heartiness in my voice.

He waves my comment away. He has other things on his mind. "We have to arrange for a funeral," he says. "For Raquel. She had a church she went to Sunday mornings. Saint Barnabas."

"I'll look into it, sir," I say.

"Thank you. I don't know if she has any family. Except for the husband, wherever he is."

The guard is stepping forward. "Is there anything I can bring you from the hotel, sir — towels, cigars?"

"You know what I want, Joseph. Find out who took her away from me."

"We've been through this, Leo," I say. I almost never call him by his first name.

Leo is standing up. "You're the only one I'd trust to do the job, Joseph." He squares his shoulders, smiles at me, and precedes his escort through the steel door.

chapter seventeen

A crowd of media people and spectators with nothing more important demanding their participation is gathered outside the police station as I make my departure. Not nearly as many as might accompany a Hollywood bad girl to rehab, but sufficient to cover the public arrest of a prominent local innkeeper. Most are there to get a quote or sound bite from Arnold Köenigsberg and I manage to elbow my way through the mob with a few pardon me pleases and no comments. Most of them wouldn't know me if I wore a nametag, which suits me fine. There is one familiar face, a camerawoman who works on location with Connie. She never warmed to me for some reason. I can feel her lens panning as I cross the street to the parking lot where a tall blonde woman is waiting beside the car.

"No comment," I say.

"Didn't ask for one," says Roselyn Hiscox.

"Force of habit," I say. "Something I can do for you?"

"I could use a lift."

"The hotel?"

"Where else?"

I unlock the passenger door. The camera across the street is still watching me.

"What's the matter with your arm?"

"Stiff."

"Want me to drive?"

"No, no thanks, it's an automatic, point and steer."

She settles herself beside me, fluffs her blonde hair. "How does he look?"

"Fine," I say.

"Really?" She sounds dubious.

The camera is swinging to follow us. It's Connie's videographer, Dee is her name. I resist the urge to stick out my tongue as we pull onto the street.

"He doesn't usually wear the same shirt all day," I say, "but he's dealing with it."

"Sounds like the least of his problems," says Roselyn.

"Still no comment."

"That's okay," she says, "it'll all come out in the wash as my mother used to say."

"Meaning your book."

"Maybe two books. It's a saga."

"Leo's past life is his business."

"His past life is likely the reason his mistress was murdered."

The word offends me for some reason and I honk at a dawdling pedestrian rather than snap at my passenger. The walker flips me the bird. Roselyn appears oblivious.

She says "He has more than one ghost in his past."

"They all in your book?"

"All? Ha! I wish. But I've got a few. Old sins cast long shadows."

"Meaning?"

"No one amasses the kind of money he has without stepping on some toes."

"Toes are one thing."

"Or stabbing someone in the back, or stealing something, or acting on inside information, or making deals under the table. You know what Balzac said?"

"Remind me."

"Every great fortune begins with a crime."

"Is any of this germane to the murder of my friend Raquel Mendez?"

"Who knows? Could be a hundred things. The shareholders of the AlBrit TV network who wound up with half of what they should have got, or Banff Action Developments which he gutted to buy AlBrit. Hell, the Lord Douglas Hotel, which he got by buying up the previous owner's IOUs for ten cents on the dollar and then foreclosing."

"Sounds like business to me. Not a world I'm familiar with."

"You will be when the book comes out."

I leave her by the front entrance and drive around to the parking garage, muttering to myself. "Invincibly Ignorant." A papal distinction for people too far gone in their primitive belief systems to accept revealed truth.

Margo is looking for me when I get back. Lloyd Gruber has had a heart attack. Better and better.

"Well, they're not sure it was a heart attack," she says. "It could be indigestion, anxiety attack, low blood sugar. He's been under a lot of stress."

"Unlike yourself," I say.

"I handle it differently," she says. "Anyway, we got him an ambulance and they took him off to Vancouver General."

"Anything I can do?"

"Oh, I've got a list. I'll make you a copy."

"Give me the top item."

"How about getting us off the front page of the newspaper? Everywhere you go your reporter pal's trotting behind with his sneaky little video phone."

"He was helping me track someone down."

"Odd how the trail of breadcrumbs always seems to end at this hotel. We're the media event of the month. We've had a murder, a dead body in the lot next door, and the boss taken out through the lobby in handcuffs."

"He'll be out on Monday."

"That's fine for Leo, but it doesn't really change the situation, does it? I've had eighty-three cancellations in the past two days," she says.

I can see the lobby through the glass partition that makes up half of her back wall. Things look normal enough, people checking in, people checking out — perhaps a few more out than in.

"Can you fix it, Joe?" she asks.

"I don't work miracles, Margo."

"Neither do I." She puts on her glasses, usually a sign that my time is up. "I've had a job offer," she says.

"I expect you get a lot of those."

"This one's tempting."

"Managing?"

"Not yet, but it's a big chain, numerous possibilities for advancement, is how they put it."

"Sounds like a great opportunity."

She takes off her glasses, rubs her eyes. "I've got a headache."

"Get you something?"

"No, I keep a big bottle in my desk these days." She helps herself to tablets, sips water, rubs her eyes again. "I don't want to leave here," she says. "I've been effectively running this place for three years, whether Lloyd acknowledges it or not. I'd rather stay — in Vancouver, in my home. I have a mother to worry about, friends, connections. But if this is a dead end ... If Leo isn't going to be able to hang onto the place ... Goddamn it, I won't work for Theodore Alexander, he gives me the creeps. And if this place gets sold to Fairmont, or, God forbid, some supermarket hotel chain, I could be out on my ear. I'm not going to wait around to go down with the ship!"

As Gritch said, if Leo goes down, the world as we know it dims and dies. "And if I can straighten it out?"

"I don't have a lot of time to decide, Joe."

"I've got the weekend."

"Think fast," she says.

"If you'd upgrade your phone and you could send me little movies," Connie says.

"Would I have to learn new buttons?"

"I saw one of you today."

"Really?"

"It was lovely."

"What was I doing?"

"Getting into your car with a long-legged blonde woman. Very stylish."

"From Dee, right? I saw her taking my picture."

"She doubts your fidelity."

"She never liked me."

"What's wrong with your arm?"

"What? Nothing. It's a bit stiff."

"Look, buster, I'm willing to accept that you can behave while chauffeuring leggy blondes around town but don't try any of that he-man guff with me. I'm a trained observer and I know what I saw. Your arm is more than stiff."

"Job-related."

"Joe."

"I got cut."

"Continue."

I come clean about the encounter, minimizing the more life-threatening aspects but admitting that the damn thing hurts.

"*How* many?"

"Thirty-six."

"I leave town for two days …"

"I changed the dressing," I say. "It's clean, neat sewing job, healing up nicely."

"Assuming you don't need both arms, what's your next move?" she asks.

"Handing in a politely worded letter of resignation has become a very appealing idea."

"You won't run out on him, big guy. It's not your style."

"Wish you weren't so far away," I say.

"I wish I had long legs," she says.

"Your legs are perfect."

"Damn right."

"God bless our Guardian Angel." I say.

"Ours?" she asks. "Yours and mine?"

I pick the card off my desk. "It's on a card," I say. "*I'm* the guardian angel. At least as far as Madge Killian is concerned. She wrote, 'God bless our Guardian Angel.' Leo just had a birthday. She figures it's because of me."

"It is, isn't it?"

"I guess."

"Notice anything about the sentiment?"

"Such as?"

"Such as, *our* Guardian Angel?"

"She was his social secretary."

"How social?" Connie wants to know.

"Maybe I should go to Victoria."

"Hey, me too," she says. "The other one."

chapter eighteen

Madge Killian lives in a rambling cottage beside a river. At the back of her house is a deck built out over the water and a floating dock where a daysailer is moored. Her flower garden is generous. The flagstone path is flanked by every perennial scheduled to show up in Victoria in early spring, which is practically all of them.

Madge is on her knees planting purple annuals along a border. She doesn't look much different from when I first met her; a bit plumper perhaps, more casually dressed, but still brisk, cheerful, and efficient. When she sees me her eyes light up and I realize that I'm happy to see her, too.

I manage to lift my left arm out of harm's way as she gives me a big hug. "I don't remember you being this tall," she says.

"Must've had a growth spurt when I hit thirty-five."

"No, that's not it," she smacks me on the chest. "Oh, I know, I wore heels back then."

She takes a step back. "Have they let him go?" she asks me.

"Not until Monday," I say. "He'll get bail."

"How ridiculous," she says. "That they could even suspect him of such a horrid thing." She looks at me fondly. "But you'll fix it, won't you, Joseph? You'll look after him. That's what you do."

"I'm trying. He hasn't given me much to go on."

"That's just Leo. Secretive man. I used to have to pry it out of him if he wanted red wine or white."

"This is a lovely place."

"Three generations, might have been four if I'd ever found time for children myself. I'll have to find someone worthwhile to leave it to."

"Historical society?"

"No, no, then you get sightseers. This is a place that should be lived in. Come in, come in, I have coffee and I have cookies."

The house is made up of many small rooms flowing in concert through a labyrinth decorated with artifacts and memories — a thousand photographs, many framed, many more leaning and curling, pinned to corkboard or held by magnets, an upright piano, full china cabinets, ceiling-tall bookshelves sagging under the complete works of anyone worthy of more than one volume.

"He sends his warmest regards," I say.

"Hmmm," she says. "You tell him I'm still waiting for that album. Cream and sugar?"

"Black, thanks. What album would that be?"

"Photographs of his ranch."

"I've never seen any."

"It's a gap in the archive," she says. "These are ginger snaps. I didn't make them, my neighbour did. These are date squares. They're mine."

"You used to bring these into the office." I have a memory of her coming out of an elevator carrying a platter, wearing a ruffled blouse and red high-heeled pumps. "Maiden cake," she is saying. "But you don't have to be one to eat one."

"You were with him a long time."

"Almost twenty-five years. Started as his secretary."

"What was he doing then?"

"Different things, real estate development, he had shares in a television station. He was an adventurer, always looking for something to conquer. I think he was looking for something he could love."

"Did he find it?"

"He loved the ranch. He liked raising horses."

"I don't know anything about that part of his life, I guess."

"Lives," she says. "I think he's had seven, at least."

"Did you know his wife? The one who was killed?"

"That was Lorraine. Yes, I knew her. She was quite mad you know."

"I didn't."

"Oh, yes. Ask anyone. Beautiful, but right off her trolley. I think it ran in her side of the family. Her daughter was odd too."

"I didn't know Leo had a third child."

"*Third*? Acknowledged perhaps. I suspect there may be a few of his 'love children' in the world — well, they wouldn't be children anymore would they? Which is one reason I never got involved with Leo Alexander in *that* way. He made a pass at me. Oh, yes. One day shortly after I started working for him. I said, 'There'll be none of *that*, Mr. Alexander.' Yes, I did. I said, 'let's remain professional.' He respected me for that."

"I understand Leo was a suspect in the matter of his wife's death."

"Not really. He was nowhere near the ranch that weekend." She deftly slices the maiden cake into neat squares and lifts one onto a plate for me. "Still, it's an awful coincidence, don't you think?"

"I haven't been able to get much information. What happened?"

"Well, I don't know, exactly. I was with Mr. Alexander at a meeting in Calgary. We were, well, *he* was, trying to acquire two new television outlets. There was a bitter round of negotiations. He was a tough horse trader. Then, in the middle of all that, he got a phone call from the ranch that Lorraine had been killed. So he went right back. It cost him the deal he was trying to make, but he didn't waste a second."

"Were Leo and his wife getting along?"

"She didn't like living on the ranch. She was always flying off to New York or Europe or somewhere she could spend a lot of money."

"Did you ever meet Raquel?"

"The maid? No, I never did. Of course I haven't been in Vancouver for quite a few years. Once Mr. Alexander closed up his businesses and moved into the hotel, I was out of a job. I don't mean that in a bad way. Mr. Alexander was very generous with my severance package, and I had a pension plan, and then when the library was established there was a yearly budget for that. But I was out of that particular job, looking after his appointments and keeping track of his social obligations. I enjoyed that job. I miss it."

She settles herself across from me. "Now don't forget," she says, "when you get a chance, mention the ranch pictures. I have the sailing years. I have his correspondence. I have just about everything except for Alberta."

"I'd love to see that collection. Is it handy?"

"Oh, Lordy, no," she laughs. "It just grew too huge. I ran out of room. Four years ago I prodded Leo into buying a nice little building not far from the University."

She hands me a brochure with a colour photograph on the cover, a two-storey house of solid Victorian aspect. "The Alexander Library," she says with pride in her voice. "It's not open to the public. By appointment only."

"I'd like to make an appointment."

"Don't be silly, I'll give you a personal tour," she says. "Finish your coffee. Have another piece of maiden cake. You don't have to be one to eat one."

Madge drives a beautifully maintained 1969 Austin-Healey Sprite, British racing green with a badge bar on the grill proudly carrying the insignia of the Victoria Sprite-Fanciers Club. It's a nimble little two-seater and she drives it well. I'm having trouble keeping up with her.

Fortunately for me it isn't far from her riverside cottage to the Alexander Library.

There's a small gravel parking lot at the side of the building and Madge motions me to occupy the space reserved for L. Alexander.

"Who's more entitled?" she asks.

I don't think the hotel's shabby sedan rates such a valued place but since Leo hasn't bothered owning a car for some time, I think I'm safe.

For a man who would throw his bronze plaque into the first available dumpster, Leo appears to have amassed an impressive collection of framed portraits, testimonials, citations, and numerous awards, medallions, statuettes, and scrolls.

"You tell Leo I'll want that Hotelier's plaque right away. I have a spot reserved right over here."

There is an open space at the end of a series of awards; one of them is similar in size and shape to the one currently in the police evidence lockup.

"You might not get it for a while," I say. "Someone defaced it."

"Why would anyone do that?"

"The police are trying to find out."

"Poor Joseph," she says. "Always tidying up, aren't you?"

"Grasping at straws is what I'm doing, Madge."

"Well, you have a look around while I check for messages. Start in there, it has the most exciting stuff."

The largest room is devoted to yachting. Model boats everywhere — racing sloops, Grand Banks schooners, square-rigged China clippers. The walls are covered with oil paintings, photographs, newspaper clippings, ship's wheels, bells, tillers, winches, and flags. Every item is accompanied by an identifying brass marker or a framed card lettered in faultless calligraphy giving dates and places and names of the vessels involved.

There are photographs of Leo surrounded by sailing crews, hoisting tankards and loving cups, helming one of his racers, wind in his hair, salt spray in his face. The man in the pictures and the Leo I'm familiar with are quite different. It's the same guy, but this version looks heroic, maybe even a bit reckless; face scoured by sun and wind, eyes bright, hands on the tiller strong and confident. The Leo I've known for the past eight years is a paler version of the buccaneer in these pictures.

"You never knew him then, did you, Joseph?" Madge has joined me in the gallery.

"No."

"Before your time." She straightens a frame that didn't need adjustment. "I crewed for him a few times, in this little boat, his first one, *Lemony*."

I can see her image in the picture she just touched, younger, quite pretty, standing behind Leo in the stern of a small sloop. They both look happy.

"That was taken so long ago," she says. "Once he started getting serious about racing he needed a real crew." She wipes an imaginary speck from Leo's image. "I just enjoyed the outings. Messing about in boats, as they say."

The next photograph looks familiar.

"I've seen this one before," I say.

"*Tyrannous*," she says.

"He has a model in his penthouse."

"Yes. She was his pride. A real racer."

"Did he sell her?"

"*Tyrannous* went down, Joseph, off Cape Flattery. Collided with a trawler in the fog. The fishermen picked them up. All but one."

Another dead body.

"He was very upset." She turns away from the picture, shakes her head. "The man's family was taken care of. He's like that. Very generous, very loyal."

"Very unlucky."

"After that he stopped racing. Bought a cabin cruiser. *Mimosa*. Said he wanted some comfort." She points to a colour photograph on the other side of the room. "Over here. Twenty-three metre Burger, sleeps six."

"Handsome vessel." It seems like an appropriate thing to say, although I'm no judge of watercraft. The identifying card reads, MIMOSA, COBBLE HILL MARINA.

"He hasn't been aboard for a long time. I'm not sure why he's hung onto her. Sentiment, I suppose."

"The crewman who drowned," I start, "do you remember his name?"

"Newton," she says. "Yarnell Newton." She turns brisk abruptly, too much memory lane, perhaps. "You have to sign the visitor's book," she says.

"Be my pleasure." I follow her into an alcove that has the unfortunate aspect of a shrine. A portrait of Leo, younger, standing in front of a building, one of his, presumably. "Do you get many visitors?" I ask.

"Well, of course the Yacht Club really covets his models, and the photographs, the trophies, there's even a movie he had commissioned of the 1987 Swiftsure race. It's quite a collection."

She opens a leather-bound visitor's book and hands me a fountain pen. "I'm very happy you showed up, Joseph. It's a comfort to me, knowing you're helping him."

"It's good to see you, too, Madge," I say. "I'm always grateful for my Christmas socks." A name has just popped out at me. Norman Weed is in the book. "Norman Weed? He's a friend of mine."

"Yes. He's mentioned your name," she says. "Nice man. He's been here a few times. Not recently, but usually once or twice a year."

Well, now.

I page backward through the book and notice Norman's name scribbled more than once.

"You said Leo had a daughter," I say. "Has she ever been here?"

"Haven't seen her in many years," says Madge. "Not since her mother was killed. Rose is her name. She had to be institutionalized after it happened. Very sad."

"Her name Alexander, too?"

"She had foster parents," she says. "I forget what they called themselves, and she was married, for a while anyway. I don't remember her married name. Something western."

"Western?"

"Like a cowboy. Buffalo Bill. Something like that. I think she met the man at a horse sale."

chapter nineteen

M*imosa* isn't the biggest yacht in the marina, not by a long stretch, but she doesn't look out of place. She has nice lines, a flying bridge, a striped canopy over the stern deck. What do I know? A yacht's a yacht. Out of my league, financially, socially, practically. Ferry rides are my preferred mode of water travel and even they make me uncomfortable. Driving off a ferry is my favourite part of the trip.

I call out "Anyone aboard?" I don't know why there would be. My investigation, if you can call it that, has run out of notions. What have I learned so far? There's another dead Newton in the mix. That's no doubt significant. And Leo has a daughter who married "Buffalo Bill." That, too, is new. Not particularly helpful, but new. If Leo's had seven lives, he seems able to leave them behind without a backward glance — wives, ranches, boats, buildings, children. "Searching for something he could love," Madge said.

Aren't we all?

A familiar figure is bulling down the wharf in my direction. Lenny Alexander has his head down and totes a two-four of Kokanee and a bag of groceries.

"Mr. Alexander. Good afternoon."

"Grundy. What the hell you doing here?"

"Working for your father."

"He still in jail? I bet that's pissing him off."

"He's asked me to look into some things. One of them was his boat." Not precisely true, but close enough.

"Tell him to relax. I needed a place to crash, figure out a few things. I'm outta the house. She can keep the damn house."

"I'm sorry, I wasn't aware you had ... difficulties at home."

"Why should you care?" He climbs aboard with his groceries. Looks around at the floating creature comforts. "See that dinghy over there? Guy just told me it's worth twenty-two million bucks. Believe that? The old man should be embarrassed. This tub only sleeps six. Ten if there's a crew. Don't think there's been one for five years. Just some dork who shows up once a month to check the bilge or whatever."

"More boat that I'll ever own," I say.

"You and me both, pal," he says. He looks me up and down with a fraction less than his usual hostility. "How's he doing?" he asks. "Ahh! He'll be all right. Water off a duck's back with that old bastard. Wears a Teflon suit. You know what he'd tell me about my marriage? Cut

her loose. That's what. Do what he did to my mother —
Here's a few bucks, go get a job."

"Do you have a lawyer?"

"Yeah, yeah," he says tiredly, "I'll survive. She'll
keep the house, good riddance, overpriced cracker box,
one of these days that hill's gonna turn to mud and the
whole piece of shit'll slide down onto Capilano Drive."
He hefts the case of beer and the groceries. "You want a
beer?" he asks.

"That'd be great. Thanks."

"Come aboard."

I make the mistake of grabbing the rail with my left
hand and feel a sharp twinge in my forearm. Woke it up.
Damn thing's been quiet most of the day.

Lenny leads the way below to a snug but well-
appointed salon with a little less headroom than I'm
at ease with. The seats are leather, the woodwork is
mahogany, the fittings are polished brass. I've seen
worse retreats.

He cracks a couple of Kokanees and slides one across
the galley table in my direction. "Goddamn lawyers
have me tied up so tight I can't piss without written
permission," he says. "My old man's richer than God,
my lard-ass brother's richer than God's uncle, and I'm on
a freakin' budget."

We sip our beers for a minute listening to gulls and
water and the slap of rigging on masts.

"You married, Grundy?"

"No."

"Smart move." He has a long pull at his bottle.
"Don't get married." Belches delicately. "My older girl

has a ring through her nose, who knows where else, failing in school, never home, I don't even want to think about what she's doing. The boy's a zombie. Spends all his time playing Mortal Kombat and Grand Theft Auto and shit where he rips people's skulls off."

"Kids grow out of things."

"Think so? He's sixteen. At his age I spent my time trying to get laid." He empties his bottle, sees that I'm still working on mine, opens another one for himself. "I don't even think he knows how to jerk off unless there's a control knob on a Playstation I don't know about." He pulls out his wallet and extracts a small colour photograph, holds it up for my inspection. "Her I miss," he says. "Melissa."

The bright-eyed schoolgirl in the picture has a tiara in her dark hair. "She's nine. Smart, pretty, plays the piano. She's the only one I wanted to come home for."

"She's lovely."

"Looks like I'm gonna be one of those weekend dads. Twice-a-month. Seen those poor bastards? Trying to do everything in one afternoon? Done it twice so far."

I'm out of platitudes. What he's going through is beyond my empathic range.

"Oh, what the hell," he says, "I'll find a place, downtown, no more driving across that damn bridge every night to the same old crap. Little joint in the west end, looking out over the water. I don't give a shit, doesn't have to be a penthouse. She's the one with all the needs. 'Oh, we need a house in West Van,' well here's a hot flash, Duchess, I can't afford a house in West Van. You married the wrong Alexander."

"What about the Warburton site?"

"*That* clusterfuck?! Jeezuss!" It's either a laugh or a sneeze, but beer comes out of his nostrils and he has to grab a dishtowel to wipe his face. "Ha! My big score. Thought I'd bought myself a piece of something huge that time, supposed to be ten, twenty stories taller than the old man's penthouse. I wanted to stand on my balcony and lob used fruit onto his patio."

"What happened?"

He laughs with a kind of rueful admiration. "The old man snapped up most of my partners' options," he says, "winds up with a controlling interest, and I'm left holding nine percent of a hole in the ground. Prick knows how to play the game. No argument there. " He looks at me. "You gonna drink that beer or what?"

I drain the first bottle, aware that I've only had coffee, painkillers, and a slice of maiden cake so far today. He opens another one for me. "Bring it up on deck," he says. "I'll put on my Commodore hat and act like I belong here."

The shadows of masts and flagpoles are lengthening over the marina and the sky to the west is getting rosier by the minute. There will be a pretty sunset before long. Lenny faces the setting sun, his yachting cap pulled low, shading his eyes. He swigs his beer and motions me to grab a seat in the stern.

"He's just making me sweat," he says. "trying to break me. He knows everything I have is tied up in that latrine." He opens his mouth and bellows across the water, "Well, FUCK HIM!"

The epithet echoes for a few seconds. There is no reply from the passing sloop easing into the marina.

Lenny turns away from the railing and joins me in the stern. He lowers his voice.

"Yeah, fuck him, thinks *he's* tough, *I'm* tough. I bet he's stretched pretty thin with all those dumbass renovations. Maybe he'll be the one looking to sell before long." He looks at the bottle in his hand, perhaps considering what to do with it — replace it with a full one or heave it at the twenty-two-million-dollar yacht across the water. "Oh, hell," he says, "I suppose I'd better go in and see the old prick. Not sure he'd do the same for me, but I owe him that much. He tossed me a few crumbs." He looks at me. "You driving?"

"Sure," I say.

"Give me a minute, I'll pack a toothbrush."

"Kinda stupid, hunh?"

"What's that?"

"Living on a yacht and riding the ferry to Vancouver. Can't drive the damn thing anyway. I'd probably hit an iceberg the way my luck's been going." He throws his spoon down in disgust. "Chowder gives me the heaves. Don't know why I order it, it's always the same crapola."

"BC Ferries signature dish."

"Yeah, people come from far and wide," he says. He turns to the window and sees his face staring back at him. Beyond are varying degrees of blackness, retreating land, water, sky.

"You ever meet Raquel?" I ask.

"Couple times. I don't speak Spanish."

"She spoke English."

"Oh, yeah? We never talked." He shakes his head. "I figured she was another one of his bimbos."

"She wasn't."

"She was pregnant?"

"Yes."

"That's rough," he says. "He knew about it?"

"They'd been trying for some time."

"Gotta hand it to the old fart. He's a stud horse." There's a note of grudging respect in his voice. "Trust me, when the old man goes, there'll be claimants popping up all over the map."

"He was going to acknowledge the child's paternity."

"More than he did when I showed up."

He pushes away from the table and heads out on deck. I clean up for the next group and throw the uneaten chowder in the garbage. The arm feels hot. My painkillers are back at the hotel and I wish I had a couple with me.

I find him standing on the upper deck looking back at the ferry's wake. He swivels his head as I get close.

"What's up with the arm?" he says.

I've slung it across my chest inside my buttoned jacket. Manny Bigalow wouldn't approve of what it's doing for the suit but it feels better that way. "A little stiff," I say.

He takes me at my word, looks out at the water. "Old man got an alibi?"

"He was with me."

"So, what's his problem?"

"They're trying hard to connect him. Because of the other one."

"Lorraine. The second Mrs. Alexander. Yeah, that one's still out there." He says. "Better it stays there."

"Who was the first?"

"That would be Theodore's dear old mum, Dorrie, who's still alive, far as I know, remarried to some English twit with a seat in the House of Lords. Theo wants to get rich enough to buy a chair for himself."

"You know where your brother's been this past week?"

"Haven't got a clue. Couldn't give a shit. Theo's a blowhard and a bully. Didn't stop pushing me around until I was seven." He laughs at the warm memory. "I broke his fucking nose. Fat prick. He was porker when he was ten."

"You grew up together?"

"Hell, no. Theo was legit. I was, let's say, semi-legit. My visits were few and far between. Suited me."

"You have the same name."

"Had to fight like a son of a bitch to keep it. My old lady, who he never got around to marrying, stuck the Alexander on when I started school. I grew up, got my driver's licence, paid taxes, married, all as an Alexander, then one day he comes after me with his suits and says I'm not entitled. Ha! One battle he lost. I threatened to take the son of a bitch to court. Blood tests, affidavits, depositions, whatever. Had him by the nuts that time."

"You two have been butting heads for a while."

"Since I could walk." He waves off any resentment. "I wasn't supposed to happen. Messed up his first marriage." He turns to lean back on the railing, spreads his arms as if accepting the inevitable. "Divorce runs in the family."

"Your brother, too?"

"Theo, Christ, he's got so much on the side he might as well have seven wives by now." He shivers, as if suddenly aware that it's chill and windy on deck. I'm feeling it now. We start back toward the warmth. "Cheaper his way in the long run. Set her up in a condo, lease her a company car, put her on the books as consultant or some such bullshit title, take her along to 'conferences' where the sun shines once in a while." He stops, looks through the cafeteria window at bright lights and family outings. "Here's the weird thing, Joe," he says quietly. "I wasn't the one who was fooling around. It was her. It was Jaqueline. It was Jackie." He shakes his head. "She should be the one out on her ass, seeing the kid, kids plural, but I'm such a stunned asshole I say, 'fine, don't want me around? Fine, I'll pack a suitcase.' What an idiot." He looks at me. "You feeling okay?"

"Few hours sleep will help."

"Figure the Douglas can comp me for a couple days?"

"Of course."

He opens the cafeteria door. "Tell you one thing," he says, "the old man gets charged with murder, some people are going to want their IOUs attended to."

Olive's is almost deserted when I show up. One couple in a far corner, heads close together, perhaps planning their future, one man at the end of the bar idly stirring his drink, maybe pondering his past. Ms. May herself is nowhere to be seen, Jimmy Hinds' bass is on the stand but in its case, Barney is checking cash and receipts. He immediately notes that I didn't come in from my usual direction.

"Late tonight, Champ," Barney says.

"Ferry from Victoria," I say.

"Beer?"

"No, I've had my quota. Quiet, for a Saturday," I say.

"Joint was rockin' till just a little while ago," Barney says. "That street-corner drummer was here, you know the one, Baba Ram-Dis, plays plastic tubs and tin pots?"

"Never heard him."

"He's a hoot. Olive loves him. They did a ninety-minute set."

"Sorry I missed it."

"Fresh coffee, Champ? Take but a minute."

"Passing through, Barney. Force of habit." I lean on the bar for a moment and pinch the worried crease between my eyes. "I think I was going to say goodnight to Olive."

"They took Baba out for moo shu pork, she and Jimmy." He pours peppermint schnapps into two ponies and pushes one toward me. "Trust me," he says. "Perk us both right up."

If Barney doesn't know, who would? We click glasses and knock them back. My nostrils open to a Christmas morning and I inhale deeply. For a moment I feel as if I've just awakened.

"Thanks," I say.

"Your friend Weed was looking for you earlier."

So much for Christmas morn. "I bet he was," I say.

"He said you got your arm carved up."

"It's not too bad," I say. I'm lying. "What did he want?"

"Didn't say. Heck, everybody except my Uncle Fred was looking for you tonight. Gritch, Larry Gormé, that blonde with the fingernails, those other two cops — the

sad-face one and Rocky three-and-a-half — and ... and ...
oh, yeah, Leo's lawyer, Arnold whatshisname ..."

"Köenigsberg."

"That's the guy. Left his card. I think they all left
cards."

"Let's pretend I haven't seen those yet."

"Yeah, they're somewhere, they'll turn up." He
gives me a careful look. "You okay, Champ? Anything
I can do?"

"I wish," I say. "Too much information and not
enough useful information."

"About?"

"Things that don't connect to what I'm supposed to
be doing."

"Which is?"

"Someone killed Raquel."

"Someone *not* Leo."

"That's the basis on which I'm functioning, Barney."
I make a concerted effort to stand up straight, button
my jacket, breathe deeply, trying to recapture that whiff
of a winter morning. "I'd better grab a few hours sleep,"
I say. "I have to go to church in the morning."

Gritch is snoring on the office couch. He has an afghan
over his shoulders and his shoes are lined up neatly. I
try not to wake him as I check for messages and memos
from Rachel.

"You gonna make coffee?" He asks without opening
his eyes.

"I was going to bed," I say.

"What time is it?"

"2:17," I say.

"Is that all? Feels like I've been out for hours. You just get in?"

"Yep." I sit in Rachel's new, extremely comfortable and supportive desk chair. "This is a great chair," I say. "You ever sit in this chair?"

"She'd brain me."

"Very ... embracing."

"So? You find out anything?"

"Oh, sure. Let's see, Lenny Alexander's in the house, he came back with me. He's been living aboard his father's yacht. And Leo has a daughter named Rose, by his second wife, the murdered one, and she's married to Buffalo Bill."

"So the trip wasn't a total loss."

"I got two beers and a slice of maiden cake."

"You watch yourself around Madge, like I said? She has the hots for you, I'm telling you."

"She's practically got a shrine set up over there. The Leo Alexander Library."

"She was a cutie, back in the day." His head swivels sharply in response to an inadvertent groan from my direction.

"I think I could use a couple of those damn painkillers," I say.

"Let me see it."

"Nothing to see, it's just sore."

"Let me see it."

He peels off my jacket.

"Oh, craps," he says. "It's leaking."

"I might've popped a stitch."

"You think?" he says. "I'm waking up Doctor Dickhead."

"I'd rather not."

"Who cares what you'd rather not? You've got shit for brains." He grabs the phone. "Raymond? It's Gritch. Get Doc Dickerson out of bed, will you? We have a small emergency. No, not a guest, it's our resident caveman. Tell the good doctor we may have to amputate."

Doctor Lionel Dickerson has been a fixture at the Lord Douglas longer than even Gritch has. A tidy little man, fastidious, well-groomed, and unfailingly polite, even when hauled out of bed at three a.m. Most of his professional expertise is applied to making certain the hotel isn't liable for lawsuits, although he has delivered at least a dozen babies over the years, and prevented more than few overindulgent guests from choking on their own vomit.

"It's infected," he says. "Those stitches have to come out."

"Can you sew it back up?"

"No, it'll have to heal from the bottom up this time."

"Oh, Lord," I say, "how long will that take?"

"Couple of weeks, I guess. What have you been doing?"

"Nothing. Driving, seeing some people."

"Well, you tore it loose somewhere down the line and it started bleeding inside. That was a deep cut."

"I guess."

"And you're running a fever. I'll get the pharmacy to send over some antibiotics."

Doctor Dickerson hums softly as he snips knots and pulls threads. I look over at Gritch to avoid staring at the widening incision. Gritch is happy to do it for me.

"Wouldn't it be simpler to take it off at the elbow?"

Doc Dickerson looks like he's considering the option. "The good news is, it'll stop hurting once it's cleaned out and packed," he says.

"Things are looking up," I say.

chapter twenty

Fevered dreams come in fragments; inner voices, other voices, my voice, all talking at the same time, switching subjects, arguing, agreeing, dismissing, never shutting up. I have a forlorn conviction that if they'd all be quiet for one minute I could make out what I was saying, but they won't, and I can't. I'm trying hard to explain something to a crowd of anonymous people, most of them faceless, the rest with dubious expressions, but I know I'm right, I'm laying it all out for them: you can't deny this fact, you can't dismiss this connection, surely to God you can see the sense in this explanation — my logic would be totally convincing if I understood a word of it.

When I wake up the sheets are damp. I feel weak and empty, but the fever has broken, my head is cool, and my arm doesn't hurt. The idea of a substantial breakfast is appealing.

I shower with my left arm encased in a plastic bag secured at the elbow by an elastic band. After that I attend to what Dr. Dickerson says will be my morning and evening ritual for a while: packing the incision with strips of surgical gauze soaked in a sterile solution. The cut runs along the top of my left forearm which means I can take care of it myself, otherwise I'd need another pair of hands. Tamp the wet gauze down the length of the wound, cover it with a thick pad and wrap the whole thing with a Tensor bandage, not too tight, just enough to make the arm feel protected and more or less functional.

The Lobby Café isn't open on Sunday, but even if it were, I'd still go to Connor's for a full breakfast. Most mornings I'm happy with coffee and toast but once in a while I feel the need of something bountiful; something with home fries and peameal bacon and a pair of basted eggs. And toast. And jam.

I slip out the side door and head down the street feeling better than I have in days; physically shaky but unusually clear-headed. My outlook is ... *positive*, no other word for it. Cheating mortality will do that to you. A jolt of euphoria generated by survival. I may not have been at death's door, but I feel as though I've been walking the corridors.

Sunday breakfast at Connor's is always well-attended; the tables are full and eggs are dancing in butter. I find a vacant stool at the counter. Duffy Connor, son of the original Connor, also named Duffy, passes me an almost-fresh copy of the Sunday *Emblem*, along with a mug of coffee. "Brown or white toast?" he asks.

"White," I say. "I'm indulging myself this morning."

Leo appears to have lost his newsworthiness. Page five devotes a few inches below the fold to a recap of Leo's arrest and his possible arraignment and/or bail hearing tomorrow. The byline is Gloria Havers, Larry Gormé's ambitious young competition on the city crime beat. Her writing style isn't quite up to Larry's standards, but she's on top of things, even manages to allude to "unresolved out-of-province legal matters" that are being "looked into." Nice.

Breakfast arrives. "Jam or marmalade?" Duffy asks.

"Both," I say.

"You're looking chipper," Gritch says, climbing onto the next stool.

"You aren't," I say.

"Yeah, well, while you were enjoying a peaceful night's repose I was composing your obit, just in case."

"Did I come off okay?"

"Oh, yeah. Except for the part where I refer to you as 'witless.' Other than that, you sound like a swell guy."

"That's a comfort."

"Your recuperative powers are the talk of the institute."

"You eating?"

"Just coffee please and thank you, Duffy." He checks the paper. "Nice to see we're off the front page," he says.

"I avoided yesterday's," I say. "Was it bad?"

"Your pal Gormé's making a career out of this one. He had pictures — a very suspicious-looking Bernard Goodier scuttling across Ultra's lot — plus indirect references to missing limos, Dysart Motors, the brothers Starryk, one Farrel Newton, deceased — you name it, he wrote it up." Gritch adds generous measures of sugar and cream to his coffee and gives it all a brisk stir. "I saved a copy for your scrapbook — 'FUBARs I have known, and other major screwups,' by J. Grundy. Madge Killian will give you a shelf in the archives."

"I'm glad someone's grasping the total picture," I say. "It's a busted mirror to me."

"Lotsa pieces," he agrees.

The eggs and extras having been efficiently attended to. I apply myself to the difficult choice between marmalade and raspberry jam. It's a weighty decision; I've only got one piece of toast left. "In my dream last night I had it all figured out," I say. "Woke up, couldn't remember any of it."

"You remember telling me Leo has a daughter named Rose who was married to Buffalo Bill?"

"Vaguely."

"How about a daughter named 'Roselyn', married, for a time, to someone who called himself 'Wild' Bill?"

"Hiscox," I say. Somehow I think I knew that. No doubt it was one of the things I was trying to explain to my faceless audience.

"That's her. Brian tracked her down. She writes for the *Star* in Toronto. 'Dear Roz'— advice-to-the-lovelorn, spice-up-your-sex-life, where to get the best manicure column."

I've decided on raspberry. It was a hard choice. "Okay," I say, "that's new information. Doesn't exactly *un*complicate things."

"Must really hate her old man."

"She still in the house?"

"Oh, yeah, one of our finer suites. She got a big advance from her publisher. Working title of the book-to-be is *Desperado Daddy*."

"Feel like going to church?"

"I feel like pretending it's my day off."

"Go ahead," I say. "I'm fine, I've got things to do."

"Exercise restraint," he says. He has a final sip of coffee and heads for the door. "It's on your tab."

"Least I can do," I say.

Been a long time since I've set foot in one, but the scent is familiar; they must buy their incense from the same store the world over. Church always smells like church.

Mass is over. A young priest has come to the front door to say goodbye to a few lingering parishioners. He has sandy hair and earnest eyes. I missed his sermon but the departing faithful look like they got something out of it.

"Father Renfrew?"

"Yes?"

"Could I talk to you for a minute?"

"Of course."

I lead him off the front steps. "My name is Joe Grundy," I say. "I work at the Lord Douglas Hotel. I'm here about Raquel Mendez."

"Oh, yes?"

"You are aware that she was killed last Tuesday night?"

"Who? Raquel Mendez? I'm not sure I know who that is."

"My apologies. I was under the impression that she came to Mass here every Sunday."

"Oh, my goodness, you don't mean Miss Santiago? Raquel? Spanish accent, dark hair?"

"I'm sure that's her," I say. Santiago. Definitely *not* a coincidence. I should share that information with Weed. He might think better of me.

"I looked for her this morning," he says. "Something happened to her?"

"She was killed Tuesday night."

"Jesus have mercy on her soul," he says.

"I'd like to arrange a funeral for her."

"Certainly," he says. "When?"

"I'm not sure, Father," I say. "The police haven't released the body yet. I should know by tomorrow."

"That's terrible," he says. "Such a nice woman. What did you call her, Mendez?"

"How did she introduce herself to you?"

"Raquel Santiago. I believe she said she was a widow."

"Okay. Sure," I say. "Would you be able to do a service for her?"

"Of course. A private service, a Mass?"

"I'll get back to you on all that," I say. "I wanted to make sure this was the right place."

"How was she killed?"

"She was murdered, Father."

"Oh, my Lord," he says. "That's tragic. She seemed so happy lately."

"You got to know her?"

"Yes, we spoke a number of times. She was concerned

about a few things."

"I don't suppose you can tell me what they were."

"I'm sorry."

"I understand. It's just that I'm trying to figure out why she, of all people, would be murdered. You knew she was going to have a baby?"

"Yes. She was very happy about that. Concerned about the circumstances, you understand, but very happy, looking forward to her wedding."

"She was going to be married here?"

"There were things yet to work out, but the child's father wanted very much to marry her, she said. She had a lovely engagement ring."

She did? I guess I'm not all that observant. Sometimes she wore earrings, I remember that. Dangling ones. And there was a jewellery box in Leo's bedroom. Rings and brooches and tangled chains. I put all that into a suitcase. Don't remember a two-carat sparkler though. Big diamond. Big enough to impress a priest, or maybe it was her excitement that touched him. She was radiant, he said.

She did seem happy that last night, satisfied with her buffet, proud of how Leo looked, perhaps secretly pleased that Vivienne Saunders was about to be given a pink slip. I'm trying to remember the last time I'd seen her before then. Han Chuen Chu. I'm standing in my underwear being measured for a tux; I see her now, across the room, in a doorway, her eyes on Leo. She smiles and complements me on my new boxers, two shades of blue, a gift from Connie. Leo tells her not to ogle. They laugh. They were a couple. She had a ring to prove it.

For the second time in as many days I'm in Raquel's apartment pawing through her privacy.

The two suitcases are on her bed where I left them. I open the smaller one; it's the one with the makeup and personal things, her magazines and creams, her jewellery box. The box itself is scuffed pink velvet with brass fittings on the corners. The key is conveniently tied to a ribbon. There are a few nice things inside, at least they look nice to me — a double strand of pearls, a delicately carved cameo set in gold, earrings with red gems dangling — rubies, or maybe garnets, how would I know? No two-carat engagement ring. Could be a lot of reasons, maybe she was wearing it, maybe it's with her personal effects at the morgue, maybe Leo has it in his safe. One thing is certain, if she was proud of it, she was taking care of it, so it should be somewhere logical. Unless it was stolen. Which would baffle me even more than I am right now.

What do I know for a fact? A real fact, not a wild guess. I know that Raquel died, in the kitchen, lying on the floor in her maid's dress, in a pool of blood ... no, that's not quite right ... it *wasn't* a maid's outfit. Her black uniform is lying on the end of the bed. Her comfortable shoes are on the floor. Her closet door is half-open and a red gown is draped across a chair beside a full-length mirror. I get a brief flash of her holding it up, deciding it wasn't exactly right, that the black cocktail number was better. She was getting ready for a party.

I remember now, bending over her, seeing only blood and broken dishes, she was wearing an apron but there was lace on her skirt, and a slip or a petticoat under that, and she was wearing stockings, and shoes with heels. She'd changed her clothes while we were away at the dinner. Changed more than her clothes. I get the feeling that she was making a statement, about to announce a change in her status. She was going to welcome Leo and his guests back to the penthouse not as hired help, but as hostess.

And for that she would definitely have worn her engagement ring, the emblem of her new position. She wasn't only the presumptive Mrs. Leo Alexander (assuming a few legal and religious snags could be negotiated), she had a trump card, she was carrying Leo's child. Raquel Mendez, *née* Santiago, was about to declare herself, to Vivienne Griese/Saunders, and to whomever else Leo brought home.

She was in earnest. She'd spoken to a priest, she was either going to get a divorce, or (less likely) an annulment or she was going to call herself a widow and go through a wedding ceremony no matter what the consequences. Her child was going to be Leo Alexander's legitimate offspring, whatever the cost to her.

That's a lot of assumption and extrapolation from one fact. What was the fact again? Raquel was murdered. And she had dressed for the occasion.

Got any other facts?

Yes. There was a dead man hanging on a piling. So? Anything you can extrapolate from that? It's a safe bet that Farrel Newton was related to Yarnell Newton, drowned off Cape Flattery while sailing with my boss. I know for a fact that Farrel was here that night. Close enough to get himself killed. Likely he was up here trying to rob the place with Dimi Starr. That's not really a fact, merely an informed guess. Okay, fact number two — Raquel wasn't the only one murdered on Tuesday night.

What else have you got?

I've got a seven-inch gash along my left pronator muscle. That's a fact. And the man who gave it to me was in the vicinity the night of the murder because he tried to run me down with his bike. And his name is Santiago. Surely that means a relative. Brother? Nephew? Another long-forgotten child? I've just remembered something else. Racing back to the Douglas in a cab, looking out the rear window to see if we were being followed, a high-revving motorcycle passes us, exceeding the speed limit. Jesus? Don't see too many dirt bikes zipping down the city streets late at night. He was headed in the same direction. And he knew where we were going.

But, big but, if he *was* following us from across town, then he wasn't up here when it happened. Not much of a fact, but Raquel's blood kin was definitely around that night. Somewhere. Sometime.

What else?

Not much. Everything else is murk. And voices in the back of my head saying *haven't you figured it out yet? It's all there in front of you.*

Perhaps. But I can't see it. Two people got killed. One person is missing. Two people are locked up. One of them tried to kill me; the other one is my boss.

Did Leo know that Raquel was dressing for the late gathering? He said he was going to tell Vivienne that they'd had their last dance. Had he done that already? When I escorted her to the cab she was in a sour mood. I'd assumed it was because of the limo mixup, or Connie joining the group, or because there wasn't a larger contingent of her sort of people invited along for nightcaps. But maybe she'd already been given the sad news. Maybe Leo had used the time in Olive's, the public conviviality, to tell her it was over. Maybe. I can ask. Who knows; he might even tell me.

The rear of Raquel's suite opens onto an enclosed patio. There is a high brick wall along the back. On the other side will be the hotel roof. No ladder out here. A chaise and an umbrella, and a table of plants. She liked African violets. A long tray of pots, all the colours. They probably need a drink. Bone dry. I find the watering can under the plant table and carry it in to the kitchen. There's a bottle with an eyedropper that says "African Violet Food" but I can't make out the dosage in the fine print. I won't feed them, I'll just water them. Might as well admit it, I need reading glasses. Need more than that. Need to re-examine my prospects.

Given Leo's battered emotional state and his precarious legal situation, it is possible that I'll be looking for another job before long. Even if Leo doesn't wind up in jail, things could change quickly. Lenny says the old man's stretched too thin. I don't know anything about finance. I know even less about Leo's financial situation. I have no idea how much he's worth, what he owns, how much he owes. Leo is at a level where such questions are irrelevant, to me at least. Leo is one of the rich people. He smokes the best cigars, he drinks the best champagne, he wears the best soup and fish, he gives his sweetheart a diamond at least half the size of the Ritz, he has a yacht, modest by Lenny's measure, but not too shabby. Rich people have cushions; what Morley Kline always referred to out of the side of his mouth, as "fuck-you money." "Gotta have it kid," he'd say. Whatever happens I'm sure Leo won't suffer too much. And if things get really tight, he can always sell out to one of the big chains. He wouldn't like it, but he might not have a choice. As far as I can project, that scenario ends with JG Security looking elsewhere for employment.

Then there are the Alexander sons, always looming, either or both of them waiting for Leo to stumble. What kind of position are they in? Not too solid, as far as I can see. Lenny's overdrawn all down the line, at least according to him. I know almost nothing about the other brother except that Theo Alexander may be ripping off his own limousines. Doesn't sound like the wheeling and dealing of a legitimate high roller, but what do I know? High finance. Not my area of expertise. Reminds me, I should open a bank account.

I give each of the violets a good soaking. Not sure what to do about them. Maybe Rachel Golden can take them home. Maybe I should set up a place in my little office. I'll think about it. If the world as we know it is dimming and dying it won't matter much where Raquel's collection of African Violets winds up.

I have the code for Leo's voice mail. I've been told to delete everything. There are thirty- seven messages waiting. A lot to delete.

"Leo, it's Frobe, I'm still getting the dickaround from Licences and Permits ..." Delete.

"Mr. Alexander? This is Virginia Newton calling. I need to talk to you. I keep getting this machine. I think you should call me pretty soon."

I jot down her number before erasing the message. There are six others from her interspersed with calls from people Leo wouldn't talk to on any occasion — newspapers, television stations ...

"This is Wendy McDonald at the CBC ..." Delete.

"Mr. Alexander, this is Cameron Marti at the *Globe and Mail* ..." Delete.

Et cetera, et cetera ... delete, delete.

And a final one from "Virginia Newton again, Mr. Alexander. You know what happened to Farrel. I can't get hold of Theodore. I need to have a few things straightened out. I'm not going to wait around like the last time."

To delete or not to delete? I have her number. I can deliver the gist of the message even though I have no idea what it's about, only that it sounds dire, possibly threatening, definitely urgent. Yarnell Newton, drowned off Cape Flattery, Farrel Newton, certainly related, Virginia Newton, likewise, and sounding impatient.

Delete.

Tomorrow, after Leo gets bail, which he no doubt will, and after he's made his way back to the relative safety of the Douglas, I will have a thorough examination of all relevant issues. It will be necessary. Who are the Newtons for God's sake? What's Farrel's connection to Theo? What's Virginia's connection to Leo? Oh, Lord, not that again. I should have been keeping score. By loose calculation I can call up six, eight, I'm not even trying. There seems to be an accepted truth among almost everyone I've bumped into that Leo is, or was, prior to Raquel, a "ladies man" or a "sultan" or a straight-ahead libertine.

I'm beginning to think that the critical mass of this situation isn't a business deal gone sour; it sounds more and more like woman trouble. Or *women* trouble. Lots of women trouble.

Leo's castle in the sky feels hollow and forlorn. The warmth and comfort I used to sense in these rooms is gone, gone with Raquel, gone with the affection and domesticity and feeling of completeness that was once here. On my first visit I remember getting a twinge of envy. Not that this was the kind of life that I wanted, but the sense that everything Leo needed in the world was in one place, safe and whole. A reminder, if I needed one, that such conditions are illusory, or temporary at best. Morely Kline reminded me regularly, "Nothing lasts forever, kid."

Leo says the wall safe wasn't touched. What else would they want? It all looks brimming to me, albeit somewhat disarrayed by various search parties — books, paintings, model boats, sculptures (*tchotchkes*, Louis Schurr would have called them), rugs, furniture, appliances, entertainments, crystal, liquor cabinet. Other than one knife missing from the wooden rack, everything looks in place. Leo's office, off his bedroom, not large, not elaborate, only the basic machinery he needs to direct his interests, stay in touch — fax, phone (four lines), printer/scanner, paper shredder. The computer is missing, probably taken under a search warrant. I can't possibly tell what discs are missing, or if they'd be significant. Leo hasn't mentioned anything he was concerned about. Of course it could be something incriminating. How would I know? He keeps secrets; he has a lot of secrets to keep.

And the bedroom, and the bathrooms, and the closets, and the guest room, and the other guest room, and the exercise room, and all his other amenities and holdings — walk-in humidor, wine vault, pantry, freezers — anything a man would need to spend his years in comfort.

"I don't care how long he lives, he'll never smoke all those," Gritch says.

"How do you get up here without a key?" I ask him.

"Lloyd's key," he says. "You'll be happy to know he didn't have a heart attack."

"Thought you were taking the day off," I say to Gritch.

"I did."

"That usually means back the next day."

"The wife's sister came over," says Gritch. "I overheard them talking about moving a few things." He stands at the door to the cigar closet like a man viewing the *Mona Lisa*. "Jeeze, you think I could smoke one of these? He's got like a thousand."

"Go ahead."

"Always wanted to try a Montecristo. Winston Churchill's brand, or so I've been told." He lights up. "So?" He puffs happily. "What are you looking for?"

"Something worth stealing, something worth risking your life for, worth falling off a building for, worth killing a —"

"And nothing's missing."

"Nothing. Except maybe a diamond ring that Dimi wouldn't have known about anyway, especially if he wasn't expecting anyone to be here."

"Wall safe?"

"Leo says it wasn't touched."

"That just means he didn't get to it."

Tyrannous off Cape Flattery swings away from the wall at a touch.

"Got the combination?" Gritch asks.

"Yep."

"You're kidding me. Why would he give that to you?"

"I don't know, he trusts me."

"Want to open it?"

"Not especially."

"Part of your commission, isn't it? Dig where you have to dig. If Dimi and the partner-who-thought-he-could-fly were up here to steal something, it was probably in there."

"Where would they get the combination?"

"Be a pretty short list," he says. "But I could see the brothers being in on it."

The combination is an easy one to remember; it's my professional record: 36 (wins) — 11 (losses) — 2 (draws).

Leo set it that way so I'd never have to tax my memory circuits. "Strictly for emergencies, Joseph," he told me over seven years ago. "In case I'm incapacitated. Or worse. A man who would stop a bullet for me can be trusted to see my wishes are carried out."

"I can see something that would motivate an intrepid cat-burglar," Gritch says. "There seems to be a whack of cash money in there."

The only other thing in the safe, besides the ostentatious bales of currency, is a large manila envelope. One of those inter-office envelopes, with a flap held closed by red string, a series of holes down the sides, and a column for the signatures of the people who received it and passed it on. There are nine signatures; three of them are Leo's. Leo had this envelope returned to him each time it went out. The other six signatures are those of Lenny Alexander, Theodore Alexander, Winston Mikela, and again, Lenny Alexander, Theodore Alexander, and Winston Mikela. Whatever's inside is family business.

The first thing that falls out is a stack of postcards held together with an alligator clip. Postcards. The notes on the back are brief. The first ones are printed in block letters, all caps. Later they switch to cursive script, becoming more fluid and confident as they progress. Seven of them. The return address is Toronto. The stamps are standard Canadian postage but the cards are images of exotic places. Whoever sent them didn't mail them from Tahiti, Honolulu, or Paris. Maybe they just collected postcards. I sort them by date. One each year for seven years.

DEAR DADDY
THANK YOU FOR THE XMAS PRES-
ENTS. I AM OK. I HOPE YOU ARE TO.
ROSE (1975)

DEAR DADDY
MERRY XMAS. DID YOU GET THE
PACKAGE? MISS YOU.
LOVE, ROSE (1976)

Daddy,
School is fine. I'm trying out for clarinet.
Rosie (1977)

Dad,
The coat is very nice. I'll grow into it.
Happy New Year.
Rose (1978)

Merry Xmas and Happy New Year,
I played a solo in the concert. I'd like
to go to the Conservatory of Music if
that's okay.
Love
Rosie (1979)

Dad,
Music isn't for me I'm afraid. I'm doing better in other areas. Thanks for
the money.
Rose (1981)

"She skipped a year."

> Happy New Year,
> I'm getting my own place. I know you
> won't approve but I need to be on my
> own for a while. I'll send you a letter
> when I know where I'll be. Don't worry.
> Rose (1983)

"Skipped another one."

That's it for father-daughter communication, at least at this end. If she was nine when her mother was killed and she was placed in the care of others, then she was seventeen or eighteen when the postcards stopped. A bit young to have left home. And they're sparse and not particularly warm, but for the first few years at least she stayed in touch. No doubt prompted by the folks who were looking after her.

"Anything else?"

"'Last Will and Testament ~ To be opened in the event of my death'. It's signed. That one I won't be opening. Marriage certificates; divorce papers. 'Dorothy Linden.' That would be Theo's mother. Birth certificate, Theo. Birth certificate and adoption papers, 'Leon Malcolm Dineen, born to Vera Maud Dineen.' Legal change-of-name to Leon Malcolm Alexander."

"You're making that up," Gritch says.

"That's what it says."

"Mrs. Dineen is Lenny's mom?"

"I'm just reading what's on the papers. 'Lorraine Cox.' Marriage certificate, death certificate. Roselyn's mother. Basic legal stuff. Private matters, but not secrets. Marriage, birth, death, divorce, adoption."

"Anything in there worth stealing?"

"Winston Mikela probably has copies. Doesn't look to me like Leo was running away from anything. He acknowledged Lenny's paternity, legally adopted him. He was keeping some sort of contact with his daughter. Paying for her upkeep, sending money, at least until she was eighteen or so."

"I vote the cash-as-motive ticket," Gritch says.

"Leo's emergency money," I say. "A little cash on hand, he calls it."

"Lock it up," he says. "I just saw myself with a walk-in humidor."

"Okay. They were after money," I say. I put the postcards back into the envelope and close the steel door, spin the dial.

"They'd need inside information," he says. "The combination. Or nitro, or a cordless drill."

"That drill wouldn't have scratched this thing," I say. I swing the painting back into place. It looks like Leo's grinning at me. "Inside information," I repeat. "Very short list, wouldn't you say?"

"I'm still trying to get my head around Mrs. Dineen being Lenny's mother," he says.

chapter twenty-one

The monthly "Scones with Jam" afternoons at Olive's are justly famous. They take place on the "middle Sunday" of every month (the dates are often arbitrary but Vancouver jazz buffs always seem to know whether she meant the 11th or the 18th) and headliners on tour make a point of dropping by. Many a chronicled concert began with the unheralded arrival of someone whose appearance elsewhere the previous night had been sold out for months. A visit to Olive's is a pilgrimage, and being invited to sit in is both an honour and a dare.

The mood is delicate and exploratory as I check in. Olive and Jimmy are on the stand with Olive's favourite guitarist, Arlen, the kid from Fretsarus music store. The trio is flipping through a medley of old MJQ classics, "Fontessa," "The Golden Striker," "Cortege." The room is half-filled, people drifting in, room at the bar for me to park my troubles two stools down from Norman Weed, who pretends I'm not in the vicinity and faces the stage, nodding, out of rhythm, but with enthusiasm. I let him have his serene moment. It's early.

There's very little chatter on Sunday afternoons. Not while the music's playing. Respectful murmuring, sighs of appreciation, an occasional "Yeah." They came to listen.

Barney wipes the bar and leans close. "What'll it be, Champ?"

"Coffee, Barney. Thanks."

"You got it. Want me to shuffle someone so you can sit with your friend?"

"Let's leave him in peace," I whisper.

Barney nods, disappears. Coffee appears. Olive launches into an impromptu fugue and variations on "No Sun in Venice" and then I see her face light up as she spots someone coming through the door, a man in a black fedora, wearing shades and carrying a trumpet case. Things are starting to get interesting.

"Is that who I think it is?" asks the guy sitting between Weed and me.

"Definitely," says Weed.

The guy and his drink move to a spot nearer the stage and I take the opportunity to sidle a notch closer to the Sergeant of Detectives.

"I suppose I have to ask," Weed says in a grumpy whisper, "how's the arm?"

"On the mend," I say. "How's the prisoner?"

"Better shape than you."

"You going to charge him with anything?"

"Yeah, sure, what do you like, attempted murder, assault with a deadly, parking on the sidewalk?" He sips his rum and Coke. "Probably be doing him a favour. They want him south of the border. He's a deserter."

"He's related to Raquel."

"How do you know that?"

"I talked to her priest. She'd started using her maiden name, Santiago."

Weed shakes his head. "I like the simple ones," he says. "Drug guys bumping each other off, domestics, stuff you can understand."

"I don't think he was involved."

"We'll see," Weed says. "They're processing that knife. Find out if there's blood on it other than yours, like maybe the guy in the hole, or the lady upstairs." He puts his drink on the bar and turns a shoulder to the music. "That's a helluva knife," he says. "Have you seen that thing?"

"Yes," I say. "May I speak to him?"

"I'll look into it," he says. He turns back to face the music.

"I need to make funeral arrangements."

"Maybe middle of the week. Not my department."

The trumpet player sticks a mute in his horn and leans against the piano for a full chorus of "Nature Boy" before lifting it to his lips to embroider Olive's melody line with gold thread. The room is hushed. If I stick around I'll ruin Weed's afternoon. I leave my coffee untouched.

He follows me, through the back door to the Lower Lobby. "Hang on a sec," he says. "That's it?"

"Don't want to break the mood," I say. "I'll track you down tomorrow. Got questions you probably won't answer anyway."

"Go ahead," he says. "I might as well not answer them now and get it over with."

"Don't want you to lose your spot at the bar."

"Barney'll hold it." There is an unoccupied banquette just inside the entrance. Can't see the bandstand from here but good sounds are reverberating. He slides into the corner and looks at me expectantly. "Well?"

"How's the massive manhunt going?"

"All effort has been made," he says. "Won't be surprised if he turns up dead like his pal."

"But you are actually looking for him, right? Questioning the brother? Goodier over at Ultra Limos? Cooperating with the Fraud Squad?"

"There's been communication."

"That's encouraging," I say.

"And we're coordinating our efforts," he says.

"Along what lines?"

"Along the lines that a murder trumps a stolen car. So we get first crack at the evidence, first crack at persons of interest."

"Tracked down any of them yet?" I ask. "Theo Alexander?"

"Away on business. Due back this very day."

"What about Newton? He have a family? Wife?"

"Mother. Lived with his mother. She thinks Dimi led him astray."

"Good to see you're making progress."

"And, of course, we've got Jesus."

"Praise the Lord," I say.

The ever-on-the-ball Kyra has noticed that Weed and I are settled in for a while and delivers Weed's drink and a fresh coffee for me.

"Thanks, Kyra," Weed says. "My mouth was getting dry."

"Two saxophones just showed up," she says. "They're settling in for a long one."

Weed shakes his head sadly.

"Don't fret," she says. "Barney's holding your spot."

Weed blows her a kiss. He turns back to me, sighs deeply, has a pull at his drink, sighs again. "Honest to God's truth, Joe," he says, "I can't connect the dots. What those Ultra idiots were up to, what Jesus was doing there. The fraud guys say Dimi and his brother could have been stealing the car. They'd done it at least once before, maybe twice, but I don't buy it. It feels like a burglary that went wrong."

"But?"

"Things aren't sitting right. Or they're sitting too right." He leans across the table and puts a hand beside his mouth. "Your friend was killed with one very nasty stab wound and most likely died where she fell. So where does all the wreckage come from? Are they trying to make it look like something else?"

"What about George?"

"We couldn't hold him for anything. Searched the dealership, invoices, phone records, emails. We're keeping a close watch but so far he's clean."

"Or smart."

"Smart enough not to wind up dead," he says.

"So why are you still holding Leo?"

"He might have staged the whole thing. He's got some history with this Newton character."

"Newton works for Theo."

"Word from Goodier is, keeping Newton on was part of the deal Theo signed with his old man."

"Oh, come on, Norman," I say with some vehemence, "you think Leo'd be stupid enough to hire a pair of idiots like that? If Leo wanted a hit man it wouldn't be Laurel and Hardy."

"Best I can say for certain is that Newton's prints are on the cordless drill, and there's bronze fragments on the drill bit, and it's a safe bet that he's the one trashed Leo's plaque thing. Don't know why he did it, but he's the one."

"And you can put Dimi in the penthouse?"

"That I can do. He must've lost his gloves somewhere. His prints are all over the joint. Maybe his blood, too. There was blood going down those fire stairs. Have to find him to make sure but she might have cut him."

"The blood on the fire stairs, does it go all the way down?"

"Yeah, smear on the street door. Why?"

"Don't tell me, just shake your head if I'm wrong," I start. "Raquel was killed sometime between 11:00 p.m. and 1:00 a.m., I'm not trying to be accurate here, just approximate. Leo and party came up from Olive's at about two-fifteen. At very least she had already been dead for an hour and fifteen minutes, maybe two hours." He's still not shaking his head. "So whoever I was chasing down the fire stairs wasn't Dimi Starr."

"Why not?"

"He wasn't on the street when I got there. I had a man covering the south side, nobody went that way, I could see left and right for ten blocks, nobody running, the cameras in the parking garage don't pick him up going in. The only one nearby was my friend Jesus. And he wasn't there when it happened."

"You know this because ..."

"Because he was following us back to the hotel from the dinner. He passed us two blocks from here. Doesn't give him much time to stash his bike, get up to the penthouse."

"It's a small window of opportunity, I'll grant you."

"Was he bleeding?"

"Split lip."

"That was from me. Was he cut and bleeding his way down the fire stairs?"

"No."

"Just shake your head if I stop making sense. I think it's possible whoever I chased down the fire stairs didn't go all the way down. They most likely exited onto another floor. Not sure how far below me they were but say seven or eight levels. When the noise stopped I figured they'd gone out the street door, but they could've got into the hotel at the sixth floor, fifth floor, mezzanine."

"They'd need a key for that, wouldn't they?"

"I think they knew their way around the hotel. Dimi didn't have a key. He came in across the roof, and exited out the fire door after he was wounded. You've got his fingerprints, blood, all the way down. All he had was the security code for the fire door on that business card of

Leo's." Norman doesn't shake his head. "I think there were three people besides Raquel that night. Jesus wasn't up there or you'd be holding him for murder. Dimi and Farrel broke in, trouble ensued, Farrel went over the edge, Dimi ran down the fire stairs leaving a blood trail, and I chased someone else entirely."

"Someone such as?"

"Time to start looking at security tapes again. You've got a time frame. Someone coming in from an emergency fire door on the east side between two and two-thirty a.m. Say from the mezzanine up to ten, to be on the safe side."

"Any idea who I'd be looking for?"

"Find the tapes. I'll probably recognize someone."

"Care to be more specific?"

"Was Raquel wearing a diamond ring?"

"You think somebody stole her ring?"

"It was a big ring, Over two carats, not cheap. Something worth stealing."

"I'll look into it," he says.

"Start looking at the tapes," I say.

"Tomorrow," he says. "Right now I'm going to listen to some music." He collects his drink and slides out of the banquette.

I stay where I am. "Went to visit Madge Killian yesterday," I say.

"Who?" he asks. He's not a very good actor.

"Nice woman. Lives on the island, Victoria, near UVic."

"Oh, yeah, I seem to recall ..."

"She says you've been nosing around there for years."

"I've been over a few times, okay."

"Still trying to find out what happened eight years ago?"

"I don't like to leave things dangling."

"This can't be the only case you have dangling after twenty years on the job."

"Try thirty-two."

"Dangling cases?"

"Years on the job, smartass."

"So?"

"Wasn't exactly the Brinks Job, pal. Somebody took a few shots and missed. Mostly. Then they bugger off. Nobody dead, Leo wasn't pounding on my door asking for answers."

"So why is it still open?"

"Call it a hobby." He smiles. "Besides, what makes you so sure that's what I was doing over there? He stands up. "Maybe I like model boats."

Weed returns to the bar. I can hear brushes on cymbals and snare; someone's brought a drum kit. Kyra notices that I haven't left and brings over the coffeepot.

"And a Martini," says Roselyn Hiscox. "Cold gin, one olive." She takes the seat across from me. She has her blonde hair pulled back tight to her skull. I can see the resemblance now, the firm jawline, the sharp blue eyes.

"Ms. Hiscox," I say. "You were on my list for today."

"I insist that you call me Roselyn," she says.

"Do you like that better than Rose?"

She smiles slowly. "Not exactly the FBI around here, are you? How long did it take you to figure it out? A week?"

"Pretty much."

"I needed a new name." She settles herself, folds her manicured fingers. She's wearing nice rings, not diamonds. "I had to reinvent myself," she says. "Get away from that shell-shocked little kid, Rose Alexander. You know, the skinny one with the murdered mother? The kid on probation from the Bogner Institute for Traumatized Toddlers? The one with the hired parents cashing monthly cheques from Alexander and Co."

Kyra delivers one of Barney's classics. I signal that it's on my tab. She gives Roselyn a closer look as she leaves.

Roselyn tries her drink. Twice. Studies the olive for a moment. "I built a new me," she says. "Not bad, huh?"

"Impressive," I say.

"Self preservation. My formative years were toxic. I got clear."

"But you came back."

"My terms, Joe. Strictly my terms. Confessionals are big sellers. Throw in psychic trauma, a high-profile villain, sex, skullduggery, high crimes and misdemeanors. Hell, I got a high six-figure advance." She nods at Kyra to set her up again. "This is all about money, Joe. Strictly a cash deal. Leo Alexander can rot in jail, or in hell, as long as he feels pain."

"He's feeling some now," I say.

"Good. Maybe not for the reasons I'd prefer, but it's a start."

"You blame him for your mother's death."

"I'm being very careful not to point any fingers. Yet. Maybe a raised eyebrow, metaphorically speaking, give it a *Black Dahlia* atmosphere. And if they charge him with this latest one, well, so much the better, don't you think?" Kyra sets a fresh drink in front of her. Picks up the empty glass. I nod that it's still my party. "Frames the story beautifully, doesn't it?" Roselyn appears to be asking the opinion of an unseen literary critic. "Two murders and a conviction. Perfect."

"What's in the middle?" I ask.

"Plenty. Drowning sailors on the high seas, stealing a hotel, boinking the head housekeeper, half her staff, too."

"Did your research take you to the Alexander Library?"

She laughs. "The little red hen didn't recognize me. No reason she should. Last time she saw me I was nine years old, huddled under a table, covered in my mother's blood." She finishes her drink. I can sense her resisting the urge to order a third.

"Didn't see your name in the visitor's book."

"I was undercover." She looks at her empty glass. "Little fussbudget never really looked at me back then anyway. Always bustling after Leo, whispering in his ear. Persuading him to lock my mother up, for a 'rest,' or a series of 'treatments.' Dumpy little Madge, Keeper-of-the-Flame." She succumbs to the impulse and signals Kyra again. "I hated her guts."

"Why?"

"He always had time for her. Not me, Lord no. And my poor ditsy mother, hell, the two of them had her on a leash — don't let her have two drinks or she'll be bouncing off the walls, keep her away from the other guests, you know what she's like, maybe she should fly to New York for a few days, do some shopping. And take Rose with her."

"This book is payback."

"Sure. I can admit that. I've had enough therapy in my life. I'll concede my baser motives. I wouldn't mind a little retribution, especially if it makes the best-seller list."

"I've never seen you take a note, Ms. Hiscox."

"I have no need. Photographic memory."

"Really?"

"Try me."

"Oh, I have no cause to doubt you," I say. "My own memory is sketchy at times, or at least slow to cough up information."

"In the privacy of my room I do make notes, go back over old ground."

"Trouble is, people tend to refine memories, put the best, or worst spin on something."

"It's a challenge," she admits. "But I can handle it."

"Even those childhood ones?"

"Those memories, painful as they are, remain clear as a bell."

"Including the night of your mother's murder."

"Oh, yes."

"Your father and Madge were in Calgary that weekend, weren't they? Some business deal?"

"So he maintained."

"How far away was the ranch?"

"Four hours, by car."

"They rushed right back?"

"Next morning."

"Where were you?"

"By then, at a neighbour's place. The police were there."

There is an almost audible click somewhere inside my head. "And yet you have a photographic memory."

"So?"

"I'm just wondering how it is that the last time Madge Killian saw you, you were huddled under a table, covered in your mother's blood."

I leave her to ponder the question over her fresh drink. Nod at Kyra and take my leave. The music is building behind me. Impressive sounds but far too demanding for a brain that could use some peace and quiet.

The afternoon shift is being handled by Todd and Roland. Roland is in the lobby when I come up from Olive's. Roland placed second runner-up (third) in the Mr. Coastal championships last year and he thinks he might have won except that he has trouble building his calves. He does much of his patrolling with his toes curled inside his shoes, claims it works the calves all day. Sometimes he walks funny. I look around the lobby. "All quiet?"

"A nice civilized Sunday afternoon," he says. "Ms. Traynor says we're about thirty percent light. How's your arm?"

"Much better, thanks, Roland."

"What did he get?"

"This one," I say, pointing at my sleeve. "The pronator."

"Here?" He shows me his own forearm. His jacket sleeve swells tight when he makes a fist. "Along here?"

"That's the spot," I say.

"Not pronator," he says. "That's the *brachioradialis*. Very important muscle. Can't turn a doorknob without it."

"Or check my watch," I say.

Margo doesn't get Sundays off. Wednesday is her usual free day, but lately, with Lloyd pretending to have a heart attack and things what they are, she's been on call seven days a week.

"Joe, come in here a minute, I need to speak to you."

"What's up?"

She looks up from the ream of paperwork spread on her desk, removes her glasses, puts on her stern expression. "Lenny Alexander's staying here?"

"Came in with me last night."

"You comped him the Beachcomber Suite?"

"He's here to visit his dad. I figured it was important. For both of them."

"So you don't recall the memo from Leo last year that neither one would be allowed to use this place as his personal hideout?"

"Check your records, Margo, I think you'll find it was Theodore abusing the privilege."

"The memo flagged both of them."

"Tell you what," I say, "put it on my tab and I'll take it up with the old man personally. So far Lenny's the only family member gives a damn."

She gives me a long, careful look. "Doctor Dickerson was in. There's a form that needs filling out."

"I'm sure it doesn't need filling out right this minute."

"The sooner the better."

"I needed my dressing changed."

"Right," she says. "And a prescription."

"Why are you fussing with this stuff, Margo? You have a staff."

She looks exasperated. "Because," she says ominously, "if I'm leaving here, I'm leaving things in good order."

"Goes without saying."

"You don't think I'll do it," she says. "Do you?"

"I think it's highly unlikely," I say. "Anyhow, it's Sunday. You can't quit until tomorrow at the earliest." I stick out my good hand. "Five bucks says you don't quit."

"You'd have to cash a paycheque."

"I can't lose," I say. "I've got twenty-four hours."

chapter twenty-two

The Beachcomber Suite is on the ninth floor, north-west corner, far from any beach.

"Oh, hey, it's you, Joe. Come on in. I just ordered some food. You hungry?"

"No, thanks. Wanted to let you know, things are straightened out with Margo."

"Not a bad-looking woman, if she wasn't wired so tight."

"She's been under the gun this week."

"I wasn't worried. Had a good talk with the old man. We're cool."

"How's he doing?"

"He's all right. Got a list of stuff he needs for court tomorrow. He wants to look sharp."

"He wants me to bring it over?"

"I'll take care of it," he says.

"When will you be heading back?"

"I don't know. I'll show up for the court appearance in the morning. See if he wants me to do anything, take care of anything."

"Happy to see you?"

"Ha! Yeah. Surprised the shit outta me. Swear to God, Joe, I think the old bastard shed a tear. I can't be sure but he looked like he was about to."

"It's good you went to see him."

"Yeah, I think so. We're never going to be best buds, but he's all right, I learned a lot butting heads with him. I sometimes got the feeling he was doing it on purpose, to see if I was tough enough, if I was really his son. He sure as shit doesn't think a lot of his first-born."

"What about his third born, he ever mention her?"

"Lorraine's kid? Never talks about her. I think she's in the loony bin."

"Actually, she's in 1214."

"Here?"

"Your sister now goes by the name Roselyn Hiscox. She's a writer, doing a biography of your father."

"No shit? Is she okay? I mean, is she crazy?"

"Seems quite sane to me."

"She killed her mother you know."

"She did?"

"That's the story we heard through the family grapevine. That's why she was sent to the cookie factory. Leo pulled some strings, got her committed. She was a basket case after it happened. At least that's the way I heard it. Police didn't have any real evidence. She was like eight or nine, just a kid, very unstable. They let it slide. Family tragedy."

"Found some other things upstairs. Your birth certificate, change of name, adoption papers."

"Oh, yeah?"

"Have you spoken to your mother since you've been here?"

"All the secrets coming out, are they? Yeah, we had breakfast. It's not something she likes to broadcast."

"She calls herself *Mrs.* Dineen. Was she married to someone else when you were born?"

"Nah, she's never been married. That's just a little fiction. She wears a ring. Keeps the staff in line."

"Are you two close?"

"I'll be honest with you, Joe. My mother's not the warmest person in the world, but to give her her due, she made sure I didn't get screwed. I was going to get my share, even if we had to fight for it."

Gritch is sitting in my personal space in the company of a chunky man wearing a Guinness windbreaker and a Blue Jays baseball cap. He looks like a cop. They're both smoking budget cigars. Gritch stands up. "Somebody I want you to meet," he says. "Ben Kaufman, Joe Grundy."

The man stands up and sticks out a meaty paw. "How do?"

"Hello, Ben," I say.

"I was going to bring him downstairs, but he hates jazz," says Gritch. He sits back down. "Ben here's an investigator for Texada Underwriters,"

"We handle the insurance for Ultra Limousine's fleet," Ben says.

"Hold on a sec," I say. I return to the outer office and crank up the smoke extractor full blast. Then I roll Rachel's new chair across the floor. "I'm definitely getting one of these," I say.

"Something the matter with one of the castors on this one," Ben says.

"Texada's on the hook for the two stolen limos," says Gritch.

"Just one, so far," Ben says. "The cheque for the second one's still in my boss's desk. Further investigation was deemed prudent."

"What can you tell me about it?"

"A bit more'n a year ago, year and a half, say, they had a car stolen. Big limo, special attachments, whatever, it's like a hundred and fifty thousand or something. It was being driven by one of the mechanics. Your dead guy, Farrel Newton. He's supposed to be taking the thing over to a specialty place to get a camera put in or something. He takes it for a ride, stops someplace to get a coffee or take a piss, and when he comes out the limo's gone. He comes back to the office, they call the cops, file a report, thing's supposed to have some kind of locator gizmo but it's not working, so yada yada, one of my pals looks into it, can't find anything fishy, my boss shuffles papers for a few weeks then coughs up the money."

"What's different about the second one?"

"Law of averages. Insurance companies live off them. Two limos, both driven by the same mechanic? Doesn't compute."

"That's when the Fraud Squad stepped in?"

"They find out the owner, Theodore Alexander, didn't

replace the first limo. He pocketed the hundred and fifty. Now he's looking to collect on a second one …?"

"Already sounds wonky," Gritch says.

"Not my department," Ben says. "His company, his accountants, as long as he's square with the taxman, no harm no foul."

"Then Farrel Newton lost another one."

"Yeah. Now this Newton mug is loopy, goes haywire from time to time, pounding walls with his head, that kind of stuff, plus he's got the IQ of a Hallmark card. Losing the *Queen Mary* in a parking lot isn't outside the realm of possibility, but it smells anyway. After the first one, who's gonna trust this jerk with another big asset? The second limo's worth even more than the first one. Armoured vehicle, drug lords and Russian Mafia guys just love that shit. So I start poking around, along with a Fraud guy I knew back on the Job.

"Grand Theft Auto's all over it too but they can't find it. Car like that's probably on its way to Shanghai or Moscow. They aren't much interested in individual cars anyway; they want the outfit that's moving them. Has to be professionals. They figure the limo is long gone, but they want the gang."

"Any luck?"

"Oh, yeah, they busted this big outfit a few months back. Very slick. Won't touch anything but expensive shit. Theft Auto rolled them up. No sign of the first limo, of course, but here's the thing — these guys are caught dead to rights so they've got no reason to bullshit about one vehicle. They say they had nothing to do with boosting the second one."

"Inside job."

"What it looks like."

"Dimi Starr."

"Me and my pal find out this Dimi has a brother who's a used-car dealer. Already it sounds promising. But his lot and showroom are clean, can't find another property in his name. Nobody's making any moves. Whole thing is dead quiet."

"Getting nervous with all the cops and dicks around," Gritch says.

"Then this Newton dude shows up seriously dead right next door to the *third* missing limo, so all bets are off. My boss says 'fuck 'em,' cheque stays in the drawer until the cops figure out what's going on."

"You still working the case?" I ask.

"Nope," he says. "Murder investigation now. Have to let Homicide handle things. But, same guy three times? No way it isn't connected."

"Did you talk to Farrel Newton's mother?"

"The first guy tried. She ran him off. Told him to stop picking on her poor little Newt."

"I'll have to pay her a visit," I say.

"Good luck."

Time to change my dressing. Gritch wanders in as I'm packing the cut.

"How's it doing?" he asks.

"Healing from the bottom up, just like the Doc said. Not that I spend a lot of time looking in there, but it isn't as deep as it used to be."

"Everlast is safe for another week."

"Or a month," I say. "Newton's mom is leaving messages on Leo's machine. Wants to talk to him right away. Sounds like a person with issues."

"Met anybody who doesn't have issues with Leo?"

"Not so far."

"Wouldn't think a guy spent the last eight years in a tree-house could stir up that much crapola."

The woman who answers the door was pretty at one time, say, twenty years ago, before sadness and mounting losses caught up with her. Her hair is an artificial shade of cherry red with pale roots visible, her rouge is vague as to where the cheekbones lie, her watery eyes are blue, unfriendly.

She leaves the chain on. "Yeah, what?" she asks.

"Mrs. Newton? Hello. My name's Joe Grundy. Leo Alexander passed on your phone messages and asked me to drop by, see if I could be of any help." When did I get to be such an accomplished liar?

"He's still in the slammer? All the lawyers he's got? Christ, he must really have stepped in it this time."

"He'll be back tomorrow. I'm sure he'll want to speak to you then. In the meantime …"

"Meantime nothing. What do you do? You write cheques? Here to negotiate?"

"I'm not exactly sure what I'd be negotiating."

"Leo didn't tell you shit, did he? You even come from him?"

"Of course. Here's my card." I pass my ID through the narrow space. "JG Security, Lord Douglas Hotel. That's me. I've worked for Mr. Alexander for eight years."

She takes her time reading it. "Doing what?" she asks. "Cleaning up his messes?"

"Hotel security," I say.

She hands it back, keeps the door on its chain. "So what are you doing here?"

"Leo wants me to find out who killed Raquel Mendez, someone he was very close to."

There is a moment of quiet and the door closes. I hear the chain being cleared and the door reopens. "She was his girlfriend, right?"

"Yes," I say.

She nods her head, accepting another inevitable cuff from life. "How old was she? There was a picture in the paper but I couldn't tell."

"I don't know exactly, Mrs. Newton. In her thirties, I imagine, possibly forty, I suppose."

Young enough to bear a child, old enough to consider it a miracle.

"That's about right for him. Thirty years difference, give or take." She leaves the door open and walks away. I take it as an invitation to follow. "He doesn't much care for old broads," she says. "'Course he never sticks around long enough to see them fall apart. He's Lo-ong Gone Leo before that ever happens." She stops in the kitchen and looks around, trying to remember what she was doing before I showed up.

"The message said that you'd been trying to contact Theo Alexander. Can I ask what that's about?"

"I just want to make sure Far's final paycheques come through on time," she says. "That fat bastard's so tight he squeaks." She opens the refrigerator door and takes out a Pepsi. She doesn't offer one to me. "And I'm sure as hell not paying for the funeral. That's the limo company's responsibility. I'll sue them if I have to."

"Raquel was killed the same night, maybe the same hour as your son," I say. "Possibly by the same person. I thought we might be able to help each other find out who did this."

"Who *did* this?!" She sits at the kitchen table holding the soda can in both hands as though wringing a neck. "I *know* who *did* this. Dimi asswipe *did* this. No goddamn mystery. Dimi, or his asshole brother, George, or that fat prick he works for, *both* fat pricks he works for. My moron son got mixed up in their shit. Got himself murdered. Dimi's the murderer. End of story."

"Mr. Starr is who I'm trying to find."

"When you do, kick him in the groin for me."

"You don't have any idea where he is?"

"I would've told the cops. Happy to help. Pick him out of a lineup, witness for the prosecution, pull the switch if they'd let me fry his ass. You know this asshole?"

"I saw him once, briefly."

"He's a Communist."

"I didn't know that."

"Oh, yeah. Big Commie. Him and his Commie brother. Far didn't know what they were talking about. Farrel wasn't too bright. Not exactly retarded, but slow. He kept coming home saying stuff like, did I think he was a slave. I told him, Far, you're lucky to have a job. If it didn't have sparkplugs he was lost. Easily lead around. Dimi tied him up so tight he didn't know what he was doing."

"Do you know what they were doing that night?"

"Stealing another car."

"Okay, I heard that maybe there was some of that going on, but I'm wondering what they were doing at the hotel later on. The cars had already been switched. If they were only stealing a car they could have taken it somewhere."

"Sure, to Georgie's."

"Dysart Motors? The used-car place."

"He's got more than one place."

"You told this to the police?"

"I told them everything I know, which is more than those Ultra pricks thought I knew."

"Would you tell me?"

"After the insurance company paid up for that first car, over a hundred thousand, Dimi hears from his brother, the Commie car-dealer, that whoever stole it walked away with fifty thousand, in cash."

"How would he know that?"

"Hey, they're all crooks. Some guy George knows brokered the deal. So Dimi says, hey, why don't we steal one of our own? Theo gets his money from the insurance company, he's happy, we put the blame on Farrel Dummy here, he won't get fired because Theo has to keep him on. So they do it again. They work it so Far does something stupid, the kind of thing he's likely to do, run out of gas, get lost, whatever, and he comes back to the office, by bus, and he tells Goodier, 'Hey, guess what, somebody stole my limo.' Again. Only this time it looks a bit suspicious. Duh. Do ya think?" She has a drink. "The insurance company sends around an investigator, the police are nosing around, questioning poor Far who can't spill anything because Dimi and George didn't tell him the plan. He's the perfect idiot. 'I don't know, one minute it was there, the next minute it was gone. Duh.' Meanwhile, the limo's sitting in Dimi's brother's junkyard somewhere down in Steveston. It's not going anywhere until things quieten down." She has another sip. "When they finally manage to unload the thing they get shit."

"They did sell the second one?"

"Not for what they wanted. They only got thirty thousand. They were supposed to split it three ways, but fatass Goodier said he wanted a piece to keep his mouth shut. Far only got two."

"He told you?"

"He had money he shouldn't have had. Two thousand dollars. Left it in his work pants, it nearly went through the wash. Two thousand dollars in hundred dollar bills. I said where'd you get this? He said 'It's my share.' Your share of what? So he told me the story. Or at least what he knew. They give Far two thousand and all he has to do is say it's his fault. He won't get fired. Theo's not allowed to fire him."

"Why not?"

"Because Leo says so."

"Leo?"

"You really don't know shit, do you?"

"Can you tell me why your son would have defaced the award Leo got last Tuesday night?"

"He did?"

"He drilled a hole through it, through Leo's eye."

She laughs. "Oh, God bless him, the poor little guy." The laugh turns into a sob. "He did that for me."

"Why?"

"He hated Leo. Leo drowned his father."

"Where would he get that idea?"

"From me, damn it! Doesn't matter any more, does it?" She pushes the empty Pepsi can away and holds her face in her hands. "After Yarnell drowned, Leo wouldn't see me any more. He blamed himself. He couldn't look at me."

"Was he to blame?"

"It was his boat. He was the captain. It was his responsibility." She wipes her eyes, shakes her head sadly. "But it wasn't his fault. They ran into a fogbank, right in the middle of a bunch of trawlers. Leo's boat got broadsided. Broke it in half. Fishing boats are made of steel. Those guys call sailboats 'Tupperware.'" She sighs. "Anyway, they never found Yarn. Big search, Leo was out there every day, but they never found his body." She looks up at me, her eyes reddened, her losses mounting. "After that he wouldn't come near me. I hated him for that. He broke my heart."

"Leo was giving you some support?"

"Oh, yeah, yeah, he made arrangements, got Farrel his job when he couldn't get anything else, made sure he hung onto it, sent me a few bucks from time to time."

"You think that will stop, now that your son is dead?"

"How should I know? That's what I want to talk to him about."

chapter twenty-three

Gritch is waiting in the car with the door open, puffing on an El Ropo.

"Enjoying your day off?" I ask.

"Reminds me why I can't stand the East End."

"You *live* in the East End."

"Tell me about it. I could be shifting furniture six blocks away."

"Virginia Newton thinks Dimi killed Farrel. Or possibly his brother George did it. They're both Commies by the way, according to her. She expects Theo to pay for her son's funeral. And she wants to talk to Leo about money. He's been supporting her for a while."

"Out of the goodness of his heart, I suppose." Gritch sounds dubious.

"They had a thing, he and Mrs. Newton, I guess, some years back."

"And then her husband drowned." Gritch blows smoke out the open window. "I don't think I could stand that much life," Gritch says. "Dead wives, sunk boats, long-lost kids cropping up, people shooting at me, no wonder he went into hiding. He needed a vacation."

"Don't we all?"

We're heading for Chinatown. I'm hungry again. I have a craving for some braised beef the way they make it at the Kom Jug. Gritch is all for the plan.

"The Gold-dust Twins'll be so pooped from shifting furniture they'll send out for pizza," he says.

"You don't like pizza?"

"Not with shrimp and pineapple," he says. He has a last puff and consigns the cigar butt to the road. "It goes against nature."

"There's probably a bylaw against that," I say.

"Pineapple on pizza?"

"Cigar butts on the street."

Gritch is unrepentant. "You know, pal," he starts, "there can't be a helluva lot of people knew Leo wasn't going to be home Tuesday night. That Dimi character had to have a floor plan or something, some way of getting in without setting off alarms. Somebody had to send him on the mission. That's got to narrow the list."

"The connection to Theo looms larger."

Braised beef with Szechuan chili oil, Chinese broccoli with black bean sauce, a bottomless pot of tea. I've never been particularly adept with chopsticks but I seem to be shovelling substantial heaps into my mouth without too much wastage. I must be on the mend.

Gritch has opted for lemon chicken and fried rice; it's as adventuresome as he's likely to get. He's using a fork. "Say he *was* acting for Theo. Theo told him how he could get in, and what he wanted. Dimi gets in but he isn't expecting Raquel to be there."

"She changed her clothes," I say. "She knew we wouldn't be back until after midnight, probably took her time — had a shower, fixed her hair, tried on at least one other dress. Maybe she wasn't in the penthouse when he got there."

"And she surprised him."

"Won't know until we find him."

"You'll never find him."

"Weed thinks he's probably dead already."

"Overly elaborate for a carjacking, don't you think?" He sounds skeptical.

"We're *assuming* they were stealing that limo." I put down my chopsticks and refill the teacups.

"Natural assumption," Gritch says. "Done it before, same MO, get Newton behind the wheel and a limo goes missing."

I shake my head at the preposterousness of the situation. "They drive to the hotel, Dimi does his cat-burglar bit, fights with Raquel, sees his partner go flying, bleeds his way down the stairs …"

"And then leaves the limo behind? How does that make sense?"

My fortune cookie says, "You will find your heart's desire". The next thing on my list isn't exactly my heart's

...esire, but it must be attended to. "They should have landed by now," I say.

"Who? Theo?"

"And Marcia. Need to talk to them."

"We going to West Van?"

"I thought we could try False Creek first," I say. "Maybe he won't go straight home."

"Nice neighbourhood," says Gritch. "Waterfront, boats, what d'ya figure a townhouse is worth down here?"

"Haven't a clue," I say.

"That'll be her place over there," he says. "The one with the Japanese maple."

"See that car?" I say. "Other side of the street? Canary yellow."

"What about it?"

"George Starryk was trying to sell one just like it out of his showroom."

"So?"

"Can't be too many of those in the city," I say. I slow down to cruise past the bright yellow Mustang. "And that one has dealer plates and most of a Dysart Motors decal on the rear bumper."

"This would be a great time to involve the authorities," says Gritch.

"I suppose. Why don't you give them a call?" I say. "Explain, if you can, that there's a possibility, very faint, that either or both of the Starryk brothers is or are in the vicinity. You might also point out that this is based on the flimsiest of evidence but that we wouldn't want anyone to think we were withholding."

"What will you be doing while I'm on the phone?" he wants to know.

"I'm here to pay my respects to Theo's girlfriend."

I back the sedan into a space recently vacated by a blue BMW, snug my Tensor bandage an extra half inch, and step out of the car, heading for Marcia Duhamel's front door. Behind me I can hear Gritch trying to locate an interested party.

No one answers the knock, or the ring. Maybe her plane hasn't landed. I cross the street to where the Mustang is notched into a tight row of vehicles. Not much is visible through the rear window, or the side window. I ill-advisedly touch the driver's side door, which sets off the world's most annoying car alarm, a relentless series of ear-jabbing beeps. There's no way for me to shut it off. I retreat to the sedan and adopt a nonchalant air while watching the buildings across the way. One by one doors open and annoyed faces peer out. A man who looks like he's been awakened from a Sunday nap yells, "Shut that damn thing off or I'm calling the police!"

I can hear Gritch muttering, "Whaddaya think I'm doing?"

Marcia's front door opens a foot and Dimi's Starr's moustache twitches in the shadows. I see his arm stick out and his thumb punch what looks to be a remote device of some kind. It isn't working; the honking goes on. He's caught between two unhappy choices — show himself, or wait for the police.

"That him?" Gritch asks.

"That's our boy," I say.

Dimi waves his keys in the air as he leaves his hideout and bolts for the car. "Sorry, sorry, sorry," he calls out to one and all. He has to squeeze between the next car, fumble with keys, all the while apologizing for the constant honking. Finally he manages to open the door, cram his upper body inside and locate the switch. Blissful silence descends upon the genteel neighbourhood. Doors are slammed, people grumble and return to their Sunday lives, and Dimi shoehorns himself into the Mustang and fires up the big motor.

Great planning, Mr. Moto, I tell myself as I clamber back behind the wheel. You might have anticipated that option. It's good of the engine to fire up without the usual complaint.

"You'll never catch him in this thing," Gritch says.

He's right about that. I'm not an intrepid driver, even with two good arms.

"No, we're not confronting," Gritch says into the phone, "we're merely tracking and observing."

"Who're you talking to?" I ask.

"I have no idea," says Gritch. "Maintai — That's right, maintaining our distance."

I don't think maintaining distance is the best plan. If he puts any distance between us it'll be game over. I decide on a more direct approach. As Dimi is backing carefully out of his parking space, I hit the gas, slide the old boat around in a tight one-eighty, and rear-end him with enough force to crumple bumpers and bodywork. I hope Dimi has insurance. I know the hotel has.

"Hello again, Detective," Gritch says into his cell, "I have an update."

There's no room for him to get out on the driver's side. He slides across to the other seat but I manage to wedge myself against a handy Forester and lean on the passenger door as he's sticking his head out.

"Hi, Dimi," I say. "Might as well sit tight, the police are on their way."

"We don't need cops," he says. "Move your car so I can back out."

"No, they need to talk to you about that other thing. Remember? Monday night?"

Dimi does the only logical thing, at least from his perspective. He slides back behind the wheel, throws the Mustang into reverse, and smashes into the long-suffering hotel sedan a few times, driving it no more than a few inches backward. It's as good as a roadblock.

Dimi smokes his tires a couple more times and then decides to have an emotional breakdown. He starts screaming and pounding the steering wheel and cursing in Macedonian or Bulgarian, I can't tell, but whatever language, I doubt the words are polite. When I squeeze in beside him he takes a couple of backhanded swings at my head.

"Take it easy now, Mr. Starr," I say. "It's all over. Might as well relax. We're not going anywhere."

He emits a groan of rage and frustration and tries to swat me again. I have a strong desire to club him on the jaw, right where the nerve endings bundle, but then he wouldn't be able to talk, and I need answers even more than payback. "Stop that!" I say, with my serious voice. I reach for the key and shut down the engine.

He slumps over the steering wheel. "What do you want?" he asks.

"Did you kill her?"

"She was dead when I got there."

"What were you doing there?"

"Lawyer up."

"What?"

"That's what I do. Lawyer up. I've got nothing to say."

"I'm not a policeman," I say. "Anything you say to me wouldn't be admissible."

"Yeah, right," he says. "I didn't kill anybody, I didn't steal anything, I was doing a favour for somebody, that's all."

"For Theo Alexander?"

"Screw him."

"Who then? Marcia?"

He shakes his head with the dead acceptance of a trapped animal. "Drive her around places, Theo says. She gets bored, he says. Take her to the shops, take her where she wants to go, keep an eye on her, report to him who she's meeting. She doesn't like it. She's a prisoner. I tell her, break free, belong to yourself, answer to nobody. She's a kept woman, but she's unsatisfied, you know? He can afford her, but he can't keep her happy, you know?"

"And you could?"

"What are you gonna do? She's bored, spends most of her time alone. 'Help me with these packages, Dimi, what do you think of this dress, Dimi, zip me up please, Dimi.' I'm human."

"I understand," I say. "You had an affair."

"Not an affair. It's serious. We were going to take off."

"But you needed money."

"She knows where the safe is. She stole the combination from Theo. The old man doesn't know he has it. There's like a million cash and Theo's bragging all he has to do is reach in and grab it. One of these days he's going to do it, he says."

"You and Marcia were going to beat him to the punch."

"It was supposed to be simple."

"What happened?"

"I get there, it's quiet, I start looking around, lights on in the kitchen, I slip on a plate of something, on the floor. Land on top of a dead woman. That's too much for me, I'm out of there. I didn't steal anything, I didn't kill anybody."

"What about Farrel?"

"That dumbass stupid dumbshit! He's supposed to bring the other car, that's *all*. I tell him to go home! He starts acting crazy. He sees that thing with the old guy's face? Grabbed it out of my hand. Payback time, he says. He's got a drill in the trunk. Puts a hole right through the eye. I say, what the fuck you do that for? Payback time, he says. I had to sneak it back inside. I'm not responsible. So I tell stupidshit to go home. He's screwing the whole thing. He says he's not a slave, he doesn't take orders, nobody's ripping him off this time. Asshole thinks we're stealing the car."

"How did he wind up dead?"

"Lawyer up."

I hear sirens approaching, but it isn't a police car honking at Gritch to move our beat up sedan. It's a black Lincoln Town Car and we're blocking his way. After a few imperious honks, the door opens and out steps Theo Alexander, fresh off the plane and looking somewhat wearied by his business trip. The passenger door opens and an attractive brunette wearing large sunglasses and a very tight T-shirt gets out and surveys the traffic snarl. Theo marches over to the sedan, recognizes Gritch, does a double take when he sees me climbing out of the Mustang. He looks back toward Marcia but she's already at her front door. I can hear Dimi pounding the steering wheel and cursing.

"Grundy! What the hell are you doing here?"

"Mr. Alexander," I say, "nice flight?"

"Get this piece of crap off the road!"

"Sorry," I say, "there's been an accident. We're waiting for certain officials to take charge of the situation."

"What situation?"

"You might want to check with your girlfriend."

"She is not my girlfriend. She's an employee. I gave her a lift from — I don't have to explain myself to you."

"No, sir, not to me," I say. "On the other hand —" police cars are arriving, two cruisers and an unmarked car —"... *they* will definitely need some clarification." Uniforms get out, Mooney gets out. Pazzano isn't with him. Suits me.

chapter twenty-four

"Now that we've caught the bad guys and solved their case for them you'd think it'd be clear sailing, wouldn't you?" says Gritch.

"Always a few last-minute details," I say.

"They'll smash the windows if they have to," he says. "I've seen them do it."

"They're waiting on the tow truck."

"Can we at least get out of here?"

"Not yet. We're what's keeping him boxed in."

Dimi is refusing to leave the Mustang. He has the doors locked, and the CD player cranking out a particularly annoying collection of rock anthems with which he is harmonizing at the top of his lungs. Every few bars he throws the car into reverse, squeals the tires and gives the uncomplaining hotel vehicle another thump. There are six police units on the scene and at least a dozen of Vancouver's finest trying to figure out a way of extricating the suspect without damaging either the Subaru Forester or the Saab 9000 on the other side.

Our street theatre has attracted a sizeable crowd of spectators who enthusiastically offer advice along the lines of, "Shoot the tires!" and "Bring out the Jaws of Life!" as well as warnings such as, "Scratch my paint and I'll sue the ass off you!"

Theo is stranded on the sidewalk, huffing and puffing and refusing to answer any questions without the presence of legal counsel. Marcia Duhamel is spurning requests to open her front door despite numerous warnings from the constabulary that they are prepared to kick it in. Some wag in the crowd once again calls for the Jaws of Life.

By this time we have also attracted a few quick-footed media people. I can spot Dee, the videographer, climbing onto the roof of a Channel 20 van some distance away. I doubt she'll be able to spot me from there. Larry Gormé, unhampered by heavy electronic equipment, is manoeuvring through the crowd in our general direction.

"Stick behind the wheel," I tell Gritch, "in case they want this thing moved. I'll be back."

Gritch pulls the cellophane off a celebratory smoke. "I'm not going anywhere," he says. "This is better than women's beach volleyball."

"Thanks for the heads-up," Larry says when I reach him. "Let me guess, argument over a parking spot."

"It isn't entirely resolved," I say.

"That's the famous fugitive, Dimi Starr, AKA Dimitar Starryk, object of a massive six-day manhunt?"

"The same."

"How'd you track him down?"

"Dumb luck."

"I doubt that."

"I was trying to talk to Theo's girlfriend, excuse me, employee, one Marcia Duhamel, currently locked inside her townhouse. Turns out she had a houseguest."

"My, my," Larry says, while quickly scratching notes. "How do you spell that? Duhamel? And what's the big fat eldest son doing here?"

"Driving her home from the airport. They'd been on a business trip."

"He doesn't look happy about the situation."

"He's going to be late for supper."

"If he's not careful he'll miss breakfast, too." Larry grabs a few shots of the tableau with his cellphone. "Get a chance to speak to the fugitive?"

"We had a chat."

"What's his story?"

"He says Raquel was dead when he got there."

"Well, what else is he going to say?" Larry grabs a picture of Theo blustering at Mooney not far away. "Fatboy's going to love this one," he says. He turns back to me. "Dimi say if his li'l buddy Farrel was also a goner when he showed up?"

"On that subject he demanded a lawyer."

"No doubt," Larry says. "That one would be harder to explain."

Mooney looks like he's had enough of Theo's guff for the moment and walks our way. Larry takes the opportunity to drift in another direction.

"Tow truck's here," Mooney says. "Your car still operational?"

"We'll soon find out," I say. "You going to arrest Theo?"

"I'd like to, but I know where to find him if his story doesn't hold up. Right now he's only guilty of taking a businessman's holiday with his secretary."

"Design consultant."

"Besides, his wife will probably give him a harder time than we can."

"I assume you'll be letting my boss go now."

"Possibly. No one's being particularly cooperative."

"No, but you can add two and two," I say. "Dimi and Marcia, Marcia and Theo. Leo won't figure into any scenario with those people."

"He still has a connection to the dead one, Farrel Newton."

"Who hated his guts."

"Well, it won't kill your boss to spend one more night at our convenience." He takes note of the cruisers making room for the arrival of the police tow truck. "See if you can detach yourself from that rear bumper without running anybody down."

"Where's your partner?"

"This is Sunday. I expect he's eating his mama's lasagna."

"How come you were available?"

"My mom lives in Wataskwin and can't cook for sour apples."

Gritch slides sideways when I open the door. "She's a cutie. Isn't she?"

"Who's a cutie?" I ask as I turn the key.

"Young Officer Chan," he says.

"She here, too?"

"Not anymore," he says. "She and her partner are off to pick up Dimi's bro." He rolls down his window to break off two inches of ash and almost makes it before it lands on his tie. "They figure he'll have a spare key for the Mustang."

There is surprisingly little damage to the front of the hotel sedan. One of the uniforms gives it a quick check and pronounces it sufficiently sound to get us back to home base, although he does strongly suggest that, until the right headlight is replaced, we not drive it at night.

As I weave us carefully out of the traffic jam, I catch a glimpse of Marcia's front door opening. It looks like she's changed out of her travelling duds.

Olive's is quiet, the jam is over, presumably all the scones have been eaten, too. The CD player is shuffling Olive May's personal heroes from Tatum to Peterson, and the lady herself is ensconced in her private corner having an unlawful Winston to go with her rum and Coke.

"Beer, Champ?" Barney asks.

"Thank you, Barney, I believe I will. I almost deserve one."

"Preference?"

"Cold, draft, you pick."

"Coming up."

"Good session?"

Barney shakes his head in wonder. "Somebody should have been recording," he says. "It was like an all-star game. If she'd booked that band it would've cost a bazillion dollars." He puts a coaster in front of me and caps it with a frosty pint. "Wall-to-wall heavyweights."

"Sorry I missed it," I say.

"Other fish to fry, I imagine."

"I ran a tab here this afternoon," I say, reaching for some money. "Martinis."

"Stuck it on your weekly. You might break fifty bucks this time."

"It's a slippery slope." The first swallow feels like victory quaff.

"Madam Queen's waving," says Barney.

All I can see of Olive is a portion of her right shoulder, with arm lifted and fingers waggling. "At you or me?" I wonder. She turns her Cleopatra *profeel* into the light and blows me a kiss.

"Both," Barney says. "Two fingers is for a fresh one, the smile is all yours."

"How you feeling, Joey darlin'?" Olive wants to know as I settle in across from her.

"Better and better," I say, almost truthfully.

She offers me a ceremonial Winston, which I take. One a day. Our little ritual. She lights me up with the gold Ronson, inscribed WARM VALLEY, which I happen to know was a gift from Billy Strayhorn, and I inhale an illicit puff and sneak a quick peek for the Smoke Police — although, to my knowledge, no one has ever had the temerity to complain, not officially anyway. Olive's dark corner is sacrosanct. A separate world. Not unlike Leo's aerie except that here I have always felt entirely welcome.

"Your arm?" she asks.

"On the mend," I say. "I'll be playing the violin again in no time."

"Saw your sweetie on the news tonight," she says. "She looked good."

"Happy, too, I bet."

"She'll be back." Barney arrives with her fresh drink — rum over ice in a tall glass, and one of his precious green Coke bottles studded with crystals. "As always, your timing is impeccable," she says to him.

Barney catches my eye and nods toward the far corner. "Lenny Alexander says they're both comped. True?"

The last banquette, just before the mall entrance, Lenny Alexander and Roselyn Hiscox are sitting side by side, heads close together.

"It's covered, Barney," I say. "Put it on my tab."

"You are definitely breaking fifty this week," he says.

"Are they sober?"

"Not entirely," he says, "but they ate well, and they're pacing themselves. Well, he is anyway."

"Old friends?" Olive asks.

"Family," I say. "Lenny's long-lost sister."

"Aww," she says, "that's so nice. You got family, darlin'?"

"Just you folks," I say.

"And your sweetie 'cross the sea."

"And my sweetie across the sea," I say.

She leans across the table and I do likewise. A generous woman's kiss — warm, not entirely platonic, out within the bounds of propriety. Olive May is what the Spanish call *un todo mujer*, all that is woman. "It's my family, too, Joey darlin'," she says.

"Hey, Joe," I hear Lenny's voice lifted. "Come on over."

Olive pats me on the back of my hand. I butt my unfinished Winston and pick up my unfinished beer. "Get some rest, hon," she says.

"Hey, now." Roselyn looks up at me from under an errant frond of blonde hair. She is obviously 'shit-faced,' as Morely Kline would have pointed out. "It's the bodyguard," she says. "Guarded any good bodies lately?"

Lenny, on the other hand, looks like a man who has had exactly as much as he requires in order to maintain a healthy glow. "Hey Joe," he says. "Sit down for a minute. You've met my sister? We've been comparing notes."

"Digging up bones," she says.

"We're going arm-in-arm into court tomorrow," he says. "United front, show the flag, all that crap."

"Don't think it'll get that far," I say. "They'll probably just turn him loose, maybe even with an apology. They arrested that limo driver."

"Yeah? All *right*!" Lenny sounds genuinely happy about the development.

"Horseshoes up his ass," says Roselyn. "If the old prick fell into a Port-A-Potty he'd find oil."

"Want to help me get her upstairs, Joe?" Lenny asks.

Roselyn flops across the bed and pulls a pillow under her cheek. Lenny and I both consider the appropriateness of removing her clothes and settle for taking off her shoes, pulling a coverlet across her shoulders and turning out the light.

"That's good they caught the guy," Lenny says when we're in the hall. "Where was he?"

"House-sitting," I say. "Ever meet a woman named Marcia Duhamel?"

Lenny laughs. "The 'design consultant'? Ha!" he presses the elevator button. "Sure. She's been his steady for a couple of years." The elevator arrives. I press L; he presses MM. "I'm having a nightcap," he says. "After tomorrow I'm back to paying my own bar bill. Join me?"

"Phone call to make," I say.

"She's involved?" he wants to know.

"It looks like Marcia and the limo driver were trying to break into Leo's safe."

"Dearie me," he says primly. "My fat-ass brother's going to have some 'splaining to do."

The doors open. "See you in the morning," I say.

Lenny sticks out a hand to hold the doors open. "Hey, Joe?" he says. "It's good you look out for the old man. He's getting on."

"It's good you two are connecting."

"Yeah, well, what the hell. Family is family no matter how fucked up it is."

The early edition of the Monday *Emblem* is being stacked by the newsstand, and for a change we aren't the top story. Larry's scoop on the arrest of Dimi Starr and

Marcia Duhamel is below the fold. The headline reads, JOURNALIST KILLED OUTSIDE KANDAHAR.

"Someone you know?"

"Jim Burrell," Connie says. "He was family."

"Aw, damn it, Connie, I'm so sorry."

"Roadside bomb," she says. "It was supposed to be a safe location."

"It's getting worse over there, isn't it?"

"Certain spots are heating up."

"I'm glad this China thing is almost over," I say. "When are you heading back? Tomorrow night? Wednesday? That'll be your Thursday, I guess."

There is a moment's silence, perhaps ten full seconds of dead air, and I know without a word being spoken what's coming next.

"Joe," she starts.

My heart sinks. "Oh, Christ," I say.

"Don't go all fatherly," she says. "You know I have to grab this."

"Of course I do," I say. "You will understand if I worry. It's my nature."

"I know. And I love it. Don't fret so much you lose your hair, okay?"

"And you'll have body-armour, right?"

"And a helmet, and a vehicle, and an armed escort."

I don't bother to state the obvious — so did Mr. Burrell. I'm sure she's far more cognizant of the situation than I. Stay positive. "When?" I ask as brightly as I can manage.

"Not sure," she says. "Have to wind up this junket and get out of here. I might get a flight to Tokyo tonight, let them figure it out from there."

"And you'll have body-armour, right?"

"You did that already."

"I know, but it's sort of important."

"And there's Saint Chris, my bulletproof boyfriend. How many missions did Uncle Victor fly?"

"Twenty."

"Missing you, big guy," she says. "This would be a good night to get cuddled and such."

Sleep is no longer an option. After we hang up, both of us reluctantly, I wander the lobby and mezzanine, walk the perimeter, check doors, and try to look like a man with purpose instead of helpless, forlorn, and on the wrong side of the world.

chapter twenty-five

"**W**ow!" says Larry. "Did she luck out. Right place, right time. Crappy way to get the job, but there'll be no stopping her now."

"Larry, she's going into a war zone."

"Tell me about it. Doesn't get any better for an up-and-comer."

Hattie brings coffee for both of us. "You sure no toast for you, Joe?"

"Not this morning, thanks, Hattie, my stomach's a little off."

"She'd better get back here soon," Hattie says. "You're showing the effects. You've got a crease between your eyes."

"Journalists are rotated out of there every six weeks at most," Larry says. "She'll be back soon."

"She'd better be," Hattie says. She heads to the other

end of the counter to flirt with the man from Coffee Central. Larry pulls a copy of the *Emblem* out of his jacket pocket. I have a sip. It tastes sour. The morning tastes sour. I reach for the cream and sugar.

"I almost asked her to turn it down," I say.

"She wouldn't have, couldn't have. Assignments like that don't come around every day."

"Why couldn't she be one of the weather ladies?"

"Nah," he says. "You like it that she's a battler. It's part of her charm. Hell, if you'd got a chance to fight Tyson would you have turned it down?"

"'Course not."

"Even though he would have handed you your head?"

"Iron Mike didn't wear high explosives strapped to his chest."

"She's in the best place," he says. "Soldiers, armoured vehicles, medical personnel."

"None of those words exactly calm my anxiety."

"You'll be okay," he says. "Just remind yourself that she's exactly where she wants to be. An assignment like that is a jump from single-A to the big show. She's playing for the Yankees, pal."

"Thought you were a Jays fan."

"Ask me again when they get over .500." He looks at the front page. "Pisses me off that we got bumped. Guy's been a fugitive for six days, half the city's police force chasing him, you bust him, and you're not even mentioned."

"Suits me."

"I'm sure I stuck your name in here somewhere. Oh, yeah, here it is, 'continued on page five'."

"How'd your friend Gloria take it?"

"Generous, professional, swears she'll cut my throat next time she gets a chance."

"Peer regard, can't beat it."

"So," he says, folding the paper and leaving it on the counter for someone else, "case all wrapped up? Leo getting out? Mission complete?"

"Still a few things to sort out."

"Such as?"

I check my watch. It's still on the wrong wrist but at least I've managed to get it facing the right way. The fingers on my left hand are functional again. Sort of. "Weed's arranged for me to see Mr. Santiago."

"How's he involved?" Larry asks. "Aside from trying to kill you?"

"Maybe he'll tell me this time," I say.

Jesus Santiago comes into the visitor's room and takes a chair on the other side of a pane of glass. He's wearing prison garb and a black eye.

¿ *Cómo está usted hoy, Señor Santiago?* I ask.

"Your Spanish sucks," he says.

"Really? Raquel always said I had a good accent."

"She didn't want to hurt your feelings."

I nod. "Yes, she was a kind person."

"Expecting somebody from Immigration to show up," he says. "Thought it was you."

"This will be a short visit," I say. "Raquel was what? Your sister?"

He waves the question aside. "How bad did I get you?" he asks.

"Just a nick," I say. "Almost healed."

"You hit pretty hard."

"Call it even?"

"Except I'm in here."

Can't argue with him there. He wouldn't be sitting on the wrong side of the Plexiglas except for my interference. "I apologize for getting in your face the other night," I say. "Raquel didn't deserve what happened to her. I've been trying to find out who did it and I thought you might —"

"Might've killed her?"

"— might have seen something that would help me find him."

"When you do, I'd like my knife back, and five minutes in a dark room with the motherfucker."

"Can't blame you for feeling that way," I tell him. "She was a lovely woman. I liked her a lot."

"Yeah," he says. "She had a good heart. My big sister. Always looked out for me. Family, right or wrong. When I told her I wasn't going back, she said 'Come up here.' No questions asked."

"Going back to the army?"

"Going back to fucking *Eye-raq*. If I wasn't in here, I'd be shipping out today." He looks around. "Fuck, this is an improvement. Three tours is plenty."

I can't even imagine what three tours in Iraq would be like and I can't bring myself to feign empathy. What he's been through makes my week look like summer camp. "Did you see the man who fell?"

"Too dark. Heard him screaming all the way down though. Didn't see him till he landed."

"Nasty way to go," I say.

"I've seen worse," he says.

"He was one of the men who was in the penthouse," I say. "We caught his partner yesterday."

His eyes go cold and hard. "He in here?"

"I don't know where they're keeping him."

"You wouldn't tell me anyway."

"Did you see Raquel when you got to town?"

"Called her. She told me to stay close. She was going to get some cash to me so I could disappear. She never showed up."

"How long were you there?"

"Just a day. Found some dude's little lean-to. I was going to call her in the morning."

"You've met Raquel's husband, I suppose?"

"Ex-husband. He divorced her for desertion two years ago. He's remarried already. Has a kid."

"I thought she couldn't get a divorce."

"Maybe she wasn't divorced according to the Pope, but according to the State of California, she was a single woman."

"I think she was wrestling with that," I say.

"She would. Hell, she wanted to be a nun for a while." He looks like he's endured as much of an interview as he's going to. He looks at the wall clock.

"I'm supposed to talk to some Immigration dude in a minute," he says.

I stand up. "My boss has some high-priced legal talent at his disposal," I say, "maybe they can help."

"Why would he do that?"

"He loved your sister very much. He wanted very

much to marry her. She was going to have his child. I think he'd probably like a chance to help."

"They'll send me back sooner or later."

"Be surprised how long a good lawyer can drag things out. War might be over by then."

"That war won't ever be over, dude. They'll just keep moving it around."

"At least you could get bail to be at your sister's funeral."

"Won't be cheap."

"I don't think the money will be a concern."

"Hell, right now all I've got is Legal Aid," he says. "A good lawyer wouldn't hurt."

"I'll get on it," I say. "Thanks for your time." I get up to leave.

He smiles. "*Hasta luego*," he says.

"*Si*," I say. "*Hasta pronto*."

"She was being kind."

"She was like that," I say. I stop and look back at him. "My girlfriend's just been sent to Afghanistan."

"Army?"

"She's a reporter."

"Tell her to stay out of the south," he says. "All bets are off down there."

"Welcome home, Mr. Alexander."

"Thank you, Andrew. I hear they tried to stick you with a new door."

"Yes, sir. Electrified," he says with a shudder.

"Turned them down, I hear."

"It wasn't worthy of your house, sir."

"Quite right," says Leo.

Andrew swings open his gleaming brass showpiece and tips his gold-braided cap a careful inch, a gesture he reserves for heads of state and visiting royalty and *never* grants to movie stars.

Margo Traynor, bless her, has organized an unobtrusive welcoming line of main floor luminaries, all of them prepared to step forward or quietly retreat depending on what they read on Leo's face. Leo makes it easy.

"Maurice, you're looking fit. New position agrees with you?"

"Settling in nicely, sir, thank you," says Maurice.

"Roy Sullivan was concierge here for thirty-seven years, did you know that?"

"Yes, sir. Taught me everything I know."

"He used to tell me a story about his first job," Leo says, raising his voice and angling his head just enough to include the rest of the welcoming committee. "His new boss said to him, 'I'll give you a hundred dollars a week. Will you *take* a hundred dollars a week? And Roy said 'Sure' and the guy said 'Okay, you got a nice *two*-hundred-dollar-a-week job; don't let me catch you takin' no more."

Leo roars with laughter and slaps Maurice on the shoulder. Maurice manages a reasonable approximation of a guffaw. Hearty chuckles resound, as much for Maurice's discomfiture as Leo's story, and the ice is broken. Rolf Kalman is embraced and engaged in a private consultation regarding Leo's evening meal. Rolf suggests a wine or two, an agreement is reached; he shakes Leo's hand formally. Leo nods at me to shake Rolf's hand as well. Mine has a hundred-dollar bill folded in the palm. Cheery greetings for Gritch and Rachel, genial waves and nods for the gathering, and I begin ushering my boss toward the elevators.

Margo steps forward holding a thin leather binder, which she hands to me. "Messages and legal papers," she says. "Nothing critical."

Leo turns and comes to her, takes both her hands in his and leans close. "Miss Traynor," he says quietly, "be assured that I am fully aware who actually runs this house."

"Kind of you to say, sir." She looks him square in the eye, doesn't curtsy, give her that.

"I take it Mr. Gruber is still under the weather?" Leo inquires.

"He's expected tomorrow."

Leo looks around at the stately expanse of the main lobby. "Looks almost as good as when she opened."

"You've done a fine job bringing her back, sir."

"It's a new age for the old girl," he says with pride. "She needs a fresh hand on the tiller." He smiles. "We will chat again, very soon."

"You owe me money," I whisper as I walk by.

"We'll see," she says. "Day's not over yet."

Roland is holding elevator number one for us. Leo plants himself like a stockman appraising a prize bull. "How are the calves coming along, young man?" he asks.

"Eighteen inches this morning," Roland says with some pride.

"Good, very good." Leo judiciously pokes one enormous bicep. "Be no stopping you this year." He enters the car, I insert the penthouse key, the doors begin to close, a manicured hand breaks the beam, and Roselyn Hiscox, perfect hair, impudent smile, steps inside and faces her father. If she's suffering a hangover, I see no evidence.

"Looks like you got away with another one, Daddy." she says.

He takes a moment to focus, or gather himself. "Rose?"

As I move forward, Leo puts out an arm to stop me. The doors close behind her, the elevator begins to rise.

"Did you get my birthday card?"

"My goodness," he says with admiration in his voice, "you look positively —"

"Sane?" she asks, brightly.

"I was going to say beautiful, elegant, confident, that sort of thing."

She's wearing a pale gold outfit, jacket and pants. No doubt a well-known designer's name is tacked on, somewhere. "But sane?" she asks again.

"I never thought you were crazy, Rose."

"Really? I could have sworn when you packed me off to the funny farm —"

"That was for your protection. Surely you know that by now."

"Oh," she says. "I thought it was for yours."

There is an awkward pause. Well, awkward for me. Roselyn appears to be enjoying the moment.

Leo retrieves his aplomb, turns to me. "You've met my daughter, haven't you, Joseph?"

"Yes, sir, we've talked a few times."

"She's turned out quite splendidly, wouldn't you say?"

"Very stylish."

"We Alexanders always knew how to shop," she says.

Leo says, "The last time I saw you —"

"Relax, Dad, I won't shoot you this time."

A sudden sense memory — a branding iron scorching my chest, Havana tobacco turned to smoldering powder in my hand. I feel the hairs on the back of my neck rise and cold beads spring to my forehead. If she so much as caresses the catch on her designer bag I'm going to deck her. I thumb the knot on my clavicle reflexively. The elevator is taking its time.

"I've found more positive ways to channel my madness," she says.

"Glad to hear it, glad to hear it," says Leo. The adrenaline rush has brightened his eyes and restored his composure. The doors open and he leads the way into the penthouse.

Roselyn looks around with the air of an interior decorator itching to be turned loose. "My, my," she says. "Positively Edwardian."

"First time you've been up here, isn't it?" Leo asks.

"Nobody would give me the secret password."

"It's a bit early, but I've had an abstemious weekend. Join me?"

"No, thanks," she says.

"Joseph?"

"No, thank you, sir. I should really be attending to things."

"Not yet," says Leo.

"He thinks I might have a gun in my bag," she says.

"Have you?"

"I've found the word processor to be mightier than the .32."

"Mind if I check?" I ask as politely as I can.

"Help yourself," she says.

The purse is soft gold leather and holds nothing lethal. I hand it back. "I never saw your face that night," I say.

"No one did," she says. "Black is invisible at a bunfight like that. It was the perfect operation. Except I missed."

"Not entirely," I say.

"Joseph tells me you're writing a book," Leo says conversationally. He pours himself a generous splash of brandy. I'm proud of him; his hand doesn't shake and he doesn't knock it back.

"Yes, I am. It should be a lulu."

"I look forward to reading it."

"Actually, I thought you might want to bid on it, before it gets between the covers, so to speak."

He laughs with genuine amusement. "You think I'm afraid of what's in it?" He shakes his head. "I don't care if my life gets plastered over the front pages." He finally takes a drink, half of it in one swallow, inhales deeply through his nose, his combative spirit restored. "My self-indulgence has cost me over the years — divorces, settlements, animosities, grudges — but I don't owe anyone. Every business deal I made was a fair fight and the people I was up against would have done the same to me." He drinks again. "But certain things ... you do certain things for family, to protect your family. You maintain a level of reserve." He looks at her. "It's your life I've been trying to protect."

"Me, too, Daddy. Catharsis. That's what it's about. Lance a few boils, bellow a few primal screams and collect a big payday."

"You've never had to worry about money. There has always been a trust fund in your name."

"Which name? Rose Alexander? Rosie Webster? Roselyn Hiscox?"

"What does it matter? You will always be my daughter."

"Will I?"

"Of course."

"If you don't need me any longer, sir ..." I start.

"Stick around, Joseph. There are a few things you should probably hear." Leo pours himself another measure of brandy and walks toward the windows. Outside, the sun is shining. "You came within an inch of killing Joseph that night, you know?"

"I didn't expect him to move that fast."

"Yes. Surprising in a man his size."

"If it's any consolation," she says, "I wasn't aiming at you."

"It isn't," I say.

"If you'd killed him I wouldn't have been able to let it go," he says. "Not this time."

"Why not? You cover up your own."

"I've never killed anyone."

"And yet they die," she says. "On second thought, I will have a drink."

"Joseph?"

"I can pour my own," she says. "Got any vodka?"

"In the freezer," Leo says.

"Juice, tonic?" I ask.

"Tonic," she says.

I open the refrigerator. A few items are still waiting for a party that will never take place — chocolate truffles and a baking tray of little cakes. I grab tonic, and a lime, just in case, ice cubes, and a frosty bottle from the freezer.

She's followed me into the kitchen. "I'll take it from here," she says.

She slides a knife out of the rack and slices the lime neatly in half. My forearm twitches. One of these days I'll add up the war wounds I've incurred while in Leo's employ. All in all I think prizefighting may have been the less hazardous profession.

"That night is still a blank, is it?" Leo asks. "Psychiatrists and therapists and now a public revelation of family secrets and you still can't face what happened that night."

"I have faced that night, Daddy dear. A thousand times. I've been hypnotized, regressed, drugged, and had my dreams picked over like pigeon entrails." She stirs her drink once with the knife blade, has a sip. And another. "I know my mother died," she says. "And I know that the only one who hated her was you."

"I never hated Lorraine."

"Could have fooled me," she says.

"Would you mind putting the knife down?" I ask.

She looks at the blade in her hand as if surprised to find she's still holding it. She smiles at me. "Do I worry you, Joseph?"

"A woman was killed in this kitchen with a knife like that," I say. "And as near as I can figure, so was your mother."

She places the knife carefully on the cutting board and steps back. "There," she says.

"Thank you."

"Terrible coincidence, don't you think?" she says.

"I doubt it was a coincidence," I say.

Leo comes toward us, his eyes cold. "If I thought you had anything to do with Raquel's death ..."

"You'd what? Ship me back to the Websters?"

"That was for your own good."

"You didn't really think I killed my own mother?"

"What was I supposed to think? You were covered in her blood. Your fingerprints were on the knife."

"I found her body."

"It doesn't matter now," he says.

Roselyn erupts. "What unmitigated horseshit!" she yells at him. "Of course it matters. You didn't defend me. You made it clear to everyone that I'd done something unspeakable and then made me disappear. I was in shock. I was practically catatonic."

"The police were going to take you into custody."

"They had nothing. I've checked. I got my hands on a copy of their file. The prints were from my left thumb and finger. I picked it up like this." The knife dangles like a dead fish.

"They didn't want to prosecute. We all thought it would be better for you ..."

"And for you."

"It had nothing to do with me. I wasn't there."

"You came back early."

"Someone did," I say.

Chocolate truffles in the refrigerator sit beside a

amiliar baking pan. Date squares.

"I'm leaving now," I say. I turn my special key and summon the elevator. "If it's any comfort to the pair of you, you're both innocent of the murder of Lorraine Alexander." The elevator bell rings. "And the murder of Raquel Santiago," I finish.

"Joseph!" Leo barks. He walks across the room and faces me. "*Who*?"

"Check the refrigerator," I say. "You'll figure it out." The elevator doors close.

"What are you doing?"

"Looking at security tapes. What are you doing?"

"Packing. I'm getting a lift to Tokyo."

"Good. That's in the opposite direction."

"Dee's coming over. I get to pick my own camera crew."

"Is she happy about it?"

"Are you mad? She's doing handsprings."

"I don't get you media types," I say. "Smart people run away from danger. If someone tried to drag me into a war zone I wouldn't be doing handsprings."

"You had your own war zones pal," she says.

"With rules," I say.

"What's on the security tapes?" she says, neatly changing the subject.

"Cars," I say. "Coming, going, coming, going."

"Sounds exciting."

"It's depressing."

"Really? Why?"

"There's a car I didn't want to see, coming an going."

After Connie goes back to packing I start on the security tapes for the fifth, sixth, and seventh floors. The most likely ones. When the cameras were made operational January 1st, they came with a monitoring station that was set up in the small office next door. I'm not sure who we ousted to get the space but these days it holds a number of TV sets and computers and the like. I rarely go in there and I'd be lost in my present pursuit if Todd wasn't handling the technical details, time codes, buttons to push, which monitor to look at.

"Roughly what time for these?" Todd asks.

"Between two and two-thirty," I say. Can't be a lot of traffic that time of the morning."

"Emergency exit cameras, east side, that's this one. Sixth floor. Nobody, nobody, and … somebody."

"That's all I need, Todd, thanks. Keep that one and the parking garage one separate okay."

"Sure," he says. "Cracked it, right?"

"I'm afraid so," I say.

Olive's is mostly quiet on Monday nights. Olive usually takes the night off. Sometimes Barney takes the night off. Not much reason for Weed to be there other than at my invitation.

"You're sure about this?" he wants to know.

"Oh, yeah," I say.

"All pretty circumstantial," he says.

"You didn't come down here because you think I'm nuts."

"I'm just saying. We don't actually have anything concrete."

"All you need," I say. "Security cameras from the parking garage, and the sixth floor emergency exit, dates and times, licence plate, and parking receipt."

"I kept thinking this had to have some connection to the Calgary thing. It was just too damn symmetrical." He's drinking coffee. This isn't a night for merriment. "Cold cases never go away," he says. "Some cops go to their graves still gnawing on something that happened fifty years back."

"Roselyn said that Madge found her huddled under a table, covered in her mother's blood. If that's true, only two possible explanations: Rose Alexander, age nine, stabbed her mother to death; or, Madge got back from Calgary a little earlier than she told the police."

"Okay," he says, "grab a couple of hours sleep. We'll get an early ferry."

"My vehicle isn't roadworthy at present," I say.

"I'll drive," he says.

chapter twenty-six

W eed is wearing a tie that boasts, I swear, the Little Mermaid swimming with a lobster.

"My granddaughter," he says. "I promised I'd wear it."

"Goes with the turquoise jacket," I say. "Nautical."

The day is perfect, the sky is blue, the water is bluer. We're portside on the promenade deck, watching the mainland slip behind.

"Pazzano's nose is out of joint that you found the bad guy while he was eating lasagna," Weed says.

"Can't please everybody."

"He asks how your arm is coming along."

"Tell him if he's really that desperate for a boxing lesson, I'll introduce him to a mechanic I know."

We count gulls and cormorants for a while.

"How much did you get from Dimi?" I ask.

He shakes his head. "The perfect crime," he says. "Poor ap. Except for his idiot accomplice tagging along."

"You can't charge him with Raquel's murder." It's not a question.

"I've got no murder weapon, no motive, and with all the other heavy crap Dimi's facing, he won't make a deal on that one. She was dead when he got there. All that wreckage and dirt and broken glass came after. When he slipped in the blood, it was already starting to dry. Lab guys say she'd been dead for a while."

"Wrong place, wrong time."

"That's his story and he's sticking to it. He tells his idiot partner to wait outside. He sneaks in, stumbles over the body, knocks down a bunch of platters. He's covered in blood and sandwiches, looks up to see his accomplice, who panics and runs for the door. Dimi can't let him do that, he'll set off alarms, so he grabs Farrel and wrestles him back across the room, smashes the French doors, gets him out onto the patio. Farrel's screaming, he won't shut up, he tears loose and falls against the railing and when Dimi tries to grab him he loses his balance and goes over." Weed shakes his head. "Or that's the story we're going with this time around."

"You buying it?"

"It sounds loony enough to be true. Might be hard to prove he deliberately tossed his pal overboard, but I wouldn't be surprised if the Crown went after First Degree for this one anyway, homicide during the commission of a felony."

"How about Dimi's other accomplice?"

"The gorgeous Ms. Duhamel? Ha! She insists s~~e~~ had nothing to do with the scheme, or with Mr. Starr. She says Starr had developed an unhealthy obsession for her. Says he must have got the inside info, combinations, and security codes et cetera by perfidious means." He laughs. "She's almost credible."

"And Theo?"

"Theodore Alexander denies that there ever existed any inappropriate relationship between he and Ms. Duhamel. He is less credible but probably not complicit. However, I understand his wife has retained a divorce lawyer."

"No happy endings."

"Not today, anyway." He turns from the rail and we start promenading aft.

The Alexander Library has three cars in the lot. Madge Killian's Austin Healey Sprite is parked to the right of the space reserved for the man who has never visited.

"Right there," I say, pointing at Leo's name. "He won't be showing up."

Madge Killian is conducting a tour. Two couples. The older man and woman have the glowing complexions and crinkled eyes of yachting enthusiasts, the pretty girl and handsome lad accompanying them are holding hands. The little group dutifully follows Madge from station to station, pausing at photos and artifacts and paying close attention to her running commentary. Weed and I stop in the foyer and keep our voices low and our presence circumspect.

"Let's wait 'til she's done with that lot," Weed says.

"Could be a while," I say. "They haven't made it past the trophies yet."

Weed goes to the visitor's book and signs in. I do the same. It seems fitting somehow.

"Now isn't this a lovely surprise," Madge says, clapping her hands together as she gives us the once-over. "Two of my favourite men showing up unannounced on the same day."

"We tried the house first," I say. "Took a chance you'd be here."

"Some nice people from Seattle," she says. "They were supposed to come last week but couldn't make it."

"You go ahead and show them around," says Weed. "We're in no rush."

"They'll do fine on their own," she says. "The older couple are the girl's parents. They're trying to get their prospective son-in-law hooked on sailing."

"If he knows what's good for him, he'll take the bait," says Weed.

"Why don't you sit in my office for a minute?" she says. "I'll be right back." She bustles off to attend to her guests. She's wearing heels. She's wearing a skirt and jacket and pearls. She's wearing a diamond ring.

Weed takes the nice leather club chair across from Madge's desk, leaving the straight-backed wooden one for me. It reminds me of a classroom.

"I'm showing them a movie," Madge says, coming back. She plops herself on the other side of the desk and settles in like a broody hen. "It's quite exciting. Should keep them occupied for twenty minutes or so."

Weed looks in my direction.

"Madge, we have a tape of your little Sprite exiting the parking garage very early Wednesday morning."

"Of course you have," she says brightly.

"And a security tape shows you on the sixth floor at 02:34, coming in through the emergency exit."

"I was so sure you were going to catch me on the stairs," she says. "Of course, I didn't know it was you at the time." She giggles like a little girl. "Oh, don't be embarrassed, Joseph," she says. "I knew this could happen sooner or later. Too many connections could be made. It wasn't planned. It was impulsive."

"You can have a lawyer, Madge," Weed says. "You don't have to say any more."

"I know my rights, Detective Weed. Maybe we can do without a big trial. I wouldn't want to put Leo through more pain."

"I don't think you can," I say.

"What about the first one?" Weed asks. "On the ranch?"

She nods at the memory. "So long ago." Her eyebrows pull together. "Impulse again," she says. "Not planned. Although I'll admit I was never fond of the woman. One time she threatened to make Leo fire me. She said she could do it."

Weed frowns. "So you came back early? That counts as planning."

"It was an accident that I came back," she says. "Leo and one of the corporate wives disappeared. He was a terrible roué in those days. I didn't really mind. I turned a blind eye. Those affairs never amounted to anything anyway. But I didn't care to wait around so I checked out of the hotel and drove back. I've always preferred having my own transportation. It's liberating." She gets up briskly and takes a stack of file folders from the top of a cabinet. "Now these," she says, placing them squarely on the desk, "are all the most important papers. I insist that they be given to Leo's lawyer for safekeeping until he can find someone to replace me." She divides the stack into two separate piles. "Now this one is the complete inventory, and this is the history. Everything comes with identification numbers. It's really quite simple to understand."

"I have to know what happened, Madge," I say.

Madge nods quietly. "I suppose so," she says. She stares into the middle distance and her expression is calm, thoughtful. "I have a key. From when he first moved in. She was very surprised to see me. I told her I'd brought a birthday present for Leo. And some maiden cake because Leo loves it so. I told her I'd give her the recipe." She sounds like she's reading a book report. "She said she'd save the date squares for some other time. Hid them away." Madge waves away the insult, resumes her account without emotion. "She told me she was getting married. To Leo. Showed me the engagement ring he gave her. It was so beautiful. I asked her if I could try it on. Please, she said. She was very happy. She told me she was pregnant, that it was Leo's son. She was putting out platters and singing something in Spanish, and I picked up the chef's knife to make her stop singing."

"And being happy," I say.

"What did you do with the knife?" Weed asks.

"The morning ferry. I threw it overboard."

"Why, Madge?" I ask her.

"I'm not sure," she says, giving it some thought. "She had so much."

"What did you do after you killed Raquel?" Weed wants to know.

"The most amazing thing happened," she says. "I thought it was another sign that it would all work out for the best, like when I found Rose under the table that time, all covered in blood, holding the knife. She couldn't make a sound. 'Well, look who's here,' I said. 'Tsk tsk,' I said. 'Now you must never ever tell anyone what you've done.'"

"Yeah, that worked out great," I say.

"Monday night," Weed prompts.

"I stayed for a while looking for the Alberta album. He promised I'd get it for years and years and never delivered. I wanted to check the bookshelves, to see if I could find it. I need it to complete the collection. And then when I was down the hall, someone came over the roof. I heard them go into the kitchen and then screams and things crashing and swearing in some foreign language. They made such a noise, I was sure they'd attract attention. There was a lot of yelling. Then they must have gone down the stairs because it was very quiet. I couldn't find the album. I looked and looked. Then I heard the elevator, so I left."

Someone's voice is echoing in the hall. Madge doesn't notice. She's twisting the ring from side to side. "I forgot I had it on until I was almost home." She grinds the ring against her knuckle. "I haven't been able to get it off," she says with a note of complaint. "It went on so easily."

Knocking on the office door. "Miss Killian? You in there?"

I open the door. It's the yachtsman. "We're smelling smoke," he says. "I don't know where it's coming from. Trev's having a look around. Have you got a fireplace going?"

Madge looks up, blinks, waking from a reverie. "No," she says, "no fireplace."

The younger man is at the far end of the hall. "I think it's coming from the basement," he says.

Weed is already on the phone.

"Get your family outside, sir," I say. "I'll have a quick look."

"What's the address?" Weed asks Madge.

"Address?" she says. "What? Here?"

I get the family group out the front door. Weed is bringing Madge out. She's trying to pull away from him. She doesn't want to leave. "There are things that I need to bring," she says.

"It's just stuff," says Weed.

She's starting to cry. "Don't be ridiculous! It's irreplaceable."

I can't see any smoke at the front. I head across the parking lot and around to the side. Basement windows, grilled and dark. Still no smoke but maybe a whiff of something scorched. There's a lane at the back, garbage cans and stacked newspapers and steps leading down a basement door where smoke is curling around the frame. A familiar figure is walking away down the lane. Long legs. Blonde hair. Not in a hurry.

"Roselyn!" I yell after her.

She turns and waves cheerily at me. "Aw," she says, "You called me by my first name."

I catch up to her. "What did you do?"

"And you call yourself a sleuth," she scoffs at me. "Smoke, fire, even you should be able to figure that one out." Behind us a basement window explodes and flames start licking up the rear of the building. "That cellar was just filled to the brim with papers and boxes," she says. "I think it will burn very nicely, don't you?" Sirens are getting closer. "Let's go around to the front, all right?" She takes my arm. "I don't want to miss the excitement."

Fire trucks are arriving; firemen are climbing out, telling people to move back. Flames have reached the ground floor. Weed is trying to get Madge into his car. "I need to move mine!" She's trying to pull away from him. "I need my keys!"

Roselyn watches it all with an expression of satisfaction. "Gone-y-gone," she says. "Clean slate."

Weed is having a difficult time controlling Madge. She's twisting out of his grasp, trying to open the door of her Sprite. "Just let me move my car," she says angrily. "It's my car."

Firemen run by heading for the front door. They are carrying axes.

"No!" Madge yells at them. "You don't have to break anything."

The head fireman tells us to clear out. The cars will have to take their chances where they are.

We lead Madge to the sidewalk. Roselyn is waiting for her.

"Hi, Madge," says Roselyn. "Like old times, isn't it?"

A main floor window explodes, billows of black smoke, flames crawling up the ivied walls. Madge screams. It is the agonized cry of a wounded child. She sinks to the ground, folding herself inside her arms and rocking back and forth. "No no no no no," she sobs. "I can't lose everything. Not everything."

"You'll get used to it," Roselyn says.

chapter twenty-seven

"**I**s that the tie you're gonna wear?" Gritch wants to know.

"Yes, it is," I say. I'm standing in front of a mirror adjusting the ends and turning down my collar. I'm pleased to see that my left hand is holding up its end of the operation.

"It's got a horse head on it."

"I'm aware," I say. "She liked it." Trigger, Roy Rogers' distinguished palomino, is nicely centred. I figure if Weed can wear a lobster for his granddaughter, I can wear a horse for Raquel. "She told me once."

"She was being kind," he says.

"That's a possibility," I say. There. A nice half-Windsor, better than I usually manage. "She was a kind person, but she wasn't insincere."

"You escorting the old man?"

"Nope," I say. "It's all family in the first car. Lenny and his wife ..."

"Together again."

"So I hear. Plus grandkids." The top button is proving uncooperative. "And there's Roselyn."

"Crowded."

"It'll be good for Leo," I say. "He can use backup that isn't hired by the hour."

"Figure Fat-Boy will show?"

"Theo will be there," I say. "He can't afford not to be." Lenny's star is definitely in the ascendant.

"I guess he's lost some traction with the old man," Gritch says.

"Plus Leo's got his daughter back."

"If he can keep her out of jail." Gritch does a little tie-adjustment of his own. "She still going to publish her book?" he wonders.

"Definitely." Success. The top button is buttoned, the tie is snug, the ends are even, my left arm isn't complaining much. My watch is back where it's meant to be. Things are looking up. "But with new details, of course."

"Look forward to it," he says.

"I'll likely give it a miss," I say. "I know too much already."

As funerals go, Raquel's ceremony at St. Barnabus was all right, I guess. Sufficient unto the occasion. Substantial turnout. I'm never completely comfortable with church funeral services — something about the setting, I suppose — it hardly ever feels like they're talking about the person I knew. Father Renfrew kept his portion brief, spoke in generalities, winging it the way clergymen do when they have few facts and abundant platitudes. Leo couldn't bring himself to say anything publicly. Tricia made a nice little speech about how Raquel's uniforms always fitted better than anyone else's because she used to sneak them home for alterations, one of the few moments that felt halfway authentic.

Theodore and his wife, Gloria, attended, their public faces proper to the gravity of the day although it was clear, even from a distance, that Theo's wife was standing an extra few inches away from his side and never deigned to glance in his direction. They didn't hold hands. Lenny and Jaqueline on the other hand looked like a married couple. Their children were in attendance, the older girl with black and red hair, a ring through her nose, supremely bored, sending private messages via the little device she kept poking with a black fingernail. The boy, too, had an electronic contraption that he stared at with intense concentration. The younger girl I recognized from the little photograph. She stood between her parents, holding their hands, keeping them linked, pleased with herself, as though she had negotiated the rapprochement.

Jesus Santiago spoke for a few minutes about his sister. His eulogy was heartfelt and not entirely coherent. He was wearing a good black suit and tie. One of Leo's, I think. They're about the same size. Jesus, like Roselyn, is out on bail, residing at the hotel while his case makes its way through various levels of bureaucracy. Leo's legal team is getting a full workout this spring.

Mrs. Dineen didn't come.

I was a pallbearer. I took a place on the left side so that I could use my good arm. Jesus was across from me. Lenny took a handle, also Maurice. Roland could have carried it on his own.

The wake is in Olive's. Invitation only. It has a sort of New Orleans/Havana feel to it. The flavours are Latin but Olive can't stop her left hand striding from time to time. I'm feeling the emotional conflict that comes with recognizing that the person being celebrated would have had a great time.

Weed is there, at the bar, enjoying the music. "Jeeze," he says, "half the people in here are out on bail."

"A slight exaggeration," I say. "How did you get in?"

"Somebody has to keep an eye on this bunch."

"Feels sort of tribal, doesn't it?"

"One way of putting it."

"Everyone here is connected, somehow. Even you."

"How about you, pal?" he asks. "You belong to this tribe?"

I lift my left arm as I head for the exit. "Blood relative," I say.

"What do you mean you have a TV in your room? When did this happen?"

"I hooked it up today," I say. "Big sucker, too. Supposed to be highly defined, I'm told."

"High Definition."

"That's what the cable guy told me. I have a clicker thing that I can almost figure out, and I'm looking at your face right now." On the screen the tiny perfect newswoman is doing her first standup from Kandahar airport. She's wearing desert camo gear and a helmet and she looks courageous, beautiful, capable, and right where she wants to be. I've seen the footage three times. They repeat the news on this channel. "If I knew how to work it I could record these for later. We could watch them from bed."

"I'll make sure you get a copy, big guy."

"Keeping your head down?"

"I may be intrepid, but I ain't stoopid."

"Atta girl. I want you to do your helmet strap tighter."

"Gotta go, slugger. You done good."

"You too."

"Love you."

"What?"

"You heard me."

On the television screen Connie is ducking her head. I can see smoke rising in the distant background. When she ducks, the helmet slips forward.

"Do up your chinstrap," I say. "I want you back."

Also by Marc Strange

Sucker Punch
A Joe Grundy Mystery
978-1-55002-702-0 $11.99

More Great Castle Street Mysteries from Dundurn

Outside the Line
by Christian Petersen
978-1-55002-859-1 $11.99

Depth of Field
A Granville Island Mystery
by Michael Blair
978-1-55002-855-3 $11.99

 DUNDURN PRESS
www.dundurn.com

Available at your favourite bookseller

Tell us your story! What did you think of this book? Join the conversation
at www.definingcanada.ca/tell-your-story by telling us what you think.